We stood awkwardly on the sidewalk in front of the hospital.

"You could always wish to get in," Ridge suggested.

"Yeah," I said. "And accept another dumb consequence?" I looked at the hospital, trying to decide how badly I wanted to spy on Tina. I had the perfect wish. Might as well see what it would cost me. "I wish to be invisible."

"Forever?" Ridge asked.

"What? No!" I answered. "Just for the next ten minutes or so. Enough to get past that security guard."

Ridge nodded in understanding. "If you want to become invisible," said Ridge, "then all your clothes will remain invisible for a day."

"Ahh!" I cried, stepping behind a shrub in case my clothes suddenly vanished. "That's terrible! What if I put on new clothes?"

Ridge shrugged. "They will also disappear."

There was no way I could accept. We were supposed to team up with Tina and Vale soon. Face it, you wouldn't accept that crazy deal, either.

Also by Tyler Whitesides

The Wishbreaker

The Janitor series

THE WISHMAKERS

TYLER WHITESIDES

ILLUSTRATED BY
JESSICA WARRICK

HARPER
An Imprint of HarperCollinsPublishers

The Wishmakers
Text copyright © 2018 by Tyler Whitesides
Illustrations by Jessica Warrick
All rights reserved. Printed in the United States of America.
No part of this book may be used or reproduced in any manner whatsoever
without written permission except in the case of brief quotations embodied in critical
articles and reviews. For information address HarperCollins Children's Books, a
division of HarperCollins Publishers, 195 Broadway, New York, NY 10007.
www.harpercollinschildrens.com
Library of Congress Control Number: 2017949556
ISBN 978-0-06-256832-8
Typography by Jessie Gang
18 19 20 21 22   BRR   10 9 8 7 6 5 4 3 2 1
❖
First paperback edition, 2018

For Chris Schoebinger

CHAPTER 1

There was a genie living inside my peanut butter jar.

I didn't see the warning label. Well, I *saw* it, but I didn't actually read it. I sort of remember glancing at the words on the lid.

WARNING: READ BEFORE OPENING

But I didn't bother to study the rest of the tiny words crammed on the small top. I didn't think it would be important. How was I supposed to know that making a sandwich would change my life?

One minute, you're trying to make lunch. Then before you know it, a genie emerges from your peanut butter jar and wants you to save the world. At least, that's what happened to me.

I looked at the open jar in my hand, then again at the strange boy who had appeared with a deafening bang and a puff of smoke.

He was on top of the dining table, standing on the slices of bread that I'd just laid out.

At that moment, I didn't know I was staring at a genie. The boy didn't seem like anything unusual, other than the fact that he had just appeared out of nowhere. He looked twelve or thirteen, about my age. He was wearing shorts and a T-shirt, with a baseball cap stuffed over his abundance of black frizzy hair. The boy was rather scrawny, had dark skin, and big unblinking eyes that stared directly at me.

Again, I looked at the jar in my hand. Where on earth had my foster parents bought it?

At this point, you are probably wondering if the peanut butter was chunky or creamy. That detail is wildly unimportant. Don't waste another moment thinking about it. Instead, think about how confused I was to find a kid living in a jar in the pantry.

"Hello," he said. If I'd known he was a genie, I might have expected his voice to be booming and ominous. It was far from that. In fact, the boy's voice was a bit squeaky.

He took a step forward, slipped on a slice of bread, and fell flat off the edge of the table.

"Yep, that hurt," cried the stranger, pulling himself to his feet and rubbing his knee. "Definitely going to feel that tomorrow."

As we stood face-to-face I realized that we were almost the same height, though he seemed taller because of his curly hair.

I was still having a hard time believing what I saw. Have you ever been so hungry that you imagine things? I once imagined that a doorknob at the orphanage was a cupcake. It did not taste good.

Deciding that this was another hallucinatory hunger moment, I slowly reached out and poked the boy's shoulder.

"Ow," he said, stepping back. "What was that for?"

I stared unblinking, finally beginning to believe what was standing before my eyes. "Had to make sure you were real."

"Of course I'm real," said the boy. "What else would I be?"

"Well," I replied, "I thought you were peanut butter." To back up my answer, I hefted the jar I had just opened.

"Hmm," he said, peering at the container. "Is it chunky or creamy?"

"You should know," I said. "Weren't you just in there?"

"Well, yes," he answered. "And no. It's not exactly a peanut butter jar. That would be ridiculous."

"That's what it looks like," I said.

"Of course," he answered. "But that's not what it *is*."

"What is it, then?" I stared skeptically at the thing I was holding.

"A genie jar," the boy said.

"A . . . genie jar?" I raised an eyebrow. "I thought genies came in lamps."

"Lamps?" He laughed. "Where would I live? In the light-bulb? Plus, you'd be tripping all over the cord. . . ." He waved off the idea. "Genies come from jars. Like that one." He pointed at the container. "The magic of the Universe disguised it as peanut butter so you'd be drawn to open it."

Genie. Magic. Universe . . . I peered into the open jar I was holding. It looked empty and vast inside, like a black hole. Definitely no peanut butter. "Is this a prank?"

The boy held up his hands. "I'm real. And I can prove it to you." He paused, then said, "I'm a genie, so . . . wish for something."

Wish for something. Hmmm. Only one way to find out.

"I wish for a lifetime supply of peanut butter and jelly sand-wiches." What? You know I was hungry.

I held out my hands as though the sandwiches might start pouring down from heaven. Instead, the genie leaped forward and slapped something around my wrist, apologizing in case it hurt.

Luckily, it didn't. It was merely a wristwatch. I couldn't help but wonder why I had gotten a watch when I had clearly wished for sandwiches. Maybe the genie was hard of hearing. Maybe his ears were full of peanut butter.

"Oops," said the genie. "I probably should have started with the rules. Now we only have thirty seconds, so listen up."

I glanced down at the watch. The band was thick leather, but instead of numbers and hands, the top was a slender hourglass, white sand pouring from the upper chamber to the bottom.

It didn't seem like a smooth design. Now I had a three-inch-tall hourglass poking up from my wrist. What if I wanted to put my hand in my pocket? Or reach inside a cookie jar?

"Okay," said the boy genie. "The world exists in a state of balance. Whenever you make a wish, the Universe has to give you a consequence to go with it."

"Wait a minute," I said, feeling cheated. "Aren't wishes supposed to be free?"

The genie shook his head. "The Universe has to keep things in balance." He pointed to my wrist. "The hourglass watch shows you exactly how long you have to accept or decline the consequence before the wish expires."

Glancing back down, I saw that the top chamber of the little hourglass was already half empty. A more positive person would have said that the bottom chamber was already half full. Either way, I was running out of time.

"You wished for a lifetime supply of sandwiches," said the genie. "If you want that wish to come true, you have to accept the consequence."

"Which is?" I asked.

"You have a smudge of peanut butter on your cheek."

I reached up instinctively, wiping both sides of my face. "I do?"

"Well, not yet," said the boy. "That's the consequence. You'll have a smudge of peanut butter on your right cheek next to your mouth."

"I'll just wipe it off," I argued.

"It doesn't work like that. Wipe it off and it will instantly reappear."

"How big is this smudge supposed to be?" I asked.

"Just a skiff," he answered, holding up his fingers to show a length shorter than an inch. "But it'll last a year. Do you accept?"

A lifetime supply of sandwiches in exchange for a smudge of peanut butter on my cheek? I doubted the scrawny kid in my kitchen could make either of those things happen.

Again, only one way to find out.

"Sure," I said, taunting him. "Prove it."

"You have to say the magic word."

"Really?" I muttered. "There's a magic word?"

"You have to say it every time you make a wish so that the Universe knows you accept the consequence," he explained. "It's like giving your final answer on a game show."

I glanced at my hourglass watch. There wasn't much sand left. "What's the word?" I asked.

"Bazang," he said.

"Bazang?" I repeated.

And just like that, I was surrounded by peanut butter and jelly sandwiches.

CHAPTER 2

When I wished for a lifetime supply of peanut butter and jelly sandwiches, I sort of thought they'd be delivered to me over the course of my life.

Nope. I got them all at once.

There were thousands of sandwiches, each individually wrapped in a little plastic bag. The entire kitchen was full, probably the entire house! I was up to my armpits in them, and the boy who had granted my wish was trying to wade toward me.

It settled one thing. The kid was a genie. A real genie!

And now I had a lot of sandwiches.

I locked eyes with the boy. He made a conspicuous gesture as though wiping at something on his cheek. It was the kind of gesture that made me do the same. As soon as my fingers touched my right cheek, I felt the promised smear of peanut butter.

For the next few seconds I tried to wipe it off. It felt slightly dried and crusty, but as I felt it flaking away, more appeared.

"It's useless," the boy said, practically swimming through sandwiches to reach me. "You can't get rid of a consequence."

As I lowered my hand in defeat, I noticed that the watch he'd given me had changed. The hourglass seemed to have collapsed, folding paper-thin across the leather band. The shiny top of the hourglass now looked very much like a regular watch, with numbers displayed on the face.

"I'm Ace," I said, reaching out for a handshake. "What's your name?"

"Ridge," he answered, giving me a high five.

"Your name is Ridge?" I clarified. I can't say it was the

strangest name I'd ever heard. I once met someone who went by Wiggy.

"Yeah," he said. "Genies get their names from wherever their jar was originally discovered."

"Someone found you on a ridge?" I asked. "Like, the top of a mountain?"

"I guess," he said.

"That seems dangerous. What were you doing up there?"

He shrugged. "I don't know. I was in a jar."

"You can't get out of the jar on your own?" I asked.

"Nope," said Ridge. "It takes a Wishmaker."

"Wishmaker?" I asked.

Ridge nodded. "Whoever opens my jar becomes the Wishmaker." He pointed at me. "That's you, now."

I was a Wishmaker. I had a genie. And I had just wasted one of my wishes on sandwiches?

"These are supposed to last a lifetime?" I said.

I set the peanut butter jar on top of the pile and picked up the nearest sandwich. I took it as a good sign that there were so many. Didn't that mean I was going to live a long time? Or maybe I was destined to eat them quickly.

"It would have been a lot nicer to get a few delivered each day," I pointed out.

"You should have mentioned that when you wished," said Ridge.

"Won't these go bad before I have a chance to eat them all?" I didn't want moldy bread.

"The sandwiches are magically preserved," the genie said. "They won't spoil."

Peeling away the bag, I began chowing down. "So, what now?"

Ridge looked at me as though it was obvious. "We begin the quest."

"Quest?" I raised one eyebrow. "What quest?"

"Didn't you read the warning label on my jar?" he asked.

Right, that. "I was too hungry to read," I said, scouring the mounds of sandwiches for the jar's lid.

"The lid's gone," Ridge said, realizing what I must have been searching for. "It puffed into smoke as soon as you opened the jar."

"Then how am I supposed to read the warning label?" I cried.

"It's a little late for that," Ridge said calmly. "The Universe likes to warn the Wishmakers about what they're getting themselves into, but if you don't read the label—"

"Who is this Universe you keep talking about?" I cut him off.

"Not who," said Ridge. "The Universe is the force that grants wishes."

Well, I had to admit, the Universe actually made a pretty

good PB and J. "And it's your job to give the consequences?" I asked.

Ridge shook his head, eyes wide. "Not me! The Universe does that, too. It has to keep things in balance," explained Ridge. "The natural choices you make every day bring about natural consequences. Same thing applies to wishes—it's just that wishes aren't really natural, so some of the consequences can be rather . . . strange."

"So the next two wishes I make will also come with consequences?" I clarified.

"Not just the next two," he answered. "All of them."

"Wait," I said. "I get more than three wishes?"

"Of course!" Ridge replied. "You have unlimited wishes. And you get thirty seconds on the hourglass to decide if you want to take the consequence."

"What happens if I don't accept?" I asked.

"Life goes on like normal," said the genie, "but you don't get your wish. And, believe me, you'll need wishes to complete your quest."

Oh, right. "So, what is this quest?" I asked.

Ridge grimaced. "It's a big one. I don't know if the Universe has ever assigned a quest with a consequence as big as this one."

"Wait a minute. Quests have consequences, too?" I asked, finishing the first of my countless sandwiches.

"Oh, yeah," answered Ridge. "The warning label on the lid explained that. When you opened the jar, you got unlimited wishes. To balance this, the Universe gave you a quest. And if you don't complete the quest, there'll be a nasty consequence."

"Like what?" I asked. "Peanut butter in my eye?"

"It's different every time," said Ridge. "Most Wishmakers have simpler quests. . . ."

"With simpler consequences," I finished for him.

Ridge nodded. "They're still bad—don't get me wrong. Usually, failing a quest means a neighborhood will burn down, or a city will get hit by a tsunami, or dolphins will go extinct. But in your case . . ." He looked grim. "Well, if you don't complete the Universe's quest, then all the cats and dogs in the world will turn into zombies and destroy mankind!"

I couldn't help but laugh out loud. All pets would turn into zombies? He had to be joking, right? "How do you make this stuff up?" I rolled my eyes.

"I don't," said Ridge. "That's the consequence that will occur if you fail to complete your quest."

"Luckily, I don't have any pets," I said.

"This isn't just about you," said Ridge. "We're talking about every human being on earth."

I didn't want to believe him. It was hard to imagine cute little kitties craving brains. But I hadn't believed him about the sandwiches, either, and now I was practically swimming in them.

"Only you can stop this from happening, Ace," said my genie. "You have seven days to complete the quest."

I took a deep breath. "All right. What do I have to do?"

CHAPTER 3

Ridge bounced up on his toes, sending a rippling wave through the sea of sandwiches. He seemed excited by the idea that we were going to try to save the world. I don't know why his excitement struck me as odd. You would be excited about saving the world, too, right?

"There's a very mean person out there," Ridge said, "trying to find the Undiscovered Genie jar. Your quest is to stop him from opening that jar."

I nodded. That seemed totally doable. "What's this bad guy's name?"

"Thackary Anderthon," said Ridge.

"Zackary Anderson?" I clarified.

"No," said Ridge. "His name is Thackary Anderthon."

"Why are you saying it that way?" I asked.

"That's his name. That's how it's pronounced," he answered.

"Thackary Anderthon?" I repeated, giggling at the way I sounded. Go ahead, you try to say it out loud. It's funny, right?

"Yep," Ridge said. "With a *T-H*."

"Where is he now?" It seemed like a perfectly good question. If I needed to stop someone, I'd have to find him first.

Ridge shrugged. "I don't know."

"Can you tell me anything about him?"

Again, Ridge shrugged cluelessly. "Not really."

"For a genie," I said, "you sure don't know very much."

"All I know is what the Universe tells me," said Ridge. "I'm simply a middleman. You make a wish, the Universe grants it and gives you a consequence. I'm just here to explain things."

"You've hardly explained anything," I pointed out. "I thought genies were supposed to be all wise and powerful. But you look an awful lot like a regular kid."

"All genies look like kids," he answered. "At least, all the ones I know about. Sure, some genies have been around for a really long time, but that doesn't mean we get older."

"Two kids trying to save the world . . ." I muttered. "I don't think I'm cut out for this."

"I know it seems like a lot," Ridge said, "but the Universe wouldn't give you a genie if it didn't believe in you. We're only talking about the fate of the world here. You'll probably do fine."

"Right!" I took a deep breath and straightened up. "I can do it. I've got unlimited wishes. I've got a genie." I turned to Ridge. "You've done this before. You've got experience."

He began to nod slowly. "Ha! Absolutely . . . saving the world is kind of my thing."

"Good," I said. "Because I have no idea what I'm doing. I'll be relying on you a lot. I mean, how am I supposed to stop this Thackary person if I don't even know where to start looking?"

"Well, let's start with what we do know," Ridge said. "Thackary has to be a kid. I can tell you that."

"How can you be sure?"

"Genie jars can only be opened by kids," Ridge said. "That's one thing I know. This Thackary character will probably be under thirteen years old."

That was something to go on, at least.

"Is he in the city?" I asked. Lincoln, Nebraska, seemed like a pretty big place to me. In the three years I'd lived here, I certainly hadn't met every resident.

"I've told you everything I know about him," said Ridge.

"This is impossible," I said. "Aren't there, like, seven billion people in the world? He could be any one of them!"

Ridge leaned over and picked up the peanut butter jar from the pile of sandwiches. He held it out to me. "Maybe it's time you start wishing for some answers."

"Do I have to have the jar to make a wish?" I asked, taking it from his hand.

"Well, no," he answered. "Technically, you don't need the jar at all. Though it should come in handy from time to time, so I'd recommend keeping it close."

"What can I do with it?" I asked.

Before he could answer me, the door that led from the kitchen to the garage flew open. I turned, watching bagged sandwiches flooding across the threshold like a dam had broken.

My foster parents were standing in the doorway. I had been so wrapped up in my conversation with Ridge that I hadn't even heard the car pull in.

"Ace!" Mr. Lindon called, a broad smile breaking over his face. "You made lunch!" He waded into the kitchen, my foster mother right behind him.

I glanced at the enormous piles around me. The man arrived home to find his house full of peanut butter sandwiches, and all he could say was "You made lunch"?

"You must have been busy," Mrs. Lindon said. "You made quite a few."

"You think I made all these?" I finally stammered. "You guys have only been gone for thirty minutes!" I turned to Ridge, my face twisted in confusion.

"Ah," Ridge said, "I should have mentioned that the Universe has a way of protecting Wishmakers from suspicion."

"Who's your friend?" Mrs. Lindon asked, lifting her arm through a mound of sandwiches to gesture at Ridge.

"Umm . . ." If the Universe was really going to protect me from suspicion, then it wouldn't hurt to tell the truth, right? "His name is Ridge. He's a magical genie, and he's here to give me unlimited wishes."

"Oh, you met at the park?" Mr. Lindon said. "How nice."

"That's not what I said," I answered. What was going on?

"It doesn't matter what you say," explained Ridge. "People around us will only hear and see what makes sense to them."

"We'll be in the living room if you need us, Ace," Mr. Lindon said, taking his wife's hand and pressing through the sandwiches. I watched speechlessly until they were almost out of sight.

"I have to go!" I suddenly blurted, causing Mr. and Mrs. Lindon to halt and look back. "I've been given a quest to save the world," I explained further, "so I'm going to be gone for a week or so."

The Lindons smiled at me. "Summer camp! That sounds like a great opportunity," Mr. Lindon said. "Have so much fun."

"And be safe," added Mrs. Lindon.

The Universe was clearly casting some pretty heavy magic over them.

"Okay," I muttered, unsure how to respond as the two adults moved into the living room.

"You'll be grateful for that," said Ridge. "Wishing can get pretty magical. It's a lot easier to have the Universe shielding us from unwanted attention. It'll help us stop Thackary without interference."

With the Lindons taken care of, I decided to turn my attention to my quest. I'd need to find Thackary if I wanted to stop him from getting that Undiscovered Genie Jar. And if I could wish for anything . . .

"I wish to teleport to wherever Thackary Anderthon is right now."

I felt a click on my wrist and I looked down to see the hourglass pop up again.

"Okay," Ridge said. "If you want to teleport to Thackary Anderthon, then you'll have to accept the consequence that goes along with the wish."

"Which is?" I prompted.

"Your legs will permanently be replaced with pogo sticks."

"What?!" I shouted. I'd seen kids bouncing around on those spring-loaded pogo sticks. They looked like fun. But I didn't want to have them in place of legs.

"The swap will be painless," Ridge said, but he wasn't helping the situation.

"No! I do not accept!" I cried. As soon as I turned the consequence down, my hourglass collapsed into a regular watch and Ridge shrugged.

"Permanent pogo stick legs?" I said. "You can tell the Universe that seems like a bit much just to teleport myself. I thought these consequences were supposed to be balanced."

"Oh, I forgot to mention that," Ridge said, holding up a finger. "Whenever you wish for something directly related to your quest, the Universe holds that at a higher value. The consequences can get pretty steep."

I parted the sea of sandwiches and looked down at my legs, grateful that they were still legs. "Pogo sticks?" I muttered. "That's so random. How does that balance against my wish to teleport, anyway?"

"The consequences don't necessarily have anything to do with the wish," Ridge answered. "Since making wishes gives you certain advantages, the consequences are meant to disadvantage. Wishes aren't exactly natural, so the Universe's consequences are kind of random."

"And wishes that will help get me closer to stopping Thackary Anderthon are going to come with bigger disadvantages?" I asked.

"Exactly," answered Ridge.

"So I have to wish to stop Thackary without ever wishing to stop Thackary?"

Ridge nodded, his face sincere. "That's the best way to do it. Wishing is tricky. If you wish to teleport directly to Thackary Anderthon, then the wish did all the work for you."

"Then what am I supposed to wish?" I asked.

"Don't wish for things directly," Ridge said. "If you make a wish that still requires some effort on your part, then the consequence might not be quite as big of a disadvantage."

"What if I wish to know where Thackary Anderthon lives?"

Ridge shrugged. "That might be better, since getting to his house would still require effort from you. But I'm guessing that'll still have a significant consequence since Thackary is the object of your quest."

Well, I could always turn down the consequence if it was too much. "I wish to know where Thackary Anderthon lives."

My hourglass watch popped open.

"If you want to know where Thackary lives," said Ridge, "then you'll never be able to find the Lindons' house again."

"This house?" I glanced toward the living room where my foster parents had gone. After two years, I was certainly calling this place home.

"This house or any house that your foster parents move to," replied Ridge.

"So I'll just wander around the neighborhood, looking for my way back?" I said. "What if someone else brings me here?"

Ridge nodded. "That would work, but you'll never be able to find it on your own."

Was it worth it? I liked this place. I was finally settling into my life here. The Lindons were good people. Maybe they'd even be willing to adopt me. If I accepted this consequence, I might never find them again.

Of course, if things worked out with this genie, I might not need to come back to the Lindons' house at all. I might finally find my real family. My real home.

My hand crept into my pocket, feeling for the only object I ever kept with me. The only object that was truly mine. My fingers curled around the tattered, folded card. My gaze was trained on Ridge—a genie, capable of granting me any wish I desired. If I went with him, my greatest wish could come true. I might finally get the answers I'd been seeking for years.

"Bazang," I said, officially accepting the wish. I suddenly knew exactly where Thackary Anderthon lived. "Let's go save the world."

CHAPTER 4

It was the strangest feeling to get lost the moment I stepped out the front door. By the time we reached the sidewalk, I couldn't remember where the Lindons' house was at all. Ridge pointed, and told me to turn around, but I guess I kept looking in the wrong direction.

I gave up after a few moments and decided to focus on getting to Thackary Anderthon's house, which I did know how to find.

"How long will it take us to get to Thackary's house?" Ridge asked, tugging at the straps on his backpack. We both wore packs so full of peanut butter sandwiches that we could barely zip them shut. I couldn't bring all of them—not by a long shot. But between the two of us, we must have had at least a hundred.

Does that seem excessive to you? I didn't know if I'd ever find my way back. And the last thing I wanted was to get hungry while I was trying to save the world.

"Thackary lives in Omaha," I said.

"How far away is that?"

"I'm not sure," I said. "People always talk about driving there."

"Then we'll need a car," replied Ridge.

"I've got something better." I pointed at him and raised the lidless peanut butter jar. "I wish I could fly to Thackary Anderthon's house."

I glanced down as the hourglass emerged from my watch.

"If you want to be able to fly," said Ridge, "then every bird you see along the way will poop on you."

Well, that wasn't going to be very pleasant. But maybe I could dodge. "Sure," I said. "Bazang."

My hourglass collapsed, and I didn't feel any different. Was I just supposed to jump into the air and see what happened? I bent my knees. Ridge shouted something, reaching out for me, but I was too excited to be stopped.

I launched upward, flying straight into the blue July sky. Laughing, I watched the ground fall away beneath me—ten feet, twenty feet, thirty . . .

Something slammed into me with so much force that the air was instantly knocked from my lungs. The peanut butter genie jar flew from my grasp, tumbling out of sight. At the same moment, I was pulled downward by a tremendous unseen force. Halfway to the sidewalk, I collided with Ridge. I didn't understand how he had managed to get twenty feet off the ground, but we smashed into each other, our bodies pressing together painfully.

For half a second, I thought we might hover there, in mid-air. Then we began plummeting toward the ground once more, this time with Ridge shrieking in my ear.

I had no idea what was happening, but I managed to get ahold of the situation just before we struck the sidewalk. I gave an upward burst of flight, but Ridge was too heavy and it was barely enough to break our fall. The two of us tumbled onto the concrete.

"What was that?" I groaned, rolling away from Ridge.

"We snapped the tether." He crawled over and picked up his fallen baseball cap. "I was going to explain, but you just took off."

"I was excited to fly!" Though I'll admit, I was much more reluctant now.

"When you opened my genie jar," Ridge said, "we got tied together for the week."

"Tied together?" I swiped my hand through the air between us. Wouldn't you notice a string if you got tied to another person?

"It's called a tether," Ridge explained. "It's invisible. As long as we stay together, it won't give us any trouble. But if you try to fly off like that . . ." He stood up slowly.

"How far apart can we get?" I asked as he helped me up.

"Forty-two feet," Ridge answered. "If we ever get more than forty-two feet apart, the tether will remind us to stick together."

"That was more than a reminder!" I felt my chest to make sure none of my ribs were broken. That invisible force had hit me like a freight train!

"If the tether snaps, it brings us both back together."

That explained why Ridge had seemed to fly upward, meeting in the middle of our invisible rope.

"What about my wish?" My ability to fly would be totally wasted if I had to stay right by Ridge's side. He was too heavy to carry.

"There is a way," Ridge said, looking both ways and then running out into the street. He stooped and picked up the peanut butter jar I had dropped when the tether snapped.

"Is it broken?" I asked as he carried it back to the sidewalk.

"You can't break a genie jar," Ridge said.

"Isn't it made of plastic?" Peanut butter jars were tough, but they didn't seem indestructible. Surprisingly, though, the thing didn't even have a scratch from the fall.

Ridge shook his head, black hair bouncing. "It's protected by the Universe. Nothing can shatter a genie jar." He handed it to me. "You can order me into the jar. It'll be a lot easier to carry me around that way."

"Another wish?" I asked, glancing down at the empty container.

"No," he said. "You just have to say 'Ridge, get into the jar,' and I'll be forced to obey. But you have to be holding the jar when you give the command."

"What about the tether?" I put a hand to my chest. "Does it still tie us together when you're in the jar?"

"Yeah," Ridge answered. "You'll have to stay within forty-two feet of the jar at all times." He gestured at the container. "Let's give it a try."

I shrugged. It seemed like the best way to fly with him. "Ridge," I said, "get into the jar."

Before my eyes, Ridge instantly turned into a puff of dark smoke and got sucked into the open jar in my hand. Suddenly alone, I peered inside but still couldn't see anything.

"You in there?" I spoke into the opening.

"YEEEOOOOW!" came Ridge's shrieking reply. "Get me out of here, Ace!"

I startled, nearly dropping the jar. What was happening to the genie in there? "How?" I shouted. "How do I get you out?"

His voice echoed out the opening. "Same way you got me in here," he answered, his voice uneasy. "Just say 'Ridge, get out of the jar.' Say it!"

"Uhh," I stammered. "Ridge, get out of the jar!"

Another puff of black smoke, and Ridge appeared. He danced across the lawn, scratching himself all over, as though his clothes were infested with ants.

"What happened to you in there?" I asked.

He finally settled, looking over at me. "It was dark," he replied. "And a very tight fit. It made me itch all over, but there was no way to scratch it."

"I thought you lived in there," I said, holding up the plastic container.

He shook his head. "The jar is usually a doorway to a peaceful place where genies are in a deep sleep and time passes quickly."

"It didn't sound too peaceful a second ago," I pointed out.

"I couldn't get there," Ridge explained. "During a quest . . ."

"I see. The Universe doesn't want you hiding away when you're supposed to be out here with me."

"It's okay for a bit," he said, shuddering. "Just don't leave me in there for a long time."

Well, that was going to put a damper on my flight to Thackary Anderthon's house. Still, flying in short bursts was better than walking.

"Ridge," I said. He gave me a pained look, and I said the next part apologetically. "Get into the jar."

CHAPTER 5

Flying was hard. Not only did we have to stop every so often so I could let Ridge out of the jar to scratch himself, but I was exhausted. Sure, flying was pretty cool, but it was also way more tiring than I thought it would be. Like a cross between swimming and running. I was glad Ridge was stuck in his jar so he couldn't see how uncoordinated I was. I couldn't fly fast or straight.

And then there were the birds.

I tried not to notice them, but if a bird so much as fluttered past my peripheral vision, it came zooming over to poop on me. I tried to dodge or outdistance them. But those birds were incredibly determined. And accurate.

It was dinnertime when we finally reached Thackary Anderthon's neighborhood. I was so splattered in bird droppings that I felt like I'd been painted white.

"Ridge, get out of the jar," I said as my feet touched down in the street. The genie appeared in his usual puff of smoke, scratching himself all over.

"Are we there yet?" It was the same question he had asked for the last few hours. Then he looked at me and cringed. "Were you always wearing a white shirt?"

I glanced down at my gooey shirt and tried not to gag. It had definitely been blue when we left my house. I ignored the comment, wiping the latest dropping from my forehead and pointing toward a dilapidated trailer home. "This is it."

The place was a dingy taupe color, like a giant Rice Krispie. Ribbons of paint peeled off the side and the tiny yard seemed to have rejected the grass. What little vegetation remained was dried and brown among patches of bare dirt.

Side by side, we approached the sagging front steps. I had just put my foot on the first one, when my eyes caught a scuffed blue cooler tipped over in the dirt. The white lid was broken, but I saw a name written in black marker across the side.

ANDERTHON

We had actually found the right place! I don't know why I was surprised—my wish had told me that this was where Thackary lived. But seeing the name written on the cooler took any doubt out of my mind.

"What's your plan?" Ridge asked quietly.

My plan was simple—get inside, tie up Thackary Anderthon, and make sure he didn't escape for a week. Then my quest would be fulfilled and the world would be saved from zombie pets.

I jogged up the trailer steps and knocked on the door.

"What are you doing?" Ridge asked, his voice shooting high-pitched. "The Universe said this Thackary kid was dangerous!"

"I'm checking to see if anyone's home," I said.

"And if they are, then you've just ruined our element of surprise!"

"Not completely," I pointed out. "I just surprised you."

Ridge was panicking over nothing. Nobody came to the door, and when I pressed my ear against it, I couldn't hear any voices.

I tried the doorknob. This also worried Ridge.

"It's locked," I said. Then, stepping back, I rubbed my hands together to build up some adrenaline.

"What are you doing?"

"I'm going to kick the door in," I said.

"With your foot?" Ridge asked.

I nodded. "That's what I usually use for kicking."

"You've done this before?" Ridge asked. "Wait a minute! Are you a criminal?" He threw his hands up. "Oh, great. The Universe assigned me to a delinquent!"

"I'm not a criminal," I said. "And as far as I can remember, I've never kicked down a door before. But I've seen it in movies. It can't be that hard."

I kicked. It was hard. Too hard.

I jumped back from the door, grabbing my foot and howling in pain. "The movies lied!"

Ridge tapped me on the shoulder and drew my attention to a frumpy-looking neighbor woman across the crunchy yard. She was wearing something that looked like a long, colorful housecoat, and her hair was in three-inch curlers.

"Act natural, Ace." Ridge waved at the neighbor. My attempted break-in seemed to be attracting some unwanted attention. I was ready to try a second kick now. I still had one foot that didn't hurt.

"She's watching us," said Ridge. "Maybe you should compliment her muumuu."

"What the heck is a muumuu?" I asked.

"The outfit she's wearing," he said.

"Isn't that a housecoat?"

"I'm pretty sure it's called a muumuu."

"I'm pretty sure you just made that word up," I said. "Anyway, I thought you said the Universe would shield us from being noticed."

"People can still notice us," Ridge whispered. "The Universe just makes it so that they don't get suspicious about *magical* activity. There's nothing magical going on right now."

"Right," I muttered. What was the sense in breaking down the door when I could easily wish to get through? "I'm going to make a wish."

"You don't have to announce it every time," Ridge replied.

I waved him off. "I wish that this door would disappear."

The hourglass popped up on my wrist and the seconds started ticking as Ridge explained the consequence. "If you want this door to disappear," he said, "then whenever you sit on a couch, you will instantly bounce over to the next cushion."

"That's weird," I said.

Ridge shrugged. "Hey, I'm not the one making this stuff up. I think it seems pretty fair. You wish for the advantage of getting past this door. The Universe balances it with the disadvantage of not being able to sit on a couch the right way."

"How long will this go on?" I asked.

"Until the end of the quest," answered Ridge. "The rest of the week."

Well, that didn't seem too bad. "How high will I bounce?"

"Not high," said Ridge. "Just enough to propel you onto the next cushion."

"What if there is someone already sitting on the next cushion?" If I was going to accept this consequence, I didn't want any surprises.

"Then you will land in their lap," my genie answered. He pointed to my hourglass watch, where most of the sand had already slipped away. "Do you accept?"

I'll admit, I was relieved that the payment wasn't more severe. And, who knows, bouncing around on couch cushions might actually be kind of fun! I looked at the door, thought about my quest to save the world, and made a decision.

"Bazang."

My hourglass watch clicked out of sight and I stood on the slanted porch, grinning. The door to Thackary Anderthon's trailer home had vanished.

CHAPTER 6

I moved into the trailer, passing a ripped, overstuffed recliner, until I reached the middle of the room. There was garbage and junk scattered everywhere. The whole place was filled with an unpleasant smell. Wet dog, I think.

I glanced back at Ridge, who crinkled his nose as he stood in the open doorway. "We should get out of here," he said in a voice so soft it was barely audible.

"Why are we whispering?" I whispered back. Have you ever noticed that when one person starts to whisper, other people join in for no apparent reason? I certainly didn't see a reason for it. I had proven that no one was home when I knocked and kicked.

"I'm just saying, I don't want to be here if Thackary returns," said Ridge. "Need I remind you that the Universe said he is a very horrible kid?"

"Need I remind *you* that the Universe put me in charge of stopping him?" I said, picking up a towel and wiping the residual bird poop off my head. "I'd like to find out everything I can about this kid while we're in his home. Maybe even catch him if he decides to come back here."

If Thackary Anderthon was trying to open the Undiscovered Genie jar, then the only way I knew how to stop him was to capture him.

"Maybe I'll wish for a really big bird cage to put him in," I continued. "Or a human-size hamster ball. I'll lock him up for the week and that will complete my quest."

"That's a good idea," he said. "Hey, what are you doing?"

"Changing my shirt." I had found clothes draped over the ottoman. I carefully peeled off my filthy shirt and put on the new one. It probably belonged to Thackary Anderthon, and going by the size, the kid was just a little bit smaller than me. Still, wearing the bad guy's shirt was way better than wearing a poo-poo shirt.

"Much better," I commented. There were a few splotches on my pants, but my head and shirt had definitely taken the brunt of the attack.

A table in the corner of the room caught my attention. It was cluttered with objects but somehow seemed more purposeful than the rest of the dirty home. A few pencils, a pad of sticky notes, a black notebook, and half a dozen maps marked with thick pen.

"Someone was planning something." I shuffled through the maps. "A journey."

"How can you tell?" asked Ridge, finally venturing across the room to stand by my side.

"Isn't it obvious?" I pointed to the stuff on the table.

Ridge shrugged. "How do you know Thackary Anderthon isn't just a map collector?"

I would have told him how absurd that was if the bathroom door hadn't burst open at that very moment. Something darted toward us, a large gray mass of fur and snarling teeth.

It barreled into Ridge, sending him sprawling under the table with a scream. I leaped backward as the animal turned to face me.

It was a wolf.

There was an actual wolf in the Anderthons' trailer house. Much larger than any dog I'd ever seen, it had piercing green eyes and insanely long fangs.

You'd think it might be hard to get distracted if you're facing off with a wolf. However, something else caught my eye, entering the room. It was a girl, no more than my age, with long black hair spilling down her back. She might have looked intimidating if it weren't for the strange way she was moving.

The girl hopped forward as though her ankles were fused together. She held her hands tucked up close to her chest, and I couldn't help but think that she was acting like a bunny.

"Paradiddle, Vale!" the girl shouted, two words that meant absolutely nothing to me.

My attention immediately returned to the wolf, who made an almost instantaneous transformation into a redheaded girl, tackling me to the floor.

From under the table, I heard Ridge shouting advice. "Wish, Ace! Wish!"

That was a wonderful suggestion from the hiding genie. But my mind was suddenly blank on how to get out of this ambush. The redheaded girl had successfully pinned my arms and was reaching one hand toward my face.

"Don't let her cover your mouth, Ace!" More good advice from the cowering genie.

I looked up, desperate to escape my attacker. "I wish I was on the ceiling!" I shouted. Underneath me, I heard my hourglass watch click out. I couldn't see the timer, but I knew I had less than thirty seconds to accept before the girl covered my mouth.

"If you want to be on the ceiling," Ridge called, "then every time you open a door today, it'll fall off its hinges."

That sounded sort of dangerous. What if the door fell on me? Oh, well. In the moment, it seemed like the advantage of escaping to the ceiling was definitely worth the consequence of having a few doors fall apart.

"Bazang!"

The redheaded girl's hand closed over my mouth just as the Universe granted my wish. Immediately, I was whisked upward, slamming into the ceiling as though it were the floor.

The bad news was the redheaded girl didn't let go. Now I was in essentially the same situation I had been in on the floor. Only upside down.

I tried to shout another wish, but the feisty girl had an iron grip across my mouth, her legs wrapped tightly around me in a crushing vise.

Below me, on the floor, the girl with the black hair strode forward. She no longer hopped like a deranged bunny. Her step even seemed to have a bit of strut to it.

"Who are you?" asked the girl on the floor. I tried to answer, but I was bound and gagged by her partner.

"The genie is under the table," said the redhead.

Like a child who'd been found in hide-and-seek, Ridge quietly crawled into sight. "Oh, hello," he said, as though he'd just noticed their arrival.

"You're the genie?" asked the dark-haired girl.

Ridge nodded, and my captor laughed. "I can see why you have a hard time believing it. They both seem equally incompetent."

"Excuse me," Ridge replied to the insult. "We are on a quest to save the world, and I'd say we're doing a pretty good job of it so far."

"Umm," said the girl on the floor. "We just captured your Wishmaker."

"True," Ridge said, looking up at me. "Maybe the ceiling trick wasn't such a good idea."

I'll admit, it wasn't the best wish. I panicked in the moment. Don't tell me you could have thought of something better while getting pinned by a girl who used to be a wolf.

"What are you doing here?" asked the girl below.

I burned Ridge with my gaze, trying to tell him not to speak. We didn't need to give in to the demands of these bullies. Ridge must have interpreted my defiant expression as a cry of defeat, because he promptly told the girls everything they wanted to know.

"My name is Ridge. That's Ace." He pointed up at me. "We're tracking a kid named . . ." Ridge's eyes suddenly grew huge. He clapped his hands together. "You're Thackary Anderthon?!"

"What?" said the dark-haired girl, her face scrunching in confusion. "No. Who's Zackary Anderson?"

"Thackary Anderthon," Ridge corrected. "Hmm. If you're not Thackary, then what are you doing here?"

"Martina Gomez," the girl introduced herself. "Call me Tina. I was led here by a wish." She looked up at me. "I'm a Wishmaker, too."

I raised my eyebrows, hoping I would soon have the opportunity to speak for myself.

"Who is . . . Thackary?" Tina asked.

"A bad guy," answered Ridge. "There's an Undiscovered Genie out there. Thackary is searching for the jar, but it's our quest to stop him."

Tina furrowed her eyebrows. "Undiscovered Genie?" she said. "Tell me more."

"We don't know more. But the genie must be special," answered Ridge. "There's a pretty scary consequence if we fail. The Universe is counting on us."

"It's counting on me, too." Tina looked up at me and the redheaded girl who was working overtime as a human clamp. "You can let him go, Vale."

Vale (I gathered that was her name) took her hand away from my mouth and swung down my shoulders, dropping to the floor next to her Wishmaker.

Ridge looked upward. "Are you coming down, Ace?"

I smiled tightly, attempting to jump from the ceiling. Instead of falling down, I miraculously fell up, my feet contacting the ceiling once again. "Well, I'm trying."

Vale shook her head at my failure. I guess I'd have to wish myself down and accept another consequence.

"Hey, Ridge," I said. "I wish I could come down from the ceiling."

"Sorry, Ace," answered my genie. "You can't wish that."

"I thought you said I could wish for whatever I want!" Of course he was contradicting himself now that we had company.

"You can't unwish something you wished for earlier," Ridge said. "I should have mentioned that before."

"Yeah, you should have," I answered. "So now I'm stuck on the ceiling for the rest of my life?"

"Just this ceiling," Ridge replied. "Once we leave the trailer, you'll be able to come back to the ground."

Tina looked up at me thoughtfully. "When did you get your genie?"

"Today," I answered. "Around lunchtime."

"About the same time as me," she said. "And you have him for seven days?" I nodded. Tina's hopeful expression seemed to fall a little. "I was hoping your time might expire soon," she said to me.

"Why would you hope that?" I asked.

"Because then I could save your life," she answered.

"Save my life?" I said. "Didn't you just attack me?"

"We didn't mean you any harm," Vale said. "We had to pin you down to get some answers. In case you were dangerous."

"You don't live here, then?" Tina clarified.

"No way," I said. "This is Thackary Anderthon's house."

"Then he must be the ex-Wishmaker," Tina muttered.

"Ex-Wishmaker?"

"Yeah," said Tina, "somebody who had a genie in the past."

I shook my head. "Wait. You think Thackary had a genie once already?" I asked.

"The wish I made," she answered. "I wished to be led to the home of the nearest ex-Wishmaker. I ended up here, which means Thackary must have had a genie once before."

"And now he's going for the Undiscovered Genie so he can

keep wishing," Ridge surmised.

"But why are you looking for an ex-Wishmaker?"

"It's my quest," Tina replied. "I'm supposed to save the life of an ex-Wishmaker. Kind of hard to find someone if you don't know who they are."

"Tell me about it," I said. At least the Universe had given me a name.

"It seems like our quests are linked together." Ridge clapped his hands cheerfully.

I shot the genie a disapproving glance. We were trying to capture Thackary, not save his life. But Tina was nodding steadily.

"You said this Thackary kid was making plans?" she asked.

Above them all, I walked across the ceiling until I was standing over the table with the maps. I pointed down. "We think he's planning a trip," I said. "Must be to find the Undiscovered Genie."

Tina looked up at me. "Then maybe we should beat him there."

It was a good idea. If we raced Thackary to wherever he was going, we could be in position to catch him. And I could always lock him up if we got lucky enough to bump into him along the way.

I pointed down at the black notebook on the floor. It had

flown out of my grasp when a wolf had suddenly appeared out of the bathroom. "Can you pass me that?" I asked.

Tina picked up the notebook and handed it up to me. By this point, I wasn't feeling really great. After a few minutes, hanging upside down makes your head feel like it might explode. I opened the notebook, hoping to find some quick and useful information so we could get out of the Anderthons' trailer.

The pages were blank.

I thumbed through them twice, scanning every page for any sort of marking that might reveal Thackary's plan. I was about to give up when I noticed a few ripped edges tucked into the spine of the notebook. I ran my finger over them, counting how many pages had been torn out.

"There are four pages missing!" I shouted.

"That's great!" Ridge replied.

"Why is that great?" asked Tina.

"Those pages probably have Thackary's plans written all over them," I said.

"Or he likes to doodle," said Vale. "And he ripped out his favorite drawings to hang in his bedroom."

I had a feeling about those missing pages. "There has to be a way to find out." I took a deep breath. "Ridge," I said, "I wish to know what was written on the four missing pages of this notebook." For clarity, I held up the notebook. Technically, I held down the notebook, since I was still standing on the ceiling.

"Oh, that's a heavy one, I'm afraid," Ridge said as my hourglass watch popped out. "It'll last a year."

"What is it?" I urged.

"If you want to know what was written on those pages"—he took a deep breath—"then every time you make eye contact with a person, their house will burn down."

"Yikes!" I shouted. I debated it for a moment, wondering how often I actually made eye contact with people. Then I realized that being polite would turn me into an arsonist, and I simply couldn't do it.

"I can't accept," I said, feeling my watch snap back into place as the deal closed.

Vale shrugged. "Probably a waste anyway."

"I don't think so," I said. "If the pages were useless, why would the Universe give me such a heavy consequence?"

"Good point," Ridge backed me up. "I think you're onto something!"

"Now," I said, "I should get a less-severe consequence if I only wish for one of the pages. Right?"

Ridge grinned. "Probably."

I was determined not to give up on this empty notebook.

"I wish to know exactly what was on the first torn-out page of this notebook."

Again, my hourglass clicked out and Ridge explained the deal to me. "The Universe can give you the information on that first page," he said, "but in exchange, you won't be able to read for the rest of the week."

I exhaled sharply. "What about you?" I asked Ridge. "Do you know how to read?"

He clucked his tongue at me. "Of course I know how to read, Ace."

If the two of us were tethered together for the week, then I could always ask him to read for me. "What about writing? Will I still be able to write?"

"Strangely," Ridge said, "yes. You won't be able to read, but you'll still know how to write."

I glanced at my hourglass. Not much sand left. It was time to make a choice. Accept or decline? How much did I believe in those ripped-out pages?

"Bazang," I said. At once, my watch clicked away and, with it, my ability to read. In the same moment, my mind was flooded with new information. The Universe fulfilled my wish, telling me exactly what was on that first missing page of the notebook.

The knowledge deposit was over in a flash, my head

pounding from hanging upside down for so long.

"Well?" Tina asked.

I closed the empty notebook and looked down at the others.

"I got it," I said. "I know where Thackary is going."

CHAPTER 7

At last, I was standing on the ground again. It had been an awkward transition, passing through the doorway from the ceiling. It took Ridge, Tina, and Vale working together to put me right again, and they all stumbled down the trailer steps with me on their shoulders.

The muumuu neighbor had gone back inside her mobile home, so the four of us stood in the Anderthons' spotty yard, arguing.

"Just tell us what you learned about the missing page," Vale said.

"I'm not so sure I want to," I replied. I was feeling much more confident with my feet on the ground. "It's our quest to stop Thackary, but you two are trying to save his life."

"Well, you're not planning on killing him, are you?" Tina asked.

"Of course not!" I cried. Though that would surely stop him from opening the Undiscovered Genie jar.

"Then what does it hurt to let us come with you?" Tina pressed. "It's the best lead we have for our quest. And it's probably safer to go together."

Tina had a point. It might be useful to see how another Wishmaker navigated her wishes. "We've got a long ways to go," I said "Let's get started."

"A long ways?" Tina repeated.

"Yeah," I replied. "We won't be back for a couple days. Maybe longer."

Tina shifted uncomfortably. "Okay, but there's something I have to do before we leave."

"What?" I asked. Was there something more important than her quest?

Tina fidgeted under my stare. "Don't worry about it. Just something personal. I can meet you at the southeast edge of town in three hours. How about Dilly's Diner on Twelfth Street?"

I narrowed my eyes suspiciously at her. "Fine. Don't be late."

Without another word, Tina and Vale moved down the gravel road of the trailer park, leaving Ridge and me standing side by side. The girls were a mysterious team, and I felt lucky that wolf Vale hadn't eaten me when they first surprised us.

"Can you turn into a wolf?" I asked Ridge.

"I can do anything you wish for," he said.

I thought back to our encounter inside the trailer. "I never heard Tina wish it," I said. "She just said some funny word and Vale turned from a wolf into a girl."

"I don't know," Ridge said. "I've never encountered anything like that."

I took a deep breath. "Do you trust them?"

"No reason not to, so far," Ridge said.

"But they're being all secretive," I said.

"They're girls."

"Where do you think they're going?" Tina and Vale had moved out of sight now, and the most brilliant plan came to me. "Let's follow them." I bent my knees and leaped forward, sprawling clumsily on the patchy dry grass.

"Are you okay?" Ridge shouted, rushing to help me up.

"What happened to flying?" I dusted myself off.

"You didn't wish for it."

"Oh, yes I did! I wished that I could to fly to Thackary Anderthon's house."

Ridge pointed back at the Anderthons' trailer, and I realized my mistake. The way I worded my wish meant that I could no longer fly now that I had reached Thackary's house.

"Hmm," I said. "Can I wish to fly again?" I hadn't really thought about asking for the same thing more than once. But it seemed a shame, since I had just cleaned myself of the bird droppings.

"You can," Ridge explained. "But the consequence will be different every time you ask."

"So I could just keep asking until I get a consequence that I like?"

"I don't think you'll like any of them," answered Ridge. "The Universe knows you. Even though the consequences will be different, they'll be equal disadvantages."

"So if I wish to fly again, it won't result in bird poop, but it'll be something that I hate just as much?"

"Probably," answered Ridge. "Though, between you and me, I'm hoping you wish for a mode of transportation that doesn't require me to travel in the jar."

Yeah, flying wasn't all it was cracked up to be. It was tiring, messy, and punished Ridge. I was sure I could think of something else. But in the meantime, we set out on foot, sneaking up to Tina and Vale and then keeping our distance as we tracked them along.

I thought back to the trailer, when my quick wish had landed me on the ceiling. I needed to be prepared to make better wishes.

"Is there any wish you can't fulfill?" I asked Ridge as we walked.

"Well, you already know that I can't let you unwish a wish," he said. "And I can't let you wish to remove a consequence. Other than that, I think you're free to ask for anything."

"What about knowledge?" I asked. "If I wish for it, the Universe can tell me anything I want to know, right?"

"As long as you accept the consequence," Ridge said. "What do you need to know?"

The moment didn't seem right, walking down an unknown street at the edge of town. But I knew I had to ask him sooner or later. Wasn't that the reason I had accepted the Universe's quest? I mean, sure, I wanted to prevent the zombie pet apocalypse, but that wasn't what had spurred me to follow Ridge out the door of the Lindons' home.

Ridge was a genie. He could give me unlimited wishes. He could answer a question that had burned in my mind for as long as I could remember.

So why was it so hard to make the wish? Why couldn't I ask him where I came from? Who my parents were, and why I had ended up so alone?

We'd been following Tina and Vale for nearly an hour, when they arrived at their destination.

St. Mercy's Hospital.

I froze. My hand strayed into my pocket and I flicked my thumbnail across the edge of the tattered card I always carried.

"You all right?" Ridge asked me.

I looked at him. The Universe would be able to tell me.

All I had to do was ask Ridge. But part of me was too afraid. Afraid to find out my past. I pulled my hand out of my pocket. "I'm fine," I said. Taking a deep breath, I followed Tina and Vale through the front doors.

I hadn't been to this hospital before, but they all seemed so alike. Same colors, same smells, same clothing. I thought back to when I had first awakened in that hospital bed. It had been over three years ago. And I was just as confused as I was back then.

Tina paused at the stairs, conversing with a uniformed security guard. We hung back until the guard stepped aside and let the girls go up the stairs.

"Why would they come here?" Ridge asked.

"Let's find out," I said, moving across the lobby.

The same security guard stopped us at the bottom of the stairs. But he didn't seem so friendly now.

"Visiting hours are over, boys," he said.

"What about those girls?" I pressed.

"She has special arrangements with the patient in room 214," answered the guard. "You two can come back in the morning."

"Special arrangements," I muttered as Ridge and I walked back outside. A moment later, we stood awkwardly on the sidewalk in front of the hospital.

"You could always wish to get in," Ridge suggested.

"Yeah," I said. "And accept another dumb consequence?" I looked at the hospital, trying to decide how badly I wanted to spy on Tina. I had the perfect wish. Might as well see what it would cost me. "I wish to be invisible."

"Forever?" Ridge asked.

"What? No!" I answered. "Just for the next ten minutes or so. Enough to get past that security guard."

Ridge nodded in understanding as my watch clicked open. "If you want to become invisible," said Ridge, "then all your clothes will remain invisible for a day."

"Ahh!" I cried, stepping behind a shrub in case my clothes suddenly vanished. "That's terrible! What if I put on new clothes?"

Ridge shrugged. "They will also disappear."

There was no way I could accept. We were supposed to team up with Tina and Vale soon. Face it, you wouldn't accept that crazy deal, either.

"No way," I said, feeling my hourglass watch close. I stepped out from behind the shrub. "These consequences are impossible!"

"Remember what I said about making direct wishes?" Ridge said. "You always wish big, so the consequence usually seems too steep. If you walk into that hospital and turn invisible, then the wish did all the work for you. I guess what I'm saying is . . . think smaller."

"Think smaller. . . ." I repeated, a grin spreading across my face. "I wish I could be three inches tall until I get to room 214."

My hourglass popped up again, and Ridge was nodding his approval at my wish. "If you want to shrink down," he explained, "then every time you exit a bathroom, you'll have toilet paper stuck to your shoe for an hour."

Well, that would be embarrassing. "Just my shoe?" I asked. "What if I'm barefoot?"

"Bare feet count, too," said Ridge.

"How much toilet paper?" I asked. If it was just half a square, nobody might notice. Then again, if it was an entire roll dragging around, then it could be a major tripping hazard.

"About fourteen inches," Ridge answered, holding up his hands to show me the length.

"That's manageable," I said. "How long will this go on?"

"The rest of the week," Ridge said. "Once the quest ends, your shoes will be toilet paper free."

I could handle that. It would be worth a bit of embarrassment for the week so I could snoop on Tina's secret.

"Bazang." I said the magic word. And just like that, I was three inches tall.

CHAPTER 8

The world looks very different when you're the size of a mouse. The sidewalk sprawled before me like a parking lot, and the hospital loomed at such a height that I could barely see the top. It was going to take a long time to walk anywhere, since my legs were now half the length of toothpicks.

I turned to look at Ridge and found myself staring at a ginormous shoe, the white sole nearly coming to my waist. I guess I had foolishly assumed that Ridge would also shrink with me. Obviously, he had remained regular size, which was humongous to me.

"I guess I'll have to put you in the jar!" I shouted. My voice must have been too faint for Ridge to hear. He dropped to his knees on the sidewalk, his head bending low until we were nearly at the same level.

"Whoa!" I shouted, surprised by the massive size of the face before me. "I think I could crawl into your nostril!"

"Why would you do that?" Ridge whispered, but his voice was still plenty loud.

"I don't want to," I said. "I was just pointing out that your nose is huge."

"My nose is the same size it's always been," Ridge said. "You're just really tiny now."

I shrugged at him. "I'll have to put you in the jar to get past the security guard," I repeated. "But you should get me as close to the stairs as you can so I don't have so far to walk."

Ridge reached out, tucking his thumb under one of my arms and his index finger under the other. With a gentle squeeze, he lifted me off the sidewalk. I clung to his hand as Ridge took a few steps and passed through the automatic hospital doors.

Once inside, he found the corner of the lobby and took a knee, depositing me behind a fake potted plant.

I dug into my backpack and pulled out the empty peanut butter jar. "Ridge," I said, holding out the container, "get into the jar."

I was grateful that the Universe shielded us from suspicion, because Ridge instantly turned into a puff of dark smoke and got sucked into the minuscule jar in my raised hand.

I took a deep breath and focused on the giant stairs across the lobby. The security guard who had stopped us earlier wouldn't be much of a threat since I could slip past him unnoticed. But there was definitely no way for me to climb the stairs at my current height.

"Are we there yet?" Ridge asked, like an annoying child on a road trip.

I didn't have the heart to tell him that I hadn't even moved. "It takes a long time to get around when you're barely bigger than a Lego figure," I said, dropping the jar into my overstuffed backpack.

Nearby, a man was talking with someone at the front desk. His laptop bag was on the floor by his feet, and I decided this was my chance.

"Here we go!" I whispered, more to encourage myself than

to inform Ridge of my plan. I sprinted toward the man, my tiny heart racing in my miniaturized chest.

I reached my ride and skidded to a halt. The laptop bag was a mountain of thick black cloth. Above my head, I saw a pocket where I could easily stow away, but reaching it was going to be a challenge.

Jumping as high as I could, I caught the zipper and pulled myself up. Dangling precariously, I swung one leg toward the empty pocket. I probably would have been able to successfully slip inside, if the man hadn't picked up his bag in that very moment.

There was a jolt as the handles went tight. I toppled backward, barely catching the zipper pull as the floor fell away beneath me. I hung there, both of my hands gripping the loop at the end of the zipper tab.

With every step the man took, I thought I might shake loose. The floor seemed like it was fifty feet below me and the tiles were a blur as my carrier walked briskly toward the stairs.

"What's going on?" Ridge's muffled voice called from the jar in my backpack. "I don't know how much longer I can stand this."

My carrier man took the stairs two at a time, looping his laptop bag over one shoulder and increasing the distance between me and the floor.

I hoisted myself up, putting my leg through the loop at the end of the zipper tab and bracing as I pulled Ridge's jar from my backpack.

We reached the second floor and the man strode down the hallway like he was in a hurry. I saw room numbers, but they just looked like gibberish squiggles, since I couldn't read. I needed Ridge to have a look around.

"We're riding in a laptop bag," I said into the jar. It was one of those sentences I never imagined myself saying. "We've got to get down, but it's too high to jump. I'm going to pull you out of the jar when I jump, and I need you to catch me before I hit the floor."

I hoped Ridge would answer with something like, "Of course. Sounds easy. I'm an excellent catch."

Instead, he simply said, "I'm so itchy!"

I pulled my foot up to brace against the zipper, readied myself, and leaped from the man's laptop bag. As I plummeted toward the hallway tiles, I squeaked out the command.

"Ridge! Get out of the jar!"

With a puff of black smoke, the genie appeared. But not exactly how I thought he would. Maybe it was because I was holding the jar sideways that Ridge landed on his shoulders, skidding to a halt against the wall.

My flight path landed me right in his mass of curly hair. I

suppose it was still better than splatting on the floor, but the impact knocked the breath right out of my lungs.

Ridge leaped to his feet. I held on for dear life, grabbing two fistfuls of hair like horse reins. "We have to get to room 214!"

"Ace?" Ridge said, wandering down the hallway. "Where are you? I hear your voice, but I can't see you." He spun around in a dizzying circle. "I'm sorry I didn't catch you. Are you a ghost now?"

"I'm in your hair!" I shouted, sitting down right atop Ridge's head.

That's when I got big again.

Ridge crumpled to the floor with a surprised yelp as I slid down in a heap beside him.

"There you are!" he exclaimed. "This is room 214." He pointed to the door in front of us.

"Shhh!" I hissed, holding a finger to my lips. If Tina was inside that room, I didn't want her knowing that Ridge and I were sneaking around out here.

We rose to our knees, positioned with our ears to the door.

"What're they doing in there?" It really bothered me that Tina hadn't told me her reason for coming here.

I glanced at Ridge. "I wish I could hear through this door."

I was aware of my hourglass watch opening up, but I didn't

even look at it. Instead, I kept my focus on Ridge.

"If you want to hear through this hospital door," he explained, "then the next time you plug your ears, your fingers will get stuck in them."

"Seriously?" I whispered. "For how long?"

"Only half an hour."

"Only," I hissed. Did I really want to run around with my fingers in my ears for thirty minutes? That depended on how badly I wanted to know what Tina was talking about behind that door. To get this far, I'd already accepted a week of toilet paper stuck to my shoe.

I grunted. "I guess I'll take it. . . . Bazang."

Suddenly, I could hear everything going on inside the room as though the door were wide open. There was a soft humming, punctuated with an occasional beep from some machines. The gentle rustle of blankets on a bed. And then I heard Tina's voice as clearly as though she were talking to me. There was only one problem.

Tina was speaking Spanish.

"What's she saying?" Ridge asked. "Who's she talking to?"

What a waste of a wish! Hearing through the door was useless if I couldn't understand what they were saying!

"No comprehendo," I said to Ridge. "Tina's speaking Spanish." Then I heard a woman's voice reply in the same language.

What if the stranger and Tina were making nefarious plans to turn against me? "I wish I could understand Spanish." It seemed like my best option.

"Well, if you want to know Spanish," said Ridge, "then you'll only be able to speak French for the rest of the week."

"Do you speak French?" I asked.

"*Sí, señor,*" he answered.

"I'm pretty sure that was Spanish," I pointed out.

"Hmm," said Ridge. "Then, nope. I guess I don't speak French."

"But you speak Spanish?" I was rather impressed.

"*Uno, dos, tres, cuatro, cinco, seis.*" Ridge paused. "That's all I've got."

I was less impressed.

"Well?" Ridge gestured to my hourglass. "Are you going to take the consequence?"

Something told me that would be a bad idea. Stopping Thackary was probably going to be hard enough even with Ridge and me speaking the same language.

"I don't accept," I said, my shoulders sagging slightly in defeat. "Maybe if I just take a peek inside . . ." I reached out slowly and gripped the door handle. If I just cracked it open, I'd at least be able to get a glimpse of Tina's mysterious meeting.

I pushed the door inward, just enough to see Tina and Vale

standing at the foot of a hospital bed. I got a clear glimpse of the patient, too. I didn't know what sort of illness she had, but the Hispanic woman looked like she was in pain. Even breathing caused her face to wince from the discomfort.

She had a dozen tubes draped around her, an oxygen mask on her face. Her hair was matted back, and her ear . . . I squinted to make sure I was seeing it correctly. The woman's ear looked like it was attached upside down.

Tina didn't seem to notice my intrusion, so I risked pushing the door open just a little farther to see if anyone else was in there.

And then the door came off its hinges and crashed to the floor with a deafening bang.

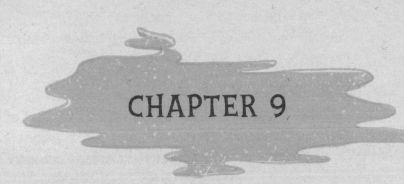

CHAPTER 9

I was just grateful that the heavy door didn't crush anyone when it came off its hinges. You see, I had sort of forgotten about that consequence. So Ridge and I did the sensible thing as soon as the door fell down.

We ran.

Of course Tina spotted us, and by the time we got outside, she and Vale had caught up.

"You followed me?" Tina shouted. "I can't believe you two!"

"It was Ace's idea," Ridge said.

I shot him a glare and tried to explain to the girls. "I had to see what you were up to. For all I know, you could be secretly working with Thackary Anderthon." I glanced back at the hospital. "Who was that woman you were talking to?"

Tina took a couple of deep breaths. When she spoke, it didn't answer my question at all. "We're basically down to six days now. If we want to complete our quests, then we'd better get moving!" She set off at a brisk pace in the opposite direction from the hospital, Vale jogging to stay close.

"Hey!" I shouted. "Where are you going?"

"You tell me," Tina called back. "You're the one with all the information on how to find Thackary."

I sighed, moving hastily to catch up to her. Arguing and distrusting was going to make for a long quest. As I moved, I swung my backpack around and pulled out a couple of sand-wiches. If Tina was as hungry as I was, then maybe she'd take this as a peace offering.

I handed one to Ridge and extended two others to Tina and Vale. "You want a sandwich?" I asked. "I have plenty." To prove my point, I pulled open my backpack so they could see how stuffed it was.

"What's with the sandwiches?" Vale asked, taking one.

I shrugged, shouldering my backpack. "I like peanut butter. Is that a crime?" I didn't feel like explaining how my first wish had been for something so ridiculous. I peeled back the plastic bag and took a bite.

"Mmm . . ." Ridge muttered behind me. "These are good!"

Tina glanced at me from the side of her eyes, and then snatched the sandwich that I still held out for her.

"Who'd have thought . . ." I said with a chuckle, trying

desperately for conversation. "Peanut butter . . ." I took another bite. "Was Vale's creamy or chunky?"

"Hey!" Vale cut in. "You calling me chunky?"

"No," I stammered. "I mean the jar."

"What are you talking about?" Tina finally said through a mouthful.

I fumbled in my backpack once more, producing Ridge's jar for her inspection. "Didn't Vale come out of one of these?"

Tina reached into her pocket and withdrew a small object. It was a little jar of lip balm, raspberry flavored. The lid was missing, but the red balm didn't appear to smudge onto anything.

"This is Vale's genie jar."

I felt a tiny pang of jealousy. Not that I wanted to carry around a jar of raspberry lip balm, but look at that size! It was a fraction of the peanut butter jar I had to lug around.

"But . . ." I stammered. "Your lips are chapped."

"Really?" Tina smirked and tucked the jar back into her pocket. "We should talk about where we're going. What did you learn from that page of the notebook?"

"I learned that we've got a long ways to go," I said. "Anybody been to Mount Rushmore?"

Tina shook her head. "Have you?" she asked me.

"Not that I remember," I said, giving my standard reply. I knew I hadn't been to Mount Rushmore in the last three years.

But before that . . . I really had no idea what I'd done. It was frustrating to have a blank memory.

"What about you two?" I asked Ridge and Vale. She took a bite of sandwich and kept walking.

"Mount Rushmore," Ridge said. "That's the one with the big faces carved in the mountainside, right?"

"Yeah," I said. "Four presidents of the United States."

"Ever wonder what happened to the rest of their bodies?" Ridge asked. "I mean, it's kind of freaky that it's just a bunch of floating heads."

"How are we going to get there?" Tina asked. "Mount Rushmore's in South Dakota. That's way too far to walk."

"We'll have to wish for something," I said.

"Ugh," Tina grunted. "I figured out within the first hour that it's better to do as little wishing as possible. I can't deal with these consequences."

"You seem to be doing fine," I said, polishing off my sandwich and stuffing the empty bag into my pocket. "What have you got so far?"

Tina shot me a disapproving glance. "Seems kind of impolite to ask another person about her consequences."

"Sorry," I replied. But my apology seemed to spur Tina into telling me anyway.

"Next time I eat ice cream, it'll taste like olives. One of my fingernails can't be trimmed for a year, and I can't tell blue

70

from orange for the rest of the week."

"So the sky looks orange to you?" I asked. Not at that moment, of course—it was practically dark.

She nodded. "It's weird."

I couldn't help but chuckle at Tina's misfortune. "What did you wish for?"

"Lots of things," she answered thoughtfully. "But there were only a few that I could accept."

"I know what you mean."

Tina looked at me and conspicuously wiped her cheek. She kept staring, persistently scraping at a spot next to her mouth. "You've got some leftovers," she finally said.

My hand shot up to my face, only to encounter the everlasting smudge of peanut butter. "That's a flavor saver," I said.

"Gross," she replied, but it got her to smile.

"You think your consequences are bad," said Vale, "you should hear about some of my previous Wishmakers."

"I bet you've got a lot of stories," Tina said.

Vale nodded. "I once had a Wishmaker who grew an upside-down mustache for a year."

"What's an upside-down mustache?" I asked.

"You know, the hair grows up instead of down."

"That would be awful," I said, unconsciously scratching my upper lip.

"Yeah." Vale took the last bite of her sandwich. "She hated it."

"How many Wishmakers have you had?" I asked the question to both genies, but only Vale responded.

"Too many."

"Do most of them succeed at their quests?" I asked.

"Most," she answered. That was reassuring, at least. Odds were in our favor.

I turned to Tina. "You never told me your quest's consequence," I said. "You're supposed to save the life of an ex-Wishmaker, but what happens if you don't?"

"Bad stuff," she answered. "Basically, the end of the world."

"Hey, me, too!" I said it like we had the same pair of shoes, not like we were talking about the world ending.

"If I don't succeed," said Tina, "the whole world will be flooded with lemonade."

"I happen to like lemonade," I said.

Tina gave me a deadpan look. "Not if it causes the end of the world. Floods can destroy huge cities. Not to mention that lemonade is acidic. Nothing will survive for long."

She had a good point. I never would have thought the world could end by lemonade.

"If I don't stop Thackary Anderthon," I said, "then all the cats and dogs in the world will turn into zombies and eat everyone. You have any pets?"

"I had a poodle," she replied.

"Undead poodle," I said. "Sounds ferocious."

Tina laughed. For that brief second, whatever worries she carried seemed to melt away.

"A world-ending consequence isn't very common," Vale said. "Wishmakers often have consequences that would cause earthquakes, start wars, wreck economies, destroy chocolate . . ."

Tina and I gave her a puzzled look. "I'm serious," she said. "I once had a Wishmaker who had seven days to pick a leaf from a very old tree in Patagonia. If he failed, chocolate would go extinct."

"Hmmm," I said in mock thought. "No more chocolate"—I held up my hands as if weighing the consequences—"versus zombie pets destroying humanity."

"Don't downplay it, Ace," Ridge cut in. "Imagine a world without chocolate!" He said it with a hint of desperation in his voice.

"Imagine a world without people!" I replied, reminding him what was expected of Tina and me. It didn't seem fair that the Universe had put that kind of responsibility on us. I guess I should have read the fine print on the genie jar's warning label.

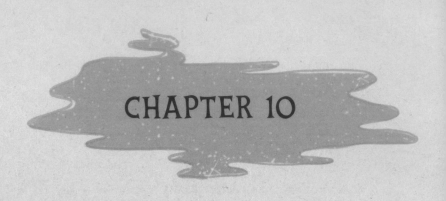

CHAPTER 10

We slept in a barn. A ray of sunlight pierced through the slats in the wall and woke me up. I sat forward abruptly, confused about where I was and what I was doing. Then it all came flooding back to me.

I had a genie. I was on a quest to save mankind.

I looked around for Ridge. He was still asleep in the corner of the barn, curled up around a barrel. It seemed odd that genies needed sleep the same way we did. More and more, I was realizing that Ridge seemed like an ordinary kid. He didn't know everything; he got blisters; and as I learned the night before when we crept into the stranger's barn, he was sort of afraid of the dark.

I spotted Tina sitting on an overturned bucket, her face toward the open door. I wondered when she had finally drifted off to sleep the previous night and how long she had been awake that morning. She seemed troubled.

There was something about Tina that I couldn't grasp. I had a lot of questions for her, starting with the woman in the hospital bed. But so far, Tina didn't seem interested in answering them. I'd have to get to know her, break down her defensive barrier. After all, if you were going on an impromptu road trip with someone to save the world, wouldn't you want to know them better?

I approached her in time to see her tinkering with the watch on her wrist. It looked nearly identical to mine. My approach must have startled her, because Tina quickly lowered her hand as though trying to hide what she'd been doing.

Her behavior caused me to turn to my own hourglass watch. I ran my thumb around the leather band, but there was no clasp. How was I supposed to take the thing off? Using my fingers, I tried to slide it over my hand.

"You can't take it off," Tina said, watching me. "That's what I was just trying."

"I guess the Universe wants us to have a fair amount of time to think about each consequence," I said, giving up on the watch.

Tina raised her eyebrows. "Not much of what the Universe does seems fair."

I thought about stepping outside and catching some fresh

air, but I didn't know how far that would put me from Ridge. I glanced back at him. Snapping the tether would be a very rude awakening.

"Have you snapped your tether yet?" I asked. Tina shook her head. "It's painful. I'd recommend staying close to Vale for the next six days."

"Six days," Tina repeated. I hoped that was enough time to complete our quests.

"How do you think it will happen?" I asked. "When our time runs out, all the pets instantly start devouring people? One minute we're walking along, and the next minute we're over our heads in lemonade?"

"The consequence might not happen immediately," Vale said, causing me to turn. I hadn't realized she was listening to our conversation. "It's not like the Universe wants it to happen. It'll be a result of someone's choice."

"My choice?" I asked. I didn't see how failing to stop Thackary would result in zombie pets.

"Think of the bigger picture," Vale continued. "If this Thackary person opens the Undiscovered Genie jar, he'll have wishes. Maybe one of those wishes will be to transform all pets into zombies."

I stood up, sighing. It didn't seem fair that my big consequence could happen as a result of someone else's choice. But then, I agreed with Tina that nothing about the Universe's methods seemed fair.

Tina glanced over at Vale. "Time's ticking. We should get moving."

I awakened Ridge, and the four of us ate a breakfast of peanut butter sandwiches from the backpacks. I could tell the day was going to be a hot one, and I was already thirsty. I was just about to wish for something to drink when Tina unzipped a backpack and handed me a bottle of cold water.

"Where'd you get the backpack?" I was pretty sure she hadn't had one yesterday.

"Wished for it this morning," Tina replied. "Full of water bottles, but it doesn't get too heavy."

She was a smart one. I probably wouldn't have thought about the weight of carrying water bottles around. I twisted off the lid and took a long drink.

"That's why we're a team, right?" Tina continued. "To share the load. I figured, you've got the sandwiches, so we should get the drinks."

"What was your consequence?" I asked.

Tina grunted. "Next time I touch someone's hand, our fingers will lock together for five minutes."

I quickly tucked my hands into my pockets. Magically holding hands with Tina would be plenty awkward.

"How are we going to get to Mount Rushmore?" Ridge asked.

I still hadn't told anyone about what Thackary was planning to do once he arrived there. His notebook had given me details, but I didn't want to share them with Tina. If she was going to keep secrets about the woman in the hospital, then I'd keep my own secrets.

"We could fly," Tina suggested.

Ridge and I both groaned.

"I tried that already," I explained. "Flying is a lot harder than it sounds."

"And may I suggest a method of transportation that doesn't require Vale and me to get stuffed into our jars?" added Ridge.

"That's a good point," said Tina. "There are two of us Wishmakers now." She looked at me. "If we take turns wishing for transportation that can accommodate all four of us, then we'll only need to make half as many wishes."

"And that means half as many consequences," I said, feeling enthusiastic about Tina's approach.

The four of us stood in awkward silence until Tina finally said, "You go first, Ace."

I took a step back. "No way! I got us sandwiches."

"And I got us water," Tina rebutted. "And technically, you wished for the sandwiches before we even met, so that doesn't count. Either way, it's your turn."

"I don't like the idea of taking turns," I replied. "Wishing for a supply of water had nothing to do with our quests. Wishing for transportation to catch Thackary will probably have a more serious consequence."

"Then I don't see how we're supposed to work together," Tina said. "If you won't wish, then we'll have to get to Mount Rushmore the old-fashioned way." She turned abruptly, moving out of the barn with Vale behind her.

I gave Ridge a puzzled look. "What's the old-fashioned way?"

CHAPTER 11

Walking.

Walking was what Tina considered the old-fashioned way of getting places. The four of us reached the interstate pretty quickly on foot. It was midmorning by now, and the summer heat seemed to be increasing with every step.

Cars whizzed by at high speed, not even slowing to acknowledge our ragtag group. Tina and Vale led the way, with Ridge and me following a few yards behind. Neither pair spoke to the other out of a stubborn determination not to be the next Wishmaker to wish.

After a long stretch in the blazing sunlight, Vale suddenly stopped under the shade of a scrubby tree. She turned around and threw her hands in the air, red hair sweaty and plastered on her forehead.

"You have the power of the Universe at your fingertips, and

we're walking!" Vale shouted. She looked at Tina, and then at me. "Would one of you please make a wish?"

As Ridge and I drew into the shade beside the girls, I could see that Tina's resolve was weakening. I completely understood her desire to avoid a consequence, but wasn't walking in the summer heat a consequence of its own?

"Rock, paper, scissors," I said to Tina.

"What?" she asked, wiping a bit of sweat from her face.

"Let's play rock, paper, scissors," I said. "The loser has to make a wish that'll help us get to Mount Rushmore."

Tina squinted out across the highway, apparently deep in thought. "Yeah, all right," she finally said. Tina held out her right fist, ready to compete for the wish.

"Best out of three?" I asked.

"Waste of time," Tina said. "First round wins."

Tina was smart and she didn't mess around. I studied her sweaty face, wondering if she was the type to play scissors or a rock. For some reason she didn't seem like a paper person to me.

"Rock, paper, scissors," I said, the two of us shaking our fists and displaying our choice on the third count. My hand was out flat, and my decision to play paper paid off.

Tina's fist was a rock. I held up my paper hand, a victorious smile tugging at my lips. Tina stepped back, scuffing the ground with her foot.

"That's never made sense," Ridge said.

"I beat Tina's rock," I replied.

"With paper?" Ridge asked. "How does paper beat a rock?"

"Paper covers rock," I answered.

"But a rock could easily rip through paper," Ridge said, "even if it was covered."

I scratched my head. "It's not supposed to make sense," I said. "It's just a game." I turned back to Tina, shrugging good-naturedly. "And I won."

Tina was biting her cheek in thought. I was anxious to see how she would handle the wish. On one hand, she could wish for something big and magical—a hover car or a giant eagle to carry us to our destination. But that was likely to have a fairly steep consequence, putting us back on Thackary's trail without any effort on our part. Ridge had said that a less direct wish would typically result in an easier consequence.

"I wish," Tina began, "that the next car to pass us will blow out a tire."

"Umm," I cut in, as the hourglass watch opened on her wrist. "Are you sure that's a good wish?" It made no sense to me. If we wanted a car to take us somewhere, it would need four tires.

"All right," said Vale, ignoring my concerns. "If you want the next passing car to lose a tire, then every time you sit down, you'll scream."

"How long will this go on?" Tina asked.

"Just until the end of the week."

"Will I constantly scream?" Tina asked. "Or just let out one little shout?"

"One short scream," answered Vale.

"How loud will I scream?"

"That's hard to describe," Vale said. "About like this." She gave a little shriek. It wasn't a full-volume bloodcurdling scream, but it certainly wasn't very quiet.

"What if I don't want to?" Tina asked. "Or if I forget?"

"The Universe won't let you miss it," answered Vale. "It will be a reaction. Like sneezing."

Tina was getting into the details, which I could appreciate, but her hourglass was nearly out of time!

"What do you decide?" Vale asked.

I don't know why Ridge thought it was a good idea to cut in with a scenario for Tina to consider. Her time was already short. "What if you get kidnapped, and someone comes to rescue you? The only way to get out is to sit down on the ground and slide through a laundry chute. But when you sit down to escape, the consequence makes you scream and the bad guy comes in and stops you."

"What are you talking about?" I asked.

"I just want her to think through all the possibilities," Ridge said. "Sometimes a consequence doesn't seem so bad at the time you accept it. Then later, you regret not thinking it through."

"You don't *think it through* when I make a wish," I pointed out.

"There usually isn't time," said Ridge. "We're under a very strict deadline before the deal expires."

"So is Tina," I said. "She doesn't get extra time to make her wishes." I paused. "Does she . . . ?"

I turned to ask Tina how long her white hourglass timer was, but in that precise moment, there was a loud bang, a screeching of tires, and a clunky blue Oldsmobile veered off to the side of the interstate. Its tire had blown to shreds, and the driver looked a mix of angry and surprised as he limped the vehicle to a stop just fifty yards ahead of where we stood.

"Our ride's here," Tina said, gesturing to the old Oldsmobile. She must have accepted the consequence while Ridge and I were debating. "And, no," she added. "I don't get extra time."

CHAPTER 12

The four of us jogged to the crippled Oldsmobile, while other vehicles continued to zoom by on the westward interstate.

"Now what?" I asked Tina. "You got a car to stop, but it only has three tires. That's not going to get us to Mount Rushmore very fast."

"It'll have a spare," Tina said. "Cars always have spare tires. We'll help put it on, and in exchange for our good deed, the nice driver will give us a ride west."

It would have been a good plan, but we quickly learned that the driver was not nice. Nor did he have a spare tire. Nor was he interested in giving us a ride anywhere.

"Ahoy, ye little scallywags!" shouted the man, as soon as we drew close. He was standing beside the blown-out tire, one hand on his bony hip, the other tracing through his stringy hair. His pants were a bit too short, his shirt a bit too long, and the expression on his face a bit too ornery. And for the life of me, I couldn't understand why the man was talking like a pirate.

"It be yer fault fer standin' around on the highway like vultures! Ye be causing me to swerve and wreck me tires." The man was ranting, his angular face sneering at the four of us. "Look what ye've done to me carrrrr!"

Looking through the back window of the car, I saw a kid in the passenger seat. He looked a little younger than me—maybe ten or eleven.

"I'm sorry, sir," Tina began. "We'd be happy to help you put on the spare."

"There be no more spares in this here vessel!" shouted the driver. "The tire that blew? That was the spare!"

I sighed. Tina had gotten us into a mess by making a tricky wish. Now she would scream whenever she sat down, and it would be for nothing, since the angry driver couldn't take us anywhere.

I quietly backed up until I was right beside my genie. "Ridge," I whispered. "I wish I had a spare tire for this car."

My hourglass watch clicked out, and I casually held it behind my back to conceal it from the man, although Ridge had explained that the Universe would shield our magic from suspicion.

"You can have the tire," said Ridge, "but for the rest of the week, you'll have to salute every time you see a white car."

"Salute?" I asked.

In response, Ridge clicked his feet together and raised a stiff hand to his eyebrow in a classic military salute.

"What if I forget to do that?" I asked.

"You won't," he answered. "It'll be like Tina's scream. If you accept the consequence, the Universe will make sure you salute. You won't even be able to control it. It'll be a reflex."

I nodded to show I understood. Saluting white cars wouldn't be too bad. I was about to accept the consequence when Ridge decided to add a little hypothetical situation.

"What if you find yourself dangling from a branch over a pool of alligators in the jungle. One arm is broken, but the other is clinging for dear life. Then a white car drives by, and the Universe forces you to salute, causing you to fall to your death."

"There are so many things wrong with that example, I don't even know where to begin," I said. "Why would there be a branch dangling over a pool of alligators? And how could a white car drive by if I'm in the middle of the jungle?"

Ridge shrugged. "I'm just talking it through with you. Isn't that what you wanted?"

I took a quick peek at my hourglass and barely hissed out, "Bazang!" before the sands expired.

Instantly, I felt a huge weight fill my backpack. Such a large weight that I was thrown backward and pinned to the ground.

My backpack also ripped, and smashed peanut butter sandwiches flew everywhere.

"Why did the spare tire appear in my backpack?" I asked,
slipping out of the straps and leaving my ruined pack in the
roadside dirt.

Ridge shrugged. "You should probably be glad it didn't
show up in your pocket."

A short distance away, Tina was arguing loudly with the
angry driver, and I saw the boy inside the car watching with
intensity.

"I only offered to help," Tina was saying. "You don't have to
be so rude about it!"

"Yar!" cried the stranger. "When I was a lad I spoke with
respect to me superiors! Yer motley crew can walk to the grave
and I'd sing a serenade as ye go!"

"Excuse me," I said, walking over to them. But the heated
argument would not be so easily interrupted.

"Looks like you'll be walking with us!" Tina retorted. She
pointed inside the car. "What kind of father drives his kid clear
out here without a spare tire for emergencies?"

"Don't ye be speakin' to me son!" said the driver, putting
his hand over the window to block the boy's view. "We be two
birds of a feather."

"Excuse me!" I shouted, stepping between Tina and the
pirate speaker. "I happen to have a spare tire."

"You do?" Tina asked.

"Ye do?" asked the man.

I pointed to my ripped backpack in the dirt, surrounded by peanut butter sandwiches. "It would be crazy to leave home without one," I said. Ridge was pulling the spare out of the pack and trying to tip it upright with all his strength. "We'd be happy to put it on your car, if you could give us a lift."

The strange man paused in thought for a moment. "Where be ye headed?"

"Mount Rushmore," I said, pointing west. "Or as far as you'll take us."

"A popular destination," answered the man. "Ye have yerself a deal."

I looked back at Ridge, who had finally managed to tip up the tire, only to have it roll down the roadside. Luckily, Vale moved in, halting the runaway spare with her foot.

It would have been easier if Tina or I had wished the tire on, but we were being stubborn again, both feeling like our latest consequences were in vain.

If you had been the driver, you would have been grateful for our help. You might have even thought we were guardian angels, waiting on the roadside with a perfect spare tire in a backpack, ready to install it and send you on your way. You certainly would have helped us install the tire.

But not this guy. He stood by, arms folded, and watched

four kids figure out how to install a spare tire. My skin crawled under his stare. It was almost like his eyeballs could shoot little invisible darts that made me feel worthless.

Twice during the gritty work, I stopped to salute a passing white car. It was the strangest sensation to lose control over my body. Just as Ridge had described it, the gesture was completely automatic. One moment, I was down on my knees in the gravel, the next moment, I was leaping up, my heels clicking together and my hand jetting up to my brow.

"That should do it," said Tina, stepping back from the tire. Her hands were completely black and her face was smudged from where she'd brushed at the sweat.

I looked up, hoping to finally get the thanks and acknowledgment we deserved for our good service. The man was nowhere in sight. I glanced into the car and saw the back of his greasy head just settling into the driver's seat.

With a few cranks, the car turned on. I reached for the handle on the back door, but before my fingers made contact, the man sped away, his new tire kicking up rocks and dirt on us.

I heard him laugh as he merged onto the freeway. His window was down and he reached out one bony arm, shaking his fist as he taunted. "Yar! That'll teach ye! The world is full of suckerfish! Maybe next time ye won't be one!"

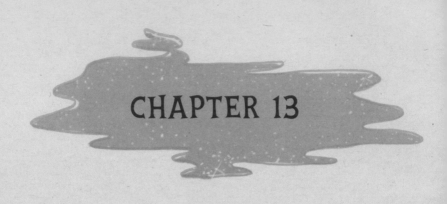

CHAPTER 13

We got to Mount Rushmore. Eventually.

Tina must have felt responsible for the way things went down with the pirate man, because after another hour of walking, she wished for a nice old granny to pick us up on the interstate. I thought she got off easy, the Universe's consequence causing Tina's socks to turn to dust.

I wished for a new backpack, for which I sang "Twinkle, Twinkle, Little Star" for a half hour straight. I think that kind of annoyed the granny who was driving.

She drove us west for several hours and dropped us off in a town I'd never heard of. From there, we used some money Tina had to catch a bus up north until we reached the national tourist destination.

"I can't believe that guy," Ridge muttered as we got off the bus. It didn't matter that it was now late in the night, and our exchange with the roadside pirate had happened almost twelve hours earlier. The insult still felt fresh and we were all feeling a little upset about it.

The moon was full, the night was warm, and there were hardly any tourists hanging around the park so late. The four of us strolled through the front entrance and down a walkway lined with flags until we stood at a big open terrace, where we got our first view of the famous mountain sculpture.

"Hmm," I said. "It's smaller than I imagined." Far out in the distance, the stone faces of George Washington, Thomas Jefferson, Theodore Roosevelt, and Abraham Lincoln were brightly illuminated by powerful unseen lights.

"It only looks small because we're far away," Tina said. "If we get closer, they'll be like giants." She turned to me. "What's next, Ace?"

Another reason that I hadn't mentioned more than our destination was because the instructions on the missing page of the notebook seemed absolutely bizarre. I wanted to make sure that Tina was committed to our quests before I explained the craziness.

"Here's what the page said," I began. "'The Undiscovered Genie jar is hidden in a cave. To reach it, you will need to pass through certain tasks. Completing each task will enable you to receive a key to enter the Cave of the Undiscovered Genie.'"

I paused.

"Is that it?" Tina asked.

"There's more. This next part is where it starts getting weird." I began to quote again. "'The first task will take place at Mount Rushmore, in the Black Hills of South Dakota. Using your hand, you must poke Theodore Roosevelt in the right eye.'"

The others waited for me to go on, but this time I was finished. There wasn't a lot of information. We'd just have to trust that the Universe had revealed the right thing. No matter how strange it seemed to poke a statue in the eye.

"Okay," Tina said, glancing toward the distantly illuminated stone faces. "So Thackary Anderthon is going to try to climb the face?"

"Unless he already did," I pointed out. "We have no way of knowing what kind of head start he had."

"We're too far behind," Ridge said, seating himself upon the low stone wall of the terrace.

"It's a waste of time sitting around here and hoping he shows up," I said. "If Thackary is ahead of us, then our best chance at stopping him might be to beat him to the cave."

"You think we should go ahead and do the task?" Tina said. "Climb up there and poke Roosevelt's eye?"

"It's the smartest move," I said. "And if we happen to run into Thackary tonight, we can nab him and sit on him for the rest of the week." How was that for a pep talk? "But Tina and

94

I should definitely poke the president's eye so we can complete the task. Otherwise we won't qualify for the key when we get to the Cave of the Undiscovered Genie."

The others were nodding their approval, which made me feel very smart for coming up with a good plan.

"Let's head over to the faces," Vale said. "They're shutting off the lights in fifteen minutes."

"How do you know everything?" Ridge asked, shaking his head in amazement at her.

Vale gestured over her shoulder. "It's not a mystery. I read the sign when we came in."

"Not all of us can read," I pointed out, as Tina led the way off the illuminated terrace.

We passed an amphitheater and stepped onto a boardwalk that led down into the trees. Even though I couldn't read, I'd seen a diagram on a sign that showed how the boardwalk would take tourists on a big loop, passing them just at the base of the sculpted mountain.

The four of us moved quickly and quietly into the dark tunnel of trees. Off both sides of the boardwalk, I could see that the terrain was littered with rocks of all sizes. The Universe would shield onlookers from strange, magical things. But if we didn't find a place to hide until the lights turned off, we'd look like four loitering delinquents.

"This is pretty exciting, don't you think?" Ridge suddenly asked at my side. "Sneaking around, saving the world . . ."

I grinned, glad that he was enjoying himself. Sure, he seemed a little clueless at times, but I was grateful that Ridge was an experienced genie. I didn't really know what we were getting ourselves into, so I'd be relying on him.

"You've got to admit," he continued, "this is probably the most exciting thing you've ever done."

Without knowing anything about my former life, I didn't know how to respond to Ridge. I stuck my hand into my pocket, flicking the edge of my card. I'd carried it with me for as long as I could remember. Maybe once we settled into our hiding place, I'd ask him my burning question. I could make the wish and finally get some answers.

"Here," said Tina, pointing off the side of the boardwalk. We were at a scenic point, at the very base of the big mountain carving. Far above, I saw the four famous faces, and I was surprised that tourists weren't allowed to get any closer. Between us and the giant heads was a sharply rising slope of loose stone chunks.

Tina vaulted over the railing, her feet crunching on the rocks as she picked her way over to a hefty boulder and small outcropping of trees. It was the perfect hiding place, allowing us to be concealed from the park rangers but stay in sight of Roosevelt's big face.

In a moment, all four of us were hunched among the fallen pieces of stone, waiting for the lights to go out so we could trespass in peace. Tina seemed careful not to sit down while we hid. I was glad she hadn't forgotten her consequence. Screaming would really blow our cover.

I glanced sideways at Tina and Vale. They were ruining the moment I thought I'd have to ask Ridge about my past. I didn't dare speak the wish in front of the girls. Learning that secret about myself was far too personal to spill in front of two people I barely knew.

The lights went out. It hadn't really occurred to me that we were hiding in a forest until it became completely dark. As far as I knew, I'd never been in a forest before. I only knew the orphanage, where they took me after I woke up in the hospital, and then two foster homes before the Lindons'.

There is something eerie about a forest at night. I decided to get a conversation going to distract myself from the rustling sounds that could possibly be bears coming to munch on us.

"What do you think is the best way to reach Roosevelt's eye?" I asked.

"It makes sense to come down from the top," said Tina. "We shouldn't have anyone trying to stop us."

"Unless Thackary's here," muttered Ridge.

"Still, he shouldn't be too hard to capture," I answered. "It's not like he's a Wishmaker."

"Hopefully, he's an ex-Wishmaker," Tina said, reminding us that she had a quest, too. In some ways it felt like we were working against each other. I was spending all my time thinking about how to stop Thackary. Tina was spending all her time thinking about how to save him.

"Enough talk," said Vale. "Let's go."

The redheaded genie was right. We had waited long enough. I stood up, peering across the slope of loose rocks toward the carved faces. I was about to say something inspiring when the boulder we were hiding behind suddenly attacked us.

CHAPTER 14

You might be wondering how a rock attacks on its own. I was also unclear on this. But I got a quick and very surprising education.

Several of the smaller rocks around us flew into the air, attaching themselves to the sides of the large boulder like arms. Then the rockman simply reached out and grabbed Ridge around the waist.

Ridge let out a squeal of alarm, as the boulder lifted him right over my head. So I did what any sensible Wishmaker would do.

I kicked the rock.

You've kicked a rock before, right? The only thing it does is hurt your toes. I don't recommend it.

Luckily, Vale responded quickly, leaping up and grabbing Ridge's ankles. The rockman must not have had a very tight grip on Ridge, because he pulled free and went tumbling to the ground with Vale.

"We've got to get to Roosevelt's eye!" I said, stumbling backward as I helped Ridge to his feet.

"That might not be so easy," Tina said, pointing toward the presidential faces.

The entire rocky slope seemed to be coming alive! The chunks of stone were fusing together and forming into creatures with legs and arms made of clustered rocks and pebbles. "Let's split up," said Tina, ducking as the rockman swiped for her. "Vale and I will go straight up the slope. You and Ridge try to circle around to the top of the mountain."

I looked up, seeing George Washington's forehead glimmering in the moonlight. Looping around was a good idea, but I wasn't sure about splitting up.

"Paradiddle!" Tina suddenly shouted as a second rockman swept down on us. Vale came bounding out of my peripheral vision, but she had somehow transformed into that huge gray wolf, just as she'd been when we first met.

Wolf Vale slammed into the rockman, slowing it down enough for her Wishmaker to hop away. And I mean hop. Like a bunny.

Tina's hands were tucked up next to her chest, her ankles seemed fused together, and she hopped carefully behind a tree. "Go!" Tina shouted back at us.

I think Ridge was just as surprised as I was. It was the second time I'd seen Vale transform without an official wish.

Another rockman came rumbling in behind me and Ridge. I whirled around, ducking as its stone arm swept over my head.

I looked at Ridge. Then, just to see if anything awesome would happen, I shouted, "Paradiddle!" I really had no idea what it meant; I was simply copying Tina and hoping that my genie turned into a fearsome animal.

He didn't.

Instead, Ridge screamed like a baby, jumping aside as the rockman pulverized the ground between us.

Wolf Vale was snarling and trying to bite the leg of a nearby rockman that was advancing on Tina. Biting rocks is very bad for your teeth. Don't try it.

"This way!" I shouted to Ridge. Pulling tight the straps of my new backpack, I leaped over the railing and back onto the boardwalk.

Ridge and I were sprinting along, minding our own business. He was about twenty feet behind me, when the boardwalk splintered into fragments between us.

"Ace!" I heard him call. I screeched to a halt, turning to see a tall pile of rocks looming over Ridge. The creature reared back and pounded its fist against the remaining bits of boardwalk.

"Ridge!" I shouted, dropping to my knees on the broken

planks. My backpack slipped off and my hand plunged inside to grab the peanut butter jar. "Get into the jar!"

There was a puff of dark smoke, and he disappeared. A fraction of a second later, the rockman destroyed the bit of the boardwalk where Ridge had been standing.

"Thanks, Ace!" Ridge shouted from inside his peanut butter jar. "I think you should have wished to stop that guy."

"There wasn't time," I said. "I had to get you out of there." Seriously? He was complaining? I had just saved his life!

"Come on," Ridge's voice moaned. "You know how itchy it is in here. Actually, no, you don't. Maybe if you did, you wouldn't be so quick to bottle me up."

The sound of our voices caused the rockman to reel around, two pebbles staring at me like beady eyes.

I didn't stick around to say hello. At a full sprint, I took off down the boardwalk, running until the pathway began to turn. Then, vaulting over the railing, I cut through the trees, heading up the dark side of Mount Rushmore.

Apparently, the rocks hadn't come alive on this side of the mountain. I wondered how Tina was faring, taking the brunt of the assault while trying to make her way up the slope.

"Would it be okay if I came out now?" Ridge said. In the heat of my sprint, I had almost forgotten about him.

"Ridge, get out of the jar," I said, not even slowing down

as I darted up the craggy slope. The genie appeared behind me, quickly falling into a sprint when he saw how fast I was moving.

He caught up to me as I ducked under a tree branch. I handed him the peanut butter jar and he dropped it into my unzipped backpack without slowing.

"What are you going to do when we reach the top?" Ridge asked.

"Find Roosevelt's forehead and look over the edge," I said. The first task was to poke Roosevelt in the eye. I wasn't sure how I'd reach it. Probably a wish.

The makeshift trail that I was blazing came to a sudden end far below the side of Abe Lincoln's head, where the untouched stone had never been carved. At least a hundred feet of vertical rock rose straight away from me.

"You have any experience with rock climbing?" I asked him.

Ridge reached back and rubbed his shoulder as if it were suddenly stiff. "I'm not supposed to put too much strain on my deltiscus."

"Your what?" I asked.

"My . . . deltiscus," he said. "It's a muscle in the shoulder. I'm surprised you haven't heard of it."

"I haven't heard of it because you just made it up." I grabbed a handhold in the rock and started to boost myself up. "Besides,"

I continued, "aren't you a little young to have a shoulder injury?"

"Shoulder injuries can happen at any age," he defended. "They're not just for old people."

I wasn't getting any higher. The rock face was surprisingly smooth and my arms were surprisingly shaky from the strain of holding myself up for just a few seconds. To add further to the situation, the rock people had sniffed us out. I could hear several of them advancing up the slope toward us.

I let go of the rock and jumped down to land beside Ridge. "I need to wish something," I said. He nodded encouragingly. Ridge always seemed a little more enthusiastic about wishing than I did. I'm not sure if my wishes gave him a sense of importance, or if he secretly enjoyed watching me pay the consequences.

"I wish I had a jet pack!" Out snapped my white-sand hourglass, thirty seconds spilling fast. Ridge clapped his hands together in excitement.

"Nice! If you want a jet pack," he said, "then every time you say hello, the sleeves of your shirt will grow an inch."

I looked down at my T-shirt, the one I'd borrowed from the Anderthons' trailer. It was a little small anyway.

"Just this shirt?" I asked. "What if I change?"

Ridge shook his head. "Any shirt you wear for the rest of the week."

"Is it specific to the word *hello*?" I asked. "What if I say *hi*, or *hey*, or *'sup*?"

"Just *hello*," Ridge said.

I could hear the enemies grating closer. *Hello* was so formal. I hardly ever said it anyway. And I'd rather have long sleeves than get smashed by rock dudes.

I nodded. "Bazang."

A sudden weight landed on my shoulders. Glancing behind me, I saw a silver canister glinting in the moonlight. The jet pack was probably smashing all the sandwiches in my backpack, but I didn't care. I looked awesome!

"Hello, jet pack!" I said. Instantly, I felt my sleeves grow an inch. Seriously? How had I already forgotten that? I had literally accepted that consequence five seconds before!

"Let's get out of here!" Ridge shouted, drawing my attention back to the approaching rock figures.

"Right!" I reached back and tapped the jet pack. Now, if I could only figure out how to turn the thing on. . . . "Uh, Ridge. Do you see a switch or something back there?"

"I see *lots* of switches!" he yelled as one of the rockmen hurled a stone. It missed us both, but shattered against the face of the cliff. "You're telling me you don't know how to use this?"

"Well, you could have at least given me a user's manual or a YouTube video or something!" I replied.

"I didn't pick the jet pack, Ace," Ridge said.

"I know, I know . . . The Universe did." I needed to remember to make my wishes more specific. What good was a jet pack if I couldn't make it work?

The first rockman reached us, swinging a massive fist. I ducked in the nick of time. In this new, hunched position, I saw a cord dangling from the bottom of the pack.

"Aha! Hold on, Ridge!" I shouted, grabbing the cord and giving it a sharp downward tug. The jet pack began to rattle and hum, but it didn't take off. Ridge had taken my advice and was kneeling on the ground, both arms clutched tightly around my legs.

The rockman circled in for another attack. I tried to lunge backward, but Ridge held me fast, causing me to topple. The jet pack crashed against the face of the cliff, but that seemed to do the trick.

In a flash, Ridge and I were rocketing into the night sky like a pair of out-of-control acrobats. In the takeoff blast, two of the rockmen were blown to bits, and the others jumped after us hopelessly.

The two of us streamed upward, Ridge swinging from my feet like a kite tail. It seemed like our flight had just begun when the jet pack began to sputter. A cloud of smoke puffed out by my left ear, and the whole device seemed to be getting hotter.

I scrambled with the straps. I had to get this thing off! Had we reached the top of the mountain? Just barely, it seemed, as I leaned forward, angling our flight to attempt a landing.

The two of us thumped down on the stone mountaintop, and I managed to slip free of the jet pack. It soared off on its own, some eighty feet higher, before it exploded like a firework.

I was feeling quite patriotic, standing on Mount Rushmore and watching fireworks—especially since we hadn't just died. We were high up, the dark sky stretching out all around us.

"Well," Ridge said, dusting himself off. "That could have gone better."

He was still gasping for breath at our near-death experience. That made me wonder. Could genies die? I'd have to remember to ask him later, when we weren't so worried about rockmen smashing us to pieces. I could hear their grinding movements far below, but they didn't seem able to climb the cliff. We'd lost them for the time being.

Ridge and I moved off in the direction of the carved faces. The rock was smooth underfoot, worn by countless years of wind and rain. We'd gone only a few steps when I realized that we'd need to scramble down a sizable boulder.

I sat down, carefully scooting forward. My backpack dragged awkwardly on the rock and I didn't want it to snag. Sliding the straps off my shoulders, I tossed it to the carved landing below and eased my way down after it.

I landed hard but didn't fall. I scooped up my bag and checked to see if Ridge needed some help, but he waved me on.

By my estimate, I was now standing on Abe Lincoln's head. Roosevelt was the next face. I peered over the edge of Lincoln's stylish hairdo. The slope below was still abuzz with rock figures, and I didn't see Tina or Vale anywhere.

But I could hear a strange voice. I couldn't make out exactly what it was saying, but the tone was unlike anything I'd heard before. I knew it didn't belong to either of the girls. It sounded . . . not quite human.

"Are we there yet?" Ridge asked, warily coming up beside me. If I had to guess, the genie wasn't as comfortable with heights as I was.

"Close," I answered, ignoring the unintelligible voice from below.

We picked our way carefully across the carved head, keeping an eye out for Tina and Vale below. In fact, our attention was so focused downward that by the time we reached Roosevelt's head, we had completely failed to see the people behind us.

"Why are you following us?" asked a voice from behind. I startled, whirling around so sharply that I nearly toppled off the edge.

There was a boy standing in the moonlight. He looked just a year or two younger than me, with slicked blond hair and a black leather jacket. I didn't know if he was trying to look cool, but the effect was ruined by the fact that he was wearing hugely oversize shoes with yellow smiley faces on them. He held something in one outstretched hand. I squinted to see it clearly in the darkness. A pickle jar?

"Scree," the boy said. "Get out of the jar."

There was a sudden puff of dark smoke and a girl appeared beside the boy, poised like she was ready for a fight. She was taller than him, and going by her thick dark hair and tanned face, I guessed she was Polynesian.

Who was I kidding? The girl obviously wasn't from Polynesia. She was from a jar! And that meant that the boy we were looking at was a Wishmaker!

The pieces fell into place. This was Thackary Anderthon. It had to be! He knew we were following him. Tina had been wrong. He wasn't an ex-Wishmaker yet. He had a genie, and he was using her to get to the cave and find another jar before his time ran out.

"That's him," Ridge whispered at my elbow. We had found the boy we were looking for.

"Hello at last," I said, and promptly felt my sleeves grow another inch. Ah. I forgot about that one again.

"Why are you following us?" the boy asked again, more urgent this time.

"Ridge," I said, trying to think up some great wish that would put Thackary Anderthon into captivity.

I probably would have said something brilliant if another voice from the cliff's edge hadn't distracted me. I whirled back around. All this whirling around was making me dizzy. And you don't want to get dizzy when you're on top of a mountain.

"Don't talk to 'em, son!" This time it was a familiar voice, and it made my blood boil. "Arrg! We done what we came here to do. Now it be time to set sail."

It was the pirate man from the interstate! As I saw him now, he was just climbing over the edge of Roosevelt's hairline. He stood, dusting off the knees of his black pants.

"You!" Ridge said, his face turning red.

"We meet again," said the pirate man.

"You won't get a hello from me," I said, and as I did, my sleeves continued to grow. They were now past my elbows.

Before I could react, the man reached out and snatched the backpack from my hand. I lunged for it, but he skirted around me. I was trying to think of something to wish, but now that the crucial moment had arrived, my mind seemed to go blank.

The man peered inside the backpack and gave a satisfactory grunt. "I should have known ye were a Wishmaker," he said, tossing the backpack to his son for further inspection.

At last, I thought of something useful. "I wish . . ." But I never got to complete that sentence. The moment I opened my mouth to speak, the pirate man reached out and pushed Ridge off the top of Lincoln's head.

CHAPTER 15

Ridge screamed. I panicked. And for a split second I had no idea what to do. If I made a wish, what were the chances that Ridge would even be able to explain the deal before he hit the ground? The bad guys had taken my backpack, and with it, the genie jar. There was only one possibility that might save his life.

The tether.

I sprinted as fast as I could, away from the edge of the cliff. I still had a vivid memory of snapping the tether in the Lindons' front yard. From what Ridge had explained, it would force both of us halfway back until we met at the central point.

That meant I had to be at least twenty-one feet from the edge of the cliff or else I would get pulled over, too.

Something hit me in the chest. It was like a punch that originated inside my body. At the same moment I felt the jarring pain, my legs were whisked out from under me and I was flung backward through the air like a puppet on a string.

Just when I thought I'd go flying off the cliff, wham! Ridge sailed upward and slammed into me with such force that we both flopped to the ground.

It worked!

The breath had been knocked from my lungs like a blow from a sledgehammer, and my head was throbbing from colliding with Ridge's bony shoulder. But it worked! The tether had snapped us both to the edge of the cliff.

Disentangling from Ridge, I clawed the ground, dragging myself away from the edge and gasping for air. I sucked in a breath, coughing. Ridge didn't seem to be doing much better, though the painful stunt had saved his life.

Someone grabbed my arm, helping me away from the dangerous drop-off. My vision was slightly blurred from the collision, but as it cleared, I saw Tina at my side.

"Thackary!" I gasped. My gaze darted around the top of the mount, but the boy, his genie, and the pirate man were nowhere to be seen.

"We've got to hurry," Tina said, hauling me up to my feet. "The rockmen are climbing."

"But Thackary was here!" I cried.

She glanced around and shrugged. "Well, he's gone now."

She pulled awkwardly at something around her neck. When I finally focused on her, I realized she was wearing a pink feather boa, wrapped around her neck like a scarf.

"Hey," I said, "what's up with the fancy boa?"

"Consequences happen," she snapped. "Now get down there and poke Roosevelt in the eye!"

"Aren't you coming with me?" I asked Tina.

"I already did it," she said, gesturing to her feather boa, as though it were evidence of the deed.

I stepped over to the edge and looked down. I couldn't simply go down it without some sort of magical help. The question was, what could I wish for that would yield me a manageable consequence?

"Anything you can do to speed things up?" Vale said, pointing across the mountaintop. The first of the rockmen were summiting George Washington's head. They'd be on us in moments.

I looked to Ridge for advice, but he was sitting far from the cliff's edge, his teeth chattering in shock.

"How far down to the eye?" I asked. "If I go over the edge alone, are we going to snap the tether again?"

Tina shook her head. "It's probably only twenty feet down to the eye."

"Okay," I said. "I wish I could walk down Roosevelt's stone face."

My hourglass watch clicked open and Ridge had to compose himself enough to fulfill his genie duties.

"If you want to be able to walk down Roosevelt's face," he said, "then your pants will be turned backward every time you put them on."

"All pants?" I asked. "Or just the ones I'm currently wearing?"

"All shorts and pants," Ridge said. "For the rest of the week."

"Take it," urged Tina. "Hurry up."

Of course she wanted me to take the deal. My backward pants would make her feather boa look normal. I glanced back at the approaching rock figures. If I didn't accept the consequence now, things would only get more complicated when the rockmen caught up.

"I'll take it," I said. "Bazang."

Poof. My pants were now backward and incredibly uncomfortable. The rear pockets of my jeans were now in the front, and the zipper was inconveniently on my backside. I looked down at my feet to see if I had suction cups on my shoes or something. But nothing seemed different.

"Let's do this," I said, taking a deep breath as I approached the edge.

"Watch out for the face," Tina said.

"Whose face?" I asked, pausing at the drop-off.

"Roosevelt's," said Tina. "I don't think he likes getting poked in the eye."

"Honestly, who does like getting poked in the eye?" Ridge asked.

But I had a more sensible comment. "He's a carving, guys. Carvings don't have feelings."

"Would you hurry up?" Vale urged.

The height was dizzying. I was putting a lot of trust in the wish as I took that first step downward. I felt my shoes suction firmly to the stone of Roosevelt's hairline. As I took another brave step, gravity seemed to shift. This actually wasn't so bad. In no time, I was standing comfortably on Roosevelt's forehead. I must have looked sideways, but I felt right side up.

"You almost there?" Ridge shouted from above. "Because the rockmen are nearly here!"

Now that I was just about in position, my mind was blanking. "Which eye was it?" I shouted.

"The right," answered Tina.

"My right?" I responded. "Or Roosevelt's right?"

"My right," Roosevelt said.

Yes. The giant stone face of Roosevelt was speaking. And now I identified it as the unnatural voice I had heard from atop the cliffs.

I gave a shriek. Roosevelt abruptly wrinkled his forehead, throwing me forward. I landed on the bridge of his nose, sliding down to the tip. My sweaty hands clutched the cold rock, and I barely got my feet under me.

"Young traveler," Roosevelt said, "I cannot let you touch my eye."

"It won't hurt!" I shouted. "I promise!"

"I am a guardian of the Ancient Consequence," he answered. "I feel no pain."

"See?" I muttered, even though I knew Ridge and Tina couldn't hear me. "I knew rocks didn't have feelings."

It would seem that Roosevelt didn't like my remark. He promptly pursed his lips, stone mustache bumping me at the end of his nose. I thought for sure I was about to get swallowed by a great American landmark. Instead, he began to blow.

For being only a head, this guy had some impressive lungs. His breath hit me like a windstorm, blasting me upward. I clung to the edge of his stone nostril, but my fingers were slipping. And apparently, Roosevelt didn't need to stop and inhale.

I quickly realized what the old president was trying to do. If I slipped, his hurricane breath would send me hurtling off the face and I'd plummet to the rockmen on the slope below.

"Ridge!" I screamed, desperate to make any kind of lifesaving wish. "I wish I could touch Roosevelt's right eye!"

I went for the direct wish—one that Roosevelt couldn't stop. There wasn't time to think of something more inventive. And I was pretty sure that whatever deal Ridge spelled out for me, I was going to accept.

"If you want to touch his eye," Ridge shouted from atop the

president's head, "then your right eye will turn yellow!"

"My eyeball is going to turn yellow?" I shrieked.

"Just accept it!" Tina's voice echoed down.

My hand began to slip. And in desperation, I shouted, "Bazang!"

I guess my eyeball changed color. Without a mirror, it was hard to tell. Luckily, it didn't affect my actual vision. It would have been pretty awful to see everything with a yellow haze.

On the plus side, my wish was answered. Roosevelt stopped blowing, and I suddenly felt myself propelled safely upward as though the Universe were giving me a huge boost. I was deposited on the lower eyelid, my hands finding a grip on the rim of the president's glasses.

I wasn't really sure about my eye-poking technique. In the end, I decided to poke it just like I would a real eye. I held out my index finger and jabbed it against the carved stone eyeball.

Nothing happened.

Except, of course, it hurt my finger. Part of me expected a secret chamber to open, displaying a magic key on a velvet pillow. But that's not what the notebook had said. The key would be presented at the cave, if I accomplished all the tasks.

"You have completed the first task," Roosevelt said. "My rock minions stand down. But you must not continue your quest," he warned. "The Undiscovered Genie has his eye set on dominion. He is stone cold, with powers great and terrible."

"If Thackary Anderthon continues," I said, "then so do I."

I stood up, my shoes adhering to Roosevelt's face as I jogged up his forehead and crested the president's hairline.

"I don't know what you did," called Ridge, "but the rocks are just rocks again."

On top of the mountain, I was surprised to see Tina and Ridge in the company of a large gray wolf. "Paradiddle," Tina said, resulting in Vale's instant transformation back into a human-looking girl.

"How do you—" I began to ask.

But Tina cut me off, pointing to the fresh piles of rock gathered around the top of the mountain. Those definitely hadn't been there when I'd gone over the edge. "The rockmen went lifeless," she said. "I'm guessing it's because you touched the eye."

"Roosevelt said the rockmen worked for him," I said. "They must have been trying to stop us from reaching his eye. But once we all completed the first task, he called them off."

"Good thing, too," Ridge said. "They were about to pulverize us."

I turned to Tina. "I didn't know Roosevelt would try to kill me. A warning would have been nice."

"I did warn you," Tina said. "Besides, the consequence wasn't that bad."

"Easy for you to say," I muttered. "Now I've got a creepy eye."

Tina stepped forward, tugging at her own eyelid. In the moonlight, I saw that the colorful part of her eye, which had previously been a dark brown, had also turned yellow. "It could have been a lot worse," she pointed out.

"You made the same wish as me?" I asked. "How long will it last?" I hadn't been able to ask for specifics while dangling like a booger from Roosevelt's nose.

"Well . . . forever," Tina muttered.

"Forever?" I shrieked.

"I'd rather have a yellow eye than get munched by Teddy Roosevelt," Tina justified.

"Did he say anything to you?" I asked.

Tina squinted in thought. "He said something about an Ancient Consequence. I didn't understand."

"Me neither," I admitted. "He said he was a guardian. And he warned me about the Undiscovered Genie."

"What did he say about it?" Tina asked.

"That he's powerful," I answered. Ridge could grant me any wish I wanted if I was willing to take the consequence. Could another genie really be *more* powerful than that?

"You said you saw Thackary?" Vale asked.

I nodded. "He was here. And he has a genie of his own."

"Then he's not an ex-Wishmaker," Tina muttered.

"Not yet," I answered. "Maybe his time is about to expire."

"I wonder if Thackary touched the eye," Ridge said.

"We saw someone climbing the faces," Tina said. "But it looked like an adult."

"Well, they must have succeeded at the first task," Vale added. "Otherwise they wouldn't have left."

"It was the pirate man from the interstate," I said with a groan. "And they stole my backpack!"

"So they got a bunch of peanut butter sandwiches," said Vale. "Big deal."

"I don't care about the sandwiches," I said. "Ridge's jar was in there, too!"

I saw Tina subconsciously reach down and touch her pocket, as if to reassure herself that Vale's lip balm jar was still in place.

"I really hate that guy," Ridge said, scuffing his shoe against the stone ground.

"Who is he, anyway?" Tina asked.

"He must be Thackary's dad," I answered. I'd heard the man refer to the boy as *son* twice.

"Poor kid," Ridge said. "No wonder the Universe described him as a very bad person. He has a horrible father for a role model."

"What do we do now?" I asked.

"We need to find out where Thackary is headed next,"

answered Tina. "We need to find out what was on the second ripped-out page of that notebook."

It took me a second to realize that everyone was staring at me. "What?" I said.

"We're just waiting for you," Ridge said.

"To do what?" I asked.

"You need to wish to learn the second page," he answered.

"Now, wait a minute," I said. "I'm not the only one here who can make wishes." I gestured toward Tina. "I thought we were in this together," I said to her. "I'm already illiterate from learning the first page. I think it's your turn."

Tina didn't seem too excited by the idea of playing fair. She put her hands on her hips in momentary thought. "Rock, paper, scissors?" she asked.

I remembered how I had squashed her last time we played. "Fine," I said. "But we're doing best out of three." She nodded and I prepared my fist to win.

I lost.

The first round, Tina crushed my scissors with her rock. The second round her scissors cut my paper.

I was pretty bummed, but I wasn't going to be a sore loser. I folded my arms and turned to Ridge. "All right, I'll make the wish," I said. "But let's do it in the morning. I want to get some sleep before we go after Thackary. What if the consequence makes it so that every time I lie down, I slide headfirst off the bed?"

"I don't think we'll be sleeping in beds tonight," Vale pointed out, brushing past me.

CHAPTER 16

Vale was right. There were no beds in the forest. We had to pick our way carefully down a crevasse in the back of Mount Rushmore before making our way several miles into the dark forest of the Black Hills.

I'm guessing it was way past midnight when we finally decided to stop for sleep. It was a good idea to put some distance between us and the national monument. I didn't know how the Universe's shield would explain the strange magical happenings at the park, but none of us wanted to stick around and find out.

Ridge and I found a comfortable spot below a pine tree where we could lie down without too many little rocks jabbing us in the back. Tina and Vale bedded down several yards away. They were close enough that I could shout for help, but not too close in case Tina snored.

Have you ever slept outside in the forest without a tent or a blanket? I didn't even have my backpack to use as a pillow anymore. I just couldn't get comfortable. And after several minutes of tossing and turning, I decided that my inability to sleep was also due to something that I couldn't get out of my mind.

"Ridge," I whispered, reaching over and poking him in the shoulder. "You awake?"

"I am now," he said.

"We could have died today," I said.

"Tell me about it," he answered. "You're not the one who got pushed off a cliff."

"I know. But we're tethered together, so I would have gone over with you," I said. "Can genies die?"

"Oh, yeah," he said, sitting up under the pine tree. "Just like you or Tina." He scratched a hand through his curly black hair.

"And it hurts to die?" I asked.

"Maybe?" he answered. "I've never done it before. This is kind of morbid, Ace. Are you all right?"

"Tomorrow probably isn't going to be any less dangerous," I said. "And there's something I have to know in case I don't make it through the week."

I sat up next to Ridge, reaching into my pocket for the only item that had ever truly been mine. It was a bit awkward to reach into a backward pocket, but in a moment I had retrieved my folded card.

"What's that?" he asked, seeing me flick the edge of the

card with my thumb—a nervous habit that had led to a worn and frayed spot.

"I don't remember anything about my family," I said.

"The Lindons?"

"Not my foster parents," I said. "My real family. My memories begin three years ago, when I was nine years old. I woke up in a hospital. The doctors said I just stumbled in. Nobody knew where I came from or what happened to me. Nobody knew who I was. Nobody knew my name."

"But . . ." Ridge stammered. "You're Ace."

I unfolded the small card and handed it to him. The moonlight glimmered on the glossy coating and Ridge held it close to his face for inspection.

"The ace of hearts," I said. "From a deck of playing cards." Ridge turned it over to look at the back, but I knew from countless hours of studying it that he wouldn't find anything. "That was the only thing I had with me when I came into the hospital."

"Ace," Ridge muttered.

"So," I began, taking a deep breath. "I guess what I want the Universe to tell me . . ." I started the sentence over, making it official. "I wish I knew my past."

At the sound of those magical words, my hourglass watch clicked open and Ridge took a deep breath.

"I had no idea," he said, still staring at the card I had handed him. "I'm sorry."

"Time's ticking," I replied, holding up my wrist so he could see the white sand spilling. "It took me two days to build up the courage to make this wish. Just tell me the consequence."

"You won't like it," Ridge said. "It seems the Universe holds that knowledge at a very high price."

"What is it?" My hands were sweating despite the coolness of the night. My throat felt tight.

"If you want to know about your past," said Ridge, "then every person who has ever seen you will cease to exist."

I felt my hopes leak out like air from a punctured balloon. I thought of all the people who had seen me in the last three years since my memories began. People at school. People around town. Thousands, if not more. "What will happen to them?" I asked.

"It'll be like they were never born," Ridge said. "Anyone who ever laid eyes on you will simply vanish. All traces of their lives will be erased. It won't change the past. What those people did will still have been done. But from this moment on, the world would go on without them. As though they never lived."

Tina, Vale, and Ridge had all seen me. If I accepted the consequence, I'd suddenly find myself alone in the forest of South Dakota. But Thackary Anderthon would also cease to exist. In a way, I would have completed my quest. But it wouldn't stop there. The Lindons and my previous foster parents would disappear. The unraveling would continue until there was no one left who knew me.

But I'd know my past. I'd know who my family was and where I came from.

I couldn't believe I was actually considering it. If the wish were anything else, I would have turned down the consequence the moment Ridge explained it. But this was the only thing I'd ever truly wanted in life. What was I willing to pay to know my past?

"Your time's almost up," Ridge said softly. Obviously, he didn't want me to take the consequence. Doing so would abruptly end his life.

My thirty seconds ran out, and I didn't answer. The little hourglass collapsed back into a shiny disk on my wrist and I slumped to the ground.

"I don't get it," I muttered. "Wishing to know my past doesn't have anything to do with stopping Thackary Anderthon. But that was the worst consequence yet!"

Ridge shrugged. "Maybe it is connected somehow. We just don't see it."

"What do you mean?"

"I don't know," he answered. "Maybe Thackary is your

brother, and that mean guy who talks like a pirate is your dad."

I shuddered. "That's a horrible thought."

"But knowing it would change the way you see the quest," answered Ridge. "If learning your past armed you with important quest-related knowledge, then it would make sense why the Universe would hold it at such a high price."

"I guess." It was frustrating. If a genie couldn't even help me, then how was I supposed to learn the truth? "Wouldn't they have recognized me?"

"Not if there was a wish in play," Ridge said.

"Or maybe they just pretended not to know me," I muttered. "Maybe they got rid of me and don't want me back." That was a depressing thought. In all the years I had imagined my family, I had never considered that they might not have wanted me.

"Hey, if those guys don't want you to be part of their family, it's probably because you're too nice," Ridge replied with a chuckle. But it didn't make me feel better. He fell quiet, then cleared his throat. "This is my first quest," Ridge said.

I turned my head to look at him, puzzled by this sudden admittance. "What?"

"You're my first Wishmaker," Ridge explained. "I'd never been out of the jar until you opened it." He sighed, as though glad to have the truth off his shoulders. "I don't really know what I'm doing."

I grinned. "I've noticed."

"I should have told you the truth before," he muttered, "but I didn't want you to think I was a bad genie."

I shook my head sympathetically. "So, why did you decide to tell me now?"

Ridge shrugged. "That wish you just made? I know it was hard for you to talk about your past." He reached out and handed me back my card. "It only seemed fair for me to tell you something that's hard for me to talk about."

I took the card from his hand, folding it along its familiar creases and tucking it into my backward pocket once more.

"I didn't want you to be disappointed," said Ridge. "I knew you were counting on me to get us through. But I don't actually have any past experience. The only stuff I know is what the Universe told me before the jar opened."

"But what about your name?" I asked. "I thought genies were named after the place where their jar was first discovered."

"Yeah," he said. "Ridge Lane. That's the address of your foster home. I saw it on an envelope when I first appeared."

Ridge Lane. The address didn't sound familiar, but that was because a consequence had forced me to forget it. "I thought you were named after a mountain ridge or something. Not some boring street in the suburbs." That seemed a little like cheating.

"Well, it could have been worse," Ridge said. "Technically, I should have named myself Kitchen."

We both laughed at that, and I settled my head back, looking up at the starry sky through interwoven branches. "We're quite a pair," I said. "A Wishmaker who doesn't know where he came from, and a brand-new genie who doesn't know what he's doing."

"We're alike, me and you," Ridge said. "Neither of us has a lot of memories to draw from. Maybe that's why the Universe put us together."

"Why?" I asked.

"So we could help each other forget about the past," said Ridge. "And move on to make our own future."

I didn't reply, partly because I didn't want to believe that my chance to learn about my past was over. Save the world from zombie pets, sure. That was a good thing. But the real reason I had gone with Ridge was to ask the question I had just asked. Now that I knew the consequence was too heavy to bear, I wondered what I had left.

Just a folded ace of hearts in my right pocket.

CHAPTER 17

Sleeping in the forest was not the way I liked to pass my nights. Sometime before dawn I woke up, freezing cold. I said hello a bunch of times, using that consequence to grow out my sleeves until they covered clear past my hands. I had hoped my newly grown shirt would be enough to warm me, but my teeth were still chattering.

So then I woke up Ridge and impulsively wished for a blanket. As a result, whenever I brushed my teeth, the toothpaste would taste like cauliflower. The consequence would only last the week, and I didn't imagine I'd have a lot of time for teeth brushing before the quest ended anyway.

I accepted the consequence, and I think secretly Ridge was grateful that the blanket was extra large so he could curl it around himself, too. By the time I was finally warm and somewhat comfortable, the sun was up and it was time to get moving.

I took a deep breath, stretched like a cat after napping, and stared off into the forest. Two days of my quest to save the world had passed. Five more to go.

"Did you make the wish yet?" Tina asked, coming over to check on us as she breakfasted on one of the peanut butter sandwiches from Ridge's backpack. I knew she was talking about the second missing page from Thackary's notebook. We were directionless without it, but I wasn't looking forward to discovering what kind of consequence I'd have to endure.

"I'm getting to it," I said, shrugging off my blanket and rolling up my extralong shirt sleeves. "I just want to be prepared for whatever the Universe is going to throw at me."

"I don't think any of us can ever truly be prepared," Tina said. "It's painfully random." She adjusted her feather boa. It looked matted and gross after a night in the forest, but I still felt like I had things worse.

I gave Tina a flat stare. "You got a fashion accessory," I said. "I forgot how to read." I waved her off. "Besides, your genie can transform into a wolf, so I don't know what you're complaining about."

"Yeah," Ridge cut in. "How does she do that?"

Tina shrugged like it was no big deal. "It was a wish," she said.

"But you didn't say it," I pressed. "I've seen Vale transform a couple of times and I've never actually heard you say the wish.

She just does it when you say that weird word."

"It's called a pay-as-you-play wish," Vale said, joining us with a sandwich of her own. "Ridge should tell you about those."

I looked at Ridge. Judging by the look on his face, he was just hearing about pay-as-you-play wishes for the first time, too.

"It works like this," Vale said, when it was apparent that Ridge wasn't going to explain it. "Sometimes you might want to wish for the same thing more than once. But when you're in the heat of the moment, you don't always have time to verbalize the wish and debate whether or not to accept a new consequence."

Tina stepped in to clarify. "So, I made a single wish that allows Vale to transform between human and wolf anytime I say a certain word."

"Paradiddle," I specified. "What does it mean?"

"It's the name of a drummer's rhythm," answered Tina.

"I didn't know rhythms had names," I said.

Tina nodded. "I took a year of percussion lessons. But it wasn't for me. Now that I quit, I'm pretty sure that's not a word I'll be using in normal conversation. I needed something that I wasn't going to say by accident."

"I get it," I said. "If you had picked 'and' as your trigger word, then Vale would have been transforming practically every time you spoke."

"Exactly," said Tina. "And while it's good to have her in wolf form for protection . . . it has an ongoing consequence. This is why it's called pay as you play."

"What's your consequence?" Ridge asked, but I had a feeling I already knew the answer.

"Every time Vale takes the wolf shape, I'm forced to hop around like a bunny."

"You should consider something like that," Vale said to me.

"Hopping like a bunny?" I asked. No thanks. I'd seen Tina do that a few times and she looked ridiculous and rather helpless.

"A pay-as-you-play wish," Vale clarified. "Pick an animal or some other form of protection that Ridge can become. Think of a trigger word, make the wish, and take the time you need to consider the consequence when it's not a crucial moment."

I glanced at Ridge, trying to imagine him as a grizzly bear or a lion. It was a stretch of the imagination, watching the skinny kid pick absently at a scab on his elbow. "Hmm," I mused. "I'll have to think about it."

"Not to pressure you, but the point is that you don't have to think about it," Tina said. "When those rock creatures attacked, I didn't have to make a wish, debate the consequence, and decide whether or not to accept it. That decision was already made. All I had to do was say the trigger word, and Vale sprang into action."

I liked the idea of a pay-as-you-play wish, but I didn't want to take another consequence right now. Especially when I was about to wish for something that the Universe considered highly important.

"While you're thinking about it," Tina said, "why don't you ask your genie what was on the second page of that notebook?"

I couldn't tell if she was just anxious to get on the road, or if she was gloating over the fact that she'd beaten me in rock, paper, scissors. Either way, I couldn't put it off any longer.

I turned to Ridge. "I wish I could know exactly what was written on the second page of that black notebook we found in the Anderthons' trailer."

"You got it," Ridge said, seeming pleased to be the middle-man between me and the Universe. I had some sympathy for the new genie since our conversation the night before. Understanding that I was his first Wishmaker made it clear why, frankly, he wasn't very good at genie-ing.

"If you want to know what was on that second page," said Ridge, "then your left arm will go missing for a day."

"Go missing?" I cried. "How does a person's arm go missing?"

"It's going to fall off," Ridge said. "But it'll be completely painless."

"Then how do I reattach it?" I asked, horrified by the thought of my arm dropping off.

"Oh, you'll just grow a new one in twenty-four hours."

"What if I don't like my new arm as much as I liked my old arm?" I asked. I couldn't believe I was actually having this conversation.

"It'll be identical," Ridge said. "You'll never know the difference."

"I think you should do it," Tina contributed.

Of course she did. It wasn't her arm that was about to fall off. I glanced down at my hourglass watch, strapped around my right wrist. Luckily, that wouldn't fall off with my arm.

"If you don't accept the consequence," Tina persisted, "then we're basically stuck out here."

It was time to make a choice. "Fine," I said, shooting a piercing glare at Tina. "I'll do this. But you're taking the consequence for the third page." She stared blankly at me and I knew my hourglass time was about to expire.

"Bazang," I said. There was a thud on the ground beside me. When I looked down, I saw that it was my arm.

The whole thing had come detached at the shoulder and dropped right out of my extralong sleeve! I was mortified by the sight of it, and for a moment I was seized with fear that the Universe could have lied, and my arm would never grow back.

At that same moment, my mind was flooded with the

knowledge of exactly what was written on the second torn-out page of the notebook.

All I had to do was open my mouth and the Universe practically spoke for me. "'The second task lies to the west, in the state of California. You must enter an amusement park known as Super-Fun-Happy Place and eat the green cotton candy, sold by a man with a pink mustache.'"

I paused, staring into the anxious faces of my three companions.

"And?" Tina prompted.

"That's all of it," I answered.

"We're just supposed to eat some green cotton candy at Super-Fun-Happy Place?" Ridge said. "That's weird."

"Weirder than poking a stone statue of President Roosevelt in the eye?" I reminded him. Nothing about this week was shaping up to be very normal. And, talk about weird . . . now I only had one arm!

We stood in a small circle, silently pondering the absurdity of our task. I'd never been to Super-Fun-Happy Place. At least, not in the last three years that I could remember. Kids were always raving about how fun the rides were, so maybe our trip there wouldn't be too bad.

Yeah, right.

CHAPTER 18

We were becoming expert hitchhikers. Once we finally staggered out of the forest and found the road, it took only a half hour before Tina made a wish for a nice mom to pick us up and take us farther west.

The consequence seemed small. For the rest of the week, anytime Tina took a drink of water, it would be warm. Not scalding, just unpleasantly warm in this July heat.

We must have seemed an odd quartet of passengers to the mom driving us. Tina screamed when she sat down, and I found myself saluting every white vehicle that we passed. Then there was my missing arm, freaky yellow eye, and backward pants. I probably looked like a zombie. Gratefully, the Universe shielded those unsightly consequences from suspicion, and the driver talked to us like we were on our way to soccer practice.

Just to be clear. You should never hitchhike. It's a risky and rather dangerous mode of transportation, and the only reason I even felt remotely safe doing it was because I was traveling with a genie who could grant my any wish.

By early afternoon we were on our own again. Tina hadn't been specific enough in her wish, and the driver suddenly seemed to realize that she had gone several hours past her exit. She dropped us in the middle of southwestern Wyoming—the middle of nowhere! So we decided to pause and have some lunch.

With one arm missing, I couldn't open the zipped bag without Ridge's help. His supply of sandwiches was dwindling, and I knew the four of us wouldn't make it to the end of the week unless we found my backpack.

The scenery here looked pretty bleak and barren, without even a spot of shade for us to eat our lunch. The landscape was so monotonous that I found myself getting excited to watch a freight train slowly approaching from behind us.

A white car drove past and I jumped up to give a swift salute, slamming my half-eaten peanut butter sandwich into my forehead. As soon as lunch was over, Tina or I would have to make a wish to get us on the road again. But I was dreading another consequence. What if my other arm fell off and I had to spend the rest of the day running around like a pencil with legs?

"Hey!" Tina stood up, her gaze directed over her shoulder to a car approaching from behind.

Her comment got my hopes up at first, like maybe someone

would pick us up without wishing for it. But I quickly realized that the vehicle speeding toward us had no intention of slowing down. The four of us were standing a safe distance off the highway, but the car was swerving like there was a first-time driver at the wheel.

Then I recognized the car.

"Hey!" It was my turn to shout. "That's the old Oldsmobile! That's Thackary Anderthon's car!"

I didn't know how we had possibly gotten ahead of Thackary and his dad. But there was no mistaking the vehicle. As it drew closer, I could see the pirate man in the driver's seat.

The Oldsmobile zoomed past us and the driver turned his head, the look of surprise on his face matching my own. In the passenger seat, I saw the boy we were after. He ran a hand through his slick blond hair, the collar of his black leather jacket turned up. I didn't spot his genie in the car, though if he was still a Wishmaker I knew she had to be within forty-two feet of him.

"We have to stop them!" I bellowed, breaking into a sprint, my single arm pumping for speed. But I knew my legs would never catch up to the speeding car. I opened my mouth to make a wish, but Tina beat me to it.

"I wish that Oldsmobile would run out of gas right now!" Tina yelled to her genie. I stopped running, turning back to hear what the consequence would be.

"If you want that car to run out of gas," answered Vale, "then every time you pass through a doorway for the next year, you have to say 'alley-oop.'"

"Bazang," said Tina, without even asking any further questions. Tina glanced at me, her face flushed from the intensity of decision-making. My attention turned up the highway to the Anderthon Oldsmobile.

"It didn't work!" Ridge shouted as the vehicle continued to move away from us.

I squinted. "It's coasting," I said. "But it's slowing down."

"I liked it better when the tire blew out," Ridge said. "Last time we didn't have so far to catch up."

The four of us ran along the roadside, anxious to reach the villains and make our long-awaited capture.

We were still forty or fifty yards away when the Oldsmobile veered suddenly, using its momentum to propel itself off the road. It went crashing down a dusty embankment and continued rolling through the desert landscape until it finally came to a halt in a cloud of dust and engine smoke.

I swerved down, making a straight run for the ruined car. The passenger door flew open and the boy stepped out, his black leather jacket zipped to his chin despite the hot afternoon. The boy's father also emerged, and when he turned, I saw that he was wearing my backpack!

The two of them left the car and took off running into the

desert. Ridge and I sprinted off the road toward them, while behind us Tina and Vale were running, too.

Basically, there was a lot of running.

I didn't know if the villainous duo had a plan. There really wasn't anywhere for them to go. Except—

"The train!" I shouted, frantically waving my one arm as I realized their plan. Cutting across the vast landscape, the freight train had finally reached us, chugging on its westward track just a hundred yards ahead.

Thackary and his dad reached the train. Sprinting alongside it, I could tell they were trying to find a way to leap aboard, but the locomotive was simply moving too fast. The man shouted something to his son. In response, the boy reached into the pocket of his leather jacket and withdrew a glass pickle jar. He must have ordered his genie out, because his words were followed by the sudden appearance of the Polynesian girl I'd seen atop Mount Rushmore.

Seeing her Wishmaker on the move, the genie girl broke into a sprint to keep up. Thackary shouted something back to her, but I couldn't make it out. It must not have taken long for him to accept the Universe's consequence, because the genie promptly disappeared and the boy slipped the pickle jar back into his pocket.

Instantly, the train began to slow. For a moment, I wondered if it might come to a halt, but that wouldn't make sense.

Would you make a wish that would stop your only means of escape?

The wish must have slowed the train just enough for Thackary and his dad to catch up. Now that it was moving at a more manageable rate, the man grasped a railing at the edge of a car and managed to hoist himself up. Bracing, he reached back and clasped hands with his son. The boy stumbled on his oversized smiley-face shoes, and I held my breath, but the man flung them both backward, pulling his son to safety on the train.

"They're getting away!" Ridge shouted. But I didn't feel like I needed to resort to wishing yet. This was a long train, and I was determined to climb aboard before it picked up full speed again.

Leaping through the sagebrush, I saw the final train car speeding along. I planned my route, picking a diagonal path across the desert that would get me to the train before the last car passed.

The huge metal wheels were thundering on the tracks and I could barely hear Ridge calling, "We're not going to make it!"

Tina had caught up to us, and her little lip balm jar was clutched in her hand. "Vale," she cried, "get into the jar!" In a cloud of smoke, the redheaded girl vanished and Tina leaped onto the ladder at the very end of the train.

"We're going to have to jump at the same time," I said to Ridge, noticing that the train was rapidly picking up speed again. Our window of opportunity was closing.

Tina, perched on the ladder of the last railway car, reached out her hand for me. Vale had reappeared at her Wishmaker's command. Now she was holding fast to the ladder beside Tina, leaning out and beckoning to Ridge.

"One, two," I counted, trying to prepare Ridge so we could leap together. "Three!"

We jumped. My one and only hand grasped Tina's and she jerked me up with as much force as she could muster. I slammed into the ladder. Unable to grip with only one arm, I dangled there, wondering how Tina managed to hold on to me.

My feet floundered underneath me for a moment, then they found the first rung of the ladder and I pushed up. Tina hauled me upward and together we spilled into the open-top railway car, an uncomfortable mound of coal beneath us.

Ridge was already there, grinning at me, Vale crouched behind him. Ridge's hands were shaking, and his face was smeared with soot from the coal. I sighed. The train was back up to full speed, the wheels thundering along the track.

I tried to pull away from Tina, but she just lay there, holding tightly to my hand, fingers interlocked with mine.

"You can let go of my hand now," I said.

Tina sat up, staring at me. "No, I can't." Before I could wonder at this sudden show of affection, she explained. "It's a consequence, remember? Our hands are stuck together for the next five minutes."

Well, this was going to be awkward. I only had one arm to start with. And now I was sitting in an open car of a freight train holding hands with Tina.

"We need to find Thackary," she said, ignoring our current situation. I didn't know what Tina planned to do with him, though. She didn't need to save Thackary's life until he became an ex-Wishmaker. Maybe she would help me capture him and wait until his genie time expired.

"With any luck," said Vale, "Thackary won't know we've gotten aboard. We might have the element of surprise. Let's go."

"Actually," I cut in, "we'll probably need to wait about five minutes. Tina and I . . ."

"Are you guys holding hands?" Vale asked.

I felt my face going red. "I can't let go of him," Tina said.

"How romantic," Ridge replied.

"It's not . . ." I trailed off with an annoyed grunt.

Thanks for embarrassing me, Universe.

CHAPTER 19

"How do we move to the front of the train?" Ridge asked, lying flat atop the load of coal. Tina and I had just released hands, after what seemed like forever. I don't know why people would ever choose to hold hands. It got all sweaty.

Ridge raised a good question. In the movies, people leaped from train car to train car as though they were on a walk in the park. Now that I was on the back of the speeding freight train, I had a feeling it might be a little more difficult than that.

"They're probably five cars ahead of us," I said. "At least." I tried to think back to where I had seen them climb aboard.

Tina lifted her head to examine the long train before us. Her black hair whipped wildly, but she didn't seem as frightened as I might have expected. Determined. That was how Tina looked with her face to the wind.

"We should be able to make our way up," she said. "Most of the rear cars are carrying coal like this one. If there's a ladder between each car, then we can try to get to the front without any unnecessary wishing."

I liked the idea of not collecting another consequence, but I was doubtful about my ability to climb forward on this speeding train with only one arm.

"Okay," I said. "But I might need some help."

"Don't worry," Ridge said, trying to suppress a smile. "I can give you a hand."

Ha.

Tina wasted no time, crawling across the lumps of coal, with Vale falling in beside her. Ridge and I began making our way also, trying to keep our heads low so the wind wouldn't push us back.

We reached the edge of the train car and watched as Tina and Vale maneuvered themselves onto the ladder. From there, they reached out to the next coal car, grasping its ladder and hoisting themselves into the open bed.

When Ridge and I followed, it was much scarier than it had looked while watching Tina. The track was thundering right below my feet and a single slip would be the end of me. If I fell, there wouldn't even be enough time to spout out a wish.

Ridge helped me get across the ladders in my one-armed state, and soon we were finding a rhythm to this dangerous maneuver.

There was no sign of Thackary or his father in the first five cars. If they had climbed aboard here, they must have moved forward, too. But it was exhausting crawling across the mounds of coal and shimmying up and down ladders, and my whole body ached.

We pressed on, three more units, until we reached a new type of freight car. It was enclosed on the top, and I guessed it wasn't hauling coal. We paused before approaching it, the four of us whipped to tatters in the wind as we knelt in the final coal car and tried to gauge what was ahead.

"There's a hole in the top of that car," Vale said, daring to rise higher than the rest of us.

"Does it look manmade?" Ridge asked.

"Isn't this whole train manmade?" I pointed out.

"I was wondering if the hole looks like it's part of the original design," Ridge said. "Or does it look like somebody broke it open?"

"No," said Vale. "The edges look ragged, like something ripped through the metal."

"Thackary's in there," I whispered, my words swept away in the rush of wind.

"Thackary's in there," said Tina, in a slightly louder voice so the others could actually hear her. I felt like she kind of stole my thunder.

"We need to get inside and secure the boy's mouth before he can make a wish," Vale said. "The father might be a challenge, so you two keep him occupied." That last bit was directed at me and Ridge.

"Why do we have to fight the pirate?" Ridge asked. "I'd rather take the boy."

"And what kind of experience do you have in capturing a Wishmaker?" Vale asked.

"It's my quest to stop him," I said. "I thought you two were supposed to save his life."

"I'm supposed to save an ex-Wishmaker," Tina clarified. "We'll have to keep him hostage until his genie time runs out. Then I can work on saving him."

"That's one way of doing it," Ridge said.

"Fine. We'll take the dad," I said, agreeing to the original plan. I wasn't crazy about it, either. I knew he could be dangerous in his own right, even without a genie. "But there's something I'd better do first."

Ridge looked at me. "What's suddenly so important?"

"Muumuu," I answered.

"Why are you talking about a muumuu right now?" he asked.

"It's a word I've never really used, and I don't think I'll ever say it by accident." I looked at him. "I'm going to use it as my trigger word."

"Trigger for what?"

"I wish," I began, "that every time I say the word *muumuu*, you will transform from your regular human form into"—I paused for dramatic effect—"a shark that swims in the air!"

I'd put a lot of thought into it, and I felt like an air shark was the right way to go. Could you have come up with anything cooler?

"Whoa!" Ridge grinned, clearly impressed by the idea. But I could tell the Universe was cooking up a good counterbalance to my wish with some sort of disadvantage. "If you want me to transform," he said, "then every time I am in shark form, you will only be able to belly scoot."

"Belly scoot?" I said, unfamiliar with that term.

"Yeah," said Ridge. "You'll have to lie on your stomach and scoot across the floor to get around. Like a baby."

I lifted my one hand to my head in thought. If I had an air shark doing battle for me, then it wouldn't really matter if I could barely move, right?

"Let's do this," I said. "Bazang."

My hourglass watch collapsed on my wrist, and I glanced over to see if the girls were impressed by my pay-as-you-play wish.

"An air shark?" Tina asked.

I grinned. "Air shark versus wolf. Who do you think would win?"

"I don't see why it matters," Tina replied. "We're on the same team."

"I'm not talking about Ridge versus Vale," I said. "Just hypothetically. Air shark and gray wolf. Who would be better?"

"An air shark isn't a real thing," Tina said.

"It is now," I replied.

"Look, we'd better get in there," Vale said, pointing to the boxcar before us. "And if you need help taking down Thackary's father, I'm sure we can do it after we've captured the Wishmaker."

"Thanks," I said, a second before realizing that she was mocking us by doubting our ability to take down the man. "We'll be just fine." I was feeling overly confident now that I could turn my genie into a shark.

"Here we go." Tina dropped over the edge of the coal car and swung to the ladder on the rear of the boxcar. In a moment, all four of us were across, perched a short distance away from the hole in the roof.

Tina and Vale shared a quick glance, their faces flushed from the afternoon heat. Then Tina muttered, "Paradiddle," and Vale became the giant gray wolf, her fur matted in the strong wind.

Wolf Vale leaped forward, disappearing as she fell through the hole in the roof of the boxcar. Tina crawl hopped the short distance, grasped the rough metal edge, and dropped out of sight.

I looked at Ridge, a smirk of awesomeness spreading across

my face at what we were about to do. "Muumuu!" I shouted.

Instantly, my genie transformed into a huge silvery shark. He turned to me, grinning with his frightening mouth, double rows of razor-sharp teeth flashing in the sunlight.

Then, without feet or hands for traction, my new shark went sliding backward across the roof of the boxcar, fins flailing.

I tensed, but even if I had wanted to jump up, I wouldn't have been able to. My stomach felt glued to the metal roof, and my only means of moving was by dragging myself forward with my single arm.

I quickly realized that Ridge was about to snap our tether, which would fling me off the train to my doom. "Swim!" I screamed. Hadn't I wished that the shark would be able to swim in the air?

"It's not that easy!" Ridge replied, his speech slurred and his shark mouth looking very odd as he formed words. "I'm a fish out of water!" He bounced across the coal in the car behind me.

"Use your fins!" I coached, wondering how absurd we must have looked.

A boy, lying on his stomach atop a speeding freight train, giving swimming lessons to a talking shark. Does it get any weirder than that?

I estimated about forty-one and a half feet of distance between us when Ridge finally figured out what his tail was for. Suddenly, he lifted into the air, swimming with purpose, though not yet with grace.

"That's it!" I called. "Now let's get in there!" I used my one arm to point to the hole in the boxcar. Ridge sped forward, fighting hard to match, and then beat, the speed of the freight train. After what seemed like ages, he had positioned his shark body directly above the hole.

I was slithering forward as quickly as I could, and I watched the air shark prepare for the dive into the boxcar. His tail tipped up, his conical nose angled downward, and he plunged into the hole. There was only one problem.

Shark Ridge was bigger than the hole in the roof.

He got wedged, just past his front fins. His tail thrashed back and forth in a hopeless attempt to dislodge himself. I put my face into my single palm and shook my head.

So much for our grand debut.

Seeing that there was only one possible way to free my genie shark, I shouted, "Muumuu," and watched him transform back into the skinny boy I knew, at the same time falling through the opening into the boxcar.

My consequence ended and I was able to rise to my knees, crawling the remaining distance and swinging down through the hole.

I nearly landed on top of Ridge, causing both of us to fall flat. As quickly as I could, I jumped to my feet, scanning the area and preparing for the worst.

There was plenty of open space in the boxcar and daylight angled down through the jagged opening in the roof. Tina was standing with her back to the wall. Vale (now returned to human form) knelt on the floor of the boxcar beside a single prisoner. I recognized his slick blond hair, black leather jacket, and oversize shoes.

We had captured Thackary Anderthon.

CHAPTER 20

Seeing the boy as Vale's prisoner gave me a swell of victory, but Ridge and I had the assignment of taking down the pirate-talking man. I raised my single hand as though I knew karate, and spun in a rapid circle, scanning all four corners for the man we despised.

"His dad's not here," Tina said.

I relaxed my ninja stance as Ridge took a step closer to the girls. "In case you guys happened to miss that," he said, a smile on his face, "I was a shark. An actual shark." He nodded. "Pretty cool."

"It would have been cooler if you'd fit through the hole in the roof," I muttered, turning back to our prisoner.

Now that my eyes had adjusted to the dim light of the car, I noticed something new about him. The boy had grown a full beard since I'd seen him on Mount Rushmore. I wondered what wish he had made to give him this new distinguished look.

"Where's your dad?" I demanded. I didn't like the idea of that cruel man out on his own.

"He's not going to answer right now," Vale said, tying off a strip of cloth around Thackary's mouth. His wrists were already tied together in front of him.

"Where's his genie?" I asked, knowing that she had to be close by.

"Right here," said Tina, holding up a glass pickle jar. "Shut away for now."

I felt much more confident knowing that Thackary was unable to access his genie. I stared down at the boy who the Universe had described as a very bad person. "It's over, Thackary," I said.

He made a sequence of grunts and groans, but nothing was intelligible with the gag in his mouth.

I grinned at Tina. "One step closer to completing my quest," I said. "Now we've just got to keep him locked up for . . ." I did the math. "About four more days."

The boy made some more sounds in an attempt to talk, but we weren't going to take such a foolish risk with a dangerous Wishmaker like him, even if Tina was holding his genie in a jar.

On his knees in the hot boxcar, Thackary looked up at me. The sunlight angled in from above, and I saw that his right eye was bright yellow. Just like Tina and me. He must have accepted the same consequence at Mount Rushmore. It gave me a twinge of satisfaction to see that Thackary also had to endure the crazy eye.

The boy made a gesture with his bound hands. He wasn't reckless enough to try to strip off the gag. Vale made it obvious that she would be on him before he could get it. He held one hand in front of him, using his other hand to draw something on the palm.

"I think he's trying to tell us that his palms are itchy," Ridge said.

"Don't be ridiculous," I replied. "I think he's offering to read our palms and tell the future. Probably a trick."

"Or," said Tina, "he wants to write us a message since we won't allow him to speak."

The boy made a few more strained speaking sounds, his eyes casting desperately around the boxcar. Then he scrambled forward, using his bound hands to grasp a small piece of coal that must have tumbled into the boxcar with our arrival.

Hunched over the dirty floor, Thackary Anderthon began scraping a message. I watched the letters appear, but I couldn't actually read it because of my consequence. When he was finished writing, the boy rocked back on his heels and let us have a clear look.

Tina and Vale shared a look of confusion. Ridge scratched his head, jaw slightly agape.

"What?" I said. "What does it say?"

Ridge pointed to the coal-scribed letters on the floor and read them aloud.

"'I am NOT Thackary Anderthon!'"

CHAPTER 21

The four of us stared in silence at the message on the floor, while the captive boy watched us.

"Did you read that wrong?" I finally asked Ridge.

"I know how to read," he said defensively. "'I am NOT Thackary Anderthon.'"

"I know you aren't," I said to Ridge. "But if he isn't"—I pointed to the stranger—"then who is?"

The boy made a bunch of sounds like he wanted to explain himself. I'll admit, I was tempted to untie his mouth so we could get to the bottom of this.

"Do you want me to untie his mouth so we can get to the bottom of this?" Ridge asked. I looked to Tina and Vale, but the girls were still silently pondering the message.

"I don't know," I said to Ridge. "What do you think?"

"It seems a little trappy to me."

"Trappy?" I asked.

"You know, like a trap?" said Ridge. "He probably just wrote that so we would let him speak. And before we can do anything, he'll grab his jar, the genie will appear, he'll make some horrible wish, and we'll be thrown through the roof before you can say 'muumuu.'"

"I won't," said the boy who claimed not to be Thackary. The sound of his voice caused me and Ridge to stagger backward in surprise.

"How did he get loose?" I swung my fist in his direction, in case he felt like pouncing at me.

Vale stepped back from him, holding the strip of cloth that had bound his mouth. "He can't do us any harm," she said. "Not while Tina has his genie in the pickle jar."

I guess that made sense. In order to grant a wish, the genie had to be out of the jar. In order to call her out of the jar, the boy would have to be holding it.

"She's in there most of the time," the boy answered.

"That's awful!" Ridge said to the prisoner. "Why would you keep your genie sealed up? Do you know what it's like inside that jar? No wonder the Universe said you were a horrible person."

"The Universe described me to you?" the boy said.

"It's our quest to stop you," I said, "from opening the

Undiscovered Genie jar." I narrowed my eyes at him suspiciously. "Unless you really aren't Thackary Anderthon, as you claim."

"I'm not," he said. "My name is Jathon."

"Jason?" I asked.

"No, Jathon."

"Come on," I said, rolling my eyes. "Thackary? Jathon?"

"I'm not making it up," the boy insisted. "My name is Jathon." He took a deep breath, and I had a feeling that he was about to say something we didn't want to hear. "My father is Thackary Anderthon."

"No!" I shouted. "That supermean pirate-talking guy that ditched us on the interstate after we changed his tire?"

"The same supermean pirate-talking guy who pushed me off a cliff?" Ridge added.

The boy nodded. "That's my dad." He looked me defiantly in the face, his yellow eye twitching.

"Where is he now?" Tina asked. "Why wasn't your father in here when we found you?"

"We got separated." Jathon studied us helplessly. "What are you going to do to my dad?" he asked.

"It's not possible," muttered Vale. "One of you must be lying." To my surprise, the redheaded genie was looking between Jathon and . . . me!

"Lying?" I cried. "What would I have to lie about?"

Vale took a step toward me, Tina watching intently from across the boxcar. "You said your quest was to stop Thackary Anderthon from opening the Undiscovered Genie jar, but only kids can become Wishmakers." She jabbed a finger in my direction. "So either you're lying about your quest"—then she pointed at Jathon, who was kneeling on the floor—"or you're lying about your dad being Thackary."

"We might both be telling the truth," Jathon said. "I can explain!"

Vale backed away from us, and I wondered if her natural angry form was even scarier than her gray wolf.

"My dad," the boy said, rising slowly to his feet, "Thackary . . . he was a Wishmaker years ago, when he was a kid. He made some bad choices and took on some tough consequences that he's had to live with forever."

"So, *he's* the ex-Wishmaker, not you," Tina exclaimed, stepping forward with interest.

Jathon nodded. "That's why my dad could see the rockmen. Since he was once a Wishmaker, he can see through the Universe's shield against magical suspicion."

"How long ago did you get your genie?" Tina followed up.

"About three days," he answered.

"Same as us," I pointed out.

"Once I became a Wishmaker," Jathon continued, "my genie changed everything. With this power . . . I have to help my dad."

"Why would you want to help that guy?" Ridge asked. "He's awful!"

"You don't understand. I have to help him," Jathon emphasized. "If I don't, it's going to rain pianos for a hundred years!"

"Pianos?" I questioned.

Jathon nodded. "That's the consequence if I fail my quest."

I found it strange that Jathon, too, was fighting to prevent such a terrible consequence. Zombie cats and dogs, lemonade flood, or raining pianos. Three unusual (and unpleasant) ways for the world to end.

"So, your quest is to help your dad?" Tina asked him.

Jathon nodded. "The Universe has instructed me to help the person I'm closest to in achieving his greatest desire." He sniffed. "My dad can be awful sometimes—pretty much all the time—but he's the only one who's always there for me."

"So what does Thackary Anderthon want so bad?" Tina said.

"He wants to make a wish," Jathon answered. "One that my genie can't grant."

"But your dad can't make wishes," I said. "He's not a Wishmaker anymore."

"And he can't be," insisted Vale. "Adults can't become Wishmakers. It's against the rules."

"The Undiscovered Genie has the power to break the rules," Jathon said.

"You're saying that your dad can become a Wishmaker?" I hated to think of what that horrible man might wish for. If anyone were to wish for the zombie pet apocalypse, it would be him.

"The Undiscovered Genie is different," Jathon said. "That's why he was locked away. I'll help my dad open that jar. Then he can finally wish for his greatest desire!"

"Not going to happen!" I shouted. "I will stop Thackary Anderthon. The world depends on it!"

"Wait a minute," Ridge cut in. "Does anyone see a problem here?"

"I can see several," Tina said.

"I'm talking about our quests," said Ridge. "Ours is to stop Thackary Anderthon from opening the jar, but Jathon's is to help him do it." The genie shook his head. "If Ace fails, the world is destroyed by zombie cats and dogs. If Jathon fails, the world is destroyed by raining the piano concerto of doom."

"And I'm supposed to save his life," Tina said. "Add lemonade into the mix."

"It's a lose-lose situation," I muttered, stepping back from Jathon. "Why would the Universe do this to us?"

"It wouldn't." Vale closed her eyes, apparently deep in thought. "There has to be some way for all of your quests to be fulfilled."

"You really think so?" I asked. "Because this just seems like another one of the Universe's demented jokes."

"This isn't about the Universe," Tina said. "It's about us."

"What do you mean?" I asked.

"It's our choices," she said. "Our wishes."

"Tina's right," said Vale. "As long as you can make your own choices, there is hope. Not even the Universe can mess with that."

I turned back to Jathon. He had to know something to help it all make sense. I was tempted to say the trigger word and use my air shark to scare some answers out of him. But if we forced Jathon to speak, couldn't he just tell us lies?

I turned to Ridge. "I wish this kid would tell us everything he knows about the Undiscovered Genie."

Jathon's face paled at my audacious wish. My hourglass flipped open and Ridge laid things out for me. "If you want Jathon to tell you more about the Undiscovered Genie," he said, "then you have to tell everyone here about your greatest desire."

I looked at him as though he had just betrayed me. Ridge already knew what my greatest desire was. I had made the wish just a few hours ago.

He shrugged apologetically, and I remembered that he

hadn't come up with that consequence. I didn't need any extra clarification on this one. I just had to think it over. Was it a good idea to let Tina and Vale know about my past? Or rather, my lack of a past? Let alone, Jathon! He was the bad guy. It felt wrong to tell them all something so personal to me.

But we really needed to know more about the Undiscovered Genie. Jathon claimed this new genie was different, and according to the Universe, Thackary was going to use him to end the world with zombie pets.

"Sorry, Ace," Ridge muttered. I looked at Tina, then Vale, and last at Jathon Anderthon.

"Fine. Bazang," I said. Part of me hoped I could keep my mouth shut and not blab about my mysterious past. But I knew that wouldn't be the case. I could already feel the Universe compelling me to tell the others. Might as well get this over with.

"Okay. I'll go first," I said, taking a deep breath. "I don't know where I came from."

Everyone stared at me in silence for a moment. Then Tina said, "Nebraska."

I rolled my eyes. "Well, obviously. But before that."

"Can't you ask your parents?" Vale responded.

"That's just it," I said. "I don't have parents. I don't have siblings. I don't even know my real name."

"Ace . . ." Tina said.

"Is what they named me because of this." I pulled the folded playing card from my pocket. "The ace of hearts. It's the only thing I have. Not even a single memory before I was nine years old. I want to know where I came from. Is my family out there, waiting for me to come home?"

I looked at Jathon and wondered again if the Universe had threatened such a heavy consequence because I was related to the Anderthons. Jathon certainly didn't seem to recognize me. And we looked nothing alike.

"I want to get some answers about who I really am," I concluded. "That's my greatest desire."

It fell awkwardly quiet in the boxcar, the only sound the rhythmic thump of the train's wheels on the track. I no longer felt the Universe urging me to say more, and I knew I had paid off the consequence by giving up the most personal bit of information I had.

"Now," Ridge said, dispelling the silence, "it's your turn, Jathon Anderthon, thon of Thackary Anderthon."

"Umm . . . you said 'thon' instead of 'son,'" I said to Ridge.

"No, I didn't," he replied. "I thaid, 'Thackary Anderthon . . .'"

"And now you just said 'thaid,' inthead of 'said.'"

"Well, you just said 'inthead' instead of 'instead,'" Ridge answered.

"Guys!" Tina yelled, abruptly ending our discussion. She

pointed at Jathon. "Tell us what else you know about the Undiscovered Genie." She seemed very interested to collect on my wish now that I had paid the consequence.

Jathon began to shake his head in defiance, but I saw the Universe work its magic and suddenly he was spewing valuable information like a fire hydrant. Except fire hydrants spew water.

"My father wants to use the Undiscovered Genie to make a wish that will remove all his old consequences," Jathon said. "Lifelong consequences that he's carried for thirty years."

Well, that would explain why he talked like a pirate all the time.

"Impossible," said Vale. "You can't wish to undo consequences."

"That's what we thought," said Jathon, "but my father convinced me to make a wish to find out if there was any way to remove them." He shrugged, an uncomfortable gesture with both hands still tied up. "Since I needed to help my dad to complete my quest, I made the wish."

"What was your consequence?" Ridge asked.

"No friends," Jathon answered. "I mean, I can make friends, but I'll never be able to spend time with them. Forever."

"So basically, you're grounded for life?" That was just cruel.

Jathon made me feel better about the consequences I'd

accepted. The thing about meeting other Wishmakers was that someone else always seemed to have it worse than you.

"I took the consequence and learned that my dad could erase his old consequences by opening the jar of the Undiscovered Genie," said Jathon. "Long ago, the original Wishmakers locked his jar into a secret cave. So I made another wish to know how I could get inside that cave."

"We know about the tasks," I said "And we know that anyone who accomplishes the tasks will be granted a key to enter the Cave of the Undiscovered Genie." I gave a victorious smirk. "We found your notebook."

"Why would you write down something so valuable?" Tina asked.

"I couldn't speak at the time," Jathon answered. "It was a consequence for . . . well, it's a long story. But my dad was too impatient to get the information that I'd learned about the tasks, so I wrote it down so he could read it." He scrunched his face in confusion. "How did you guys find out what I wrote? We ripped out the pages and burned them."

"The Universe told us," I said. "And I paid an arm and a leg to figure it out. Actually, not a leg. Just an arm . . . but still."

"What was your consequence for learning about the tasks?" Ridge asked.

"I got this jacket," Jathon answered, looking down at his black leather apparel.

"That's a pretty cool-looking consequence, if you ask me," I said. How come mine never turned out that nice?

Jathon shook his head. He looked down bitterly at the leather he was wearing. "It's not as cool as it looks. I can't take it off for the rest of the week."

"So you have to wear a black jacket," I replied. "It's not that bad."

"The inside is lined with sandpaper."

Ouch. That had to hurt.

I glared at the boy. "Go on," I demanded.

"There is only one more thing I know," said the boy. But he was trembling, trying uselessly to hold it back.

"Spill it, Jathon!" I shouted. "All of it."

"The Undiscovered Genie can grant any wish. Any wish. And once you open his jar and tether yourself to him, you get the first wish"—Jathon held his breath, as if trying not to say the next part—" consequence free."

"Consequence free?" I repeated, my voice barely a whisper. I wouldn't have believed him if he weren't obligated to speak the truth.

"That's all I'm forced to say," Jathon said, slowly bowing his bearded face into the shadows of the boxcar.

The rest of us were silent, contemplating the idea of a wish with no consequence. What would you wish for? What's that one thing that you desire more than anything else? You know what mine is, and thanks to the consequence I had just accepted, now everyone else in the boxcar knew it, too.

I could find out my past.

"My father is out there," Jathon said, his voice barely audible. "And he won't stop until he gets what he wants most."

"The Undiscovered Genie," I muttered.

A wish without a consequence.

CHAPTER 22

I couldn't help it. I wished for a mattress. Have you ever ridden in an empty boxcar for fifteen hours straight? Let me say— not comfy. In exchange for the luxurious mattress to sleep on, my left shoelace would come untied anytime someone clapped their hands. But it would only last the rest of the week, so it was totally worth it.

I awoke around dawn, suddenly remembering where I was. I leaped from my cozy mattress, my shifting weight causing Ridge to roll off the other side and land with a thump on the floor.

I blinked a few times, trying to force my eyes to adjust to the lighting. Ridge was pulling himself up off the floor. Tina was sitting in the corner, and Vale was standing beside her.

Jathon Anderthon was gone.

"Where is he?" I shouted, crossing the boxcar to face Tina.

She remained seated, her face turned upward to the jagged hole in the roof, a bit of early morning light illuminating her flat expression.

"I let him go," she said.

"You did what?" Ridge and I shouted together.

"I gave him back his genie jar and let him go," Tina said, finally rising to her feet. "You're not the only one with a quest, Ace."

"So you thought you could save Jathon's life by letting him go?" I asked. "He's not even the right person!"

"But his dad is," said Tina. "And Thackary has a better chance of surviving with his Wishmaker son. I can't let him die out there."

"And I can't let him succeed!" I shouted. We all had our quests. And it seemed none of us could succeed without the other two destroying the world. "So now what? You're on Thackary's side?"

"Maybe I should be," she answered.

Tina and I glared at each other, and I was thinking about having that epic shark versus-wolf throwdown to prove my point.

Ridge stepped up, patting me on the shoulder. "On a positive note," the genie said, "your left arm grew back!"

I looked down at my newly regrown appendage. That was

good news. In the adrenaline of waking up to find Jathon escaped, I hadn't even noticed that I was whole again.

"Are you trying to destroy the world?" I shouted, grateful I had two arms to gesture at Tina.

"I'm trying to save it!" she yelled back. "I'm trying to do what the Universe told me. I thought you'd understand!"

"How are we supposed to be a team if you do things behind my back?"

"Maybe we're not supposed to be a team, Ace," said Tina. "Maybe I should have left with Jathon."

"Maybe it's not too late," I spat.

We stared at each other for a long, awkward moment. Then Tina moved abruptly. Vale boosted her and she leaped up, catching the edge of the hole in the roof and climbing out of the railway car.

"Come on, Tina," I said. "You know I didn't mean it."

On the roof, Tina produced her genie jar and ordered Vale into it, only to remove her a second later so they were both successfully on top of the car.

"You're really leaving us?" I asked, my voice cracking.

"You helped me realize something," Tina answered. "I can't save Thackary's life if I'm not with him."

I felt the sting of betrayal. "Tina!" I shouted, but the girl and her genie were gone.

I stood in rigid disbelief. I couldn't believe Tina would just leave us like that.

"I can't believe Tina would just leave us like that," Ridge said, falling onto the mattress like he was ready to give up entirely.

"It's all right," I said, though my insides were starting to panic at the thought of being on our own. "We'll get along fine without those two."

And we did. But it wasn't easy.

It took Ridge and me almost an hour just to get out of the boxcar. I was too stubborn to make a wish after I had watched Tina escape with such ease.

First, Ridge boosted me up and I tried to pull him out. When that didn't work, I boosted him up and he tried to pull me out. Neither was strong enough to lift the other, so I had him transform into a shark and dangle his tail through the hole for me to grab on to. Problem was, once he became a shark, I had to lie on my stomach on the floor of the boxcar, so I couldn't even come close to reaching his tail.

Then we finally realized that the boxcar had a door.

By the time we figured out how to unlatch the door, the train was conveniently slowing down as it passed through a town.

Ridge and I jumped off at the same time, tumbling side

by side so we wouldn't snap our tether. The landing was much more painful than we thought it would be and both of us sat on the ground, rubbing our bruised elbows and knees for about a half hour.

We wandered down a small street and saw a woman on the sidewalk. Since I had no idea where we were or which direction we needed to go, I decided to talk to the stranger.

"Hello," I said, stopping in her path. As soon as I said the word, I felt my rolled-up sleeves grow an inch longer. My baggy sleeves and discolored eye, together with my backward pants, made me wonder if the woman was nervous to be stopped by me. I decided to put her at ease by asking a very basic question. "Can you tell me what state we are in?"

The woman looked at us like we were crazy, but the sincere looks on our faces must have persuaded her to answer. "California."

Ridge and I gave a quick high five to celebrate the fact that the train had taken us so far in the right direction. At the sound of our hands clapping, my left shoelace came untied.

"And could you point us the way to Super-Fun-Happy Place?" Ridge asked. "We need to eat some green cotton candy."

The woman gave us some useful directions to a bus station where we could catch a ride to the amusement park. By the time we arrived there, the bus we needed was ten minutes from departing.

"Can you think of any way to get on that bus without wishing?" I asked, dreading the thought of another consequence.

Ridge glanced left and right. "Sneak on," he whispered, tiptoeing backward toward the bus. In the process, he bumped into a metal garbage can and sent it clattering to the concrete. In trying to recover, he staggered sideways, knocking over a display rack of newspapers.

"You are the least sneaky person in the world," I said, realizing that the only way to get on that vehicle was to wish it. But I was going to be smart about it. The more indirect my wish, the gentler the consequence would be.

Ridge was picking up the newspapers when I noticed a middle-aged couple, clearly bound for Super-Fun-Happy Place with their fanny packs and visors, taking a selfie in front of the bus. I grinned, turning so Ridge would be sure to hear me clearly.

"I wish that couple thought we were their kids," I said. To avoid a misinterpretation from the Universe, I pointed to the couple beside the bus.

"Good plan," Ridge said, as my hourglass watch extended. "If you want them to think we are their sons, then you'll have to wear a helmet for the next twenty-four hours."

"What kind of helmet?" I asked.

"A medieval knight's helmet."

"Seriously? Cool!" I was going to look fearsome! This

was the easiest consequence so far. "Bazang," I said without hesitation.

No sooner had my watch closed than I felt the power of the Universe slipping a knight's helmet into place, causing my neck to wobble suddenly.

"Whoa!" I shouted, my voice echoing within the metal mask. "This thing is superheavy!"

"Eight pounds," Ridge answered. "That's like wearing a gallon of milk on your head."

"How do you know how heavy the helmet is?" I asked. He hadn't even touched it.

"The Universe told me when you wished for it," he answered.

"Why didn't you mention it?" I said. "I can barely keep my head up!"

"You didn't ask," Ridge said. "You usually ask a bunch of questions to clarify the consequence, but you just accepted this one right away."

"That's because I thought it would look cool," I said, grunting. "I can't see a thing through these tiny little eyeholes."

Suddenly, the woman who had been taking a selfie came racing across the station. "Ace!" she cried. "Ridge!" I was surprised that the Universe had given her our names. But then, what kind of mother would she be if she didn't know what to call her own kids?

"Hi, Mom," I said. I knew it was only pretend, but saying those words caused a little stir in my chest. I wondered if I would ever say that phrase to the person it was meant for.

"What are you two doing?" she asked. By now, her husband had arrived on the scene, a bit of unsmeared sunscreen on his earlobe. Clearly, they were ready for the hot California sun, despite the fact that Super-Fun-Happy Place was still a bus ride away.

"Where are your tickets, boys?" Dad asked. Neither of them seemed bothered by the fact that I was wearing a helmet from the Dark Ages.

I glanced at Ridge through the narrow eyeholes. "Tickets?" Then I shrugged in what I hoped was an endearing way. My new dad was not impressed. Mom shot him a look and he

jogged back to the booth to purchase two more tickets.

"Look at you both!" said Mom, her tone disapproving. I thought she might comment on my knight's helmet, but instead, she said, "How did you get so filthy?" The woman licked her thumb and used it to wipe some of the coal dust off Ridge's face. "You can't go wandering off like that. This vacation is for your father. He's been under a lot of stress at work, and I expect my boys not to add to it."

"Yes, Mommy dear," Ridge said. She turned around to check her husband's progress with the tickets.

"Mommy dear?" I whispered. "You're like the embarrassing little brother that I don't know if I have."

"Actually, they probably think we're twins," Ridge said.

"How is that possible?" I rolled up my extralong sleeve and put my arm next to his, pointing out the color difference of our skin.

Ridge shrugged. "Clearly, you were adopted," he muttered as Dad returned. The excitement I had seen in the selfie had faded to weariness as he handed us our bus tickets. I'll admit, I felt a little bad about taking his money and burdening his vacation. But this was about saving the world.

And eating cotton candy.

CHAPTER 23

Having fake parents was working out even better than I had hoped. After the bus ride, they bought us lunch at a little café outside the park. Conversation was a bit awkward, since we were practically strangers. But the magic of the Universe had made us a family. And being in a family meant getting a lunch that wasn't a smashed peanut butter sandwich.

On the downside, my new helmet made it terribly difficult to eat. With a full metal face mask, it was difficult to slide the food into my mouth. Believe me, I had tried to take it off, but the Universe had fused the helmet to the top of my head and no amount of prying could work it loose.

When we were done eating, it was time to head into the park. Apparently, passes to Super-Fun-Happy Place are rather expensive. I'm going by what Ridge told me, since I couldn't read any of the signs near the entrance. But as it was, I was once again grateful to have a stressed-out dad to pay for me.

I had seen Super-Fun-Happy Place in movies, so I thought I knew what to expect. But the bright spread of adventure seemed so much bigger as I saw it with my own discolored eye.

There were roller coasters and spinning rides, splash pads and arcade games. Vendors passed by with dripping Popsicles and candied nuts. The whole place smelled like sugar . . . with just a hint of dried vomit.

I looked at Ridge, pleased to see that I wasn't the only one gawking at this awesome place. "We've got to find the cotton candy guy," I said, remembering the real reason we had come. "And keep an eye out for Thackary and Jathon."

Before Ridge could answer, someone stepped between us, taking us both by an arm. It was our dad. Now that we had arrived, I'd forgotten all about our pseudoparents.

"Thanks for everything . . . Dad," I said. I looked at Ridge, slightly puzzled by the man's persistence at parenting. "When does my wish end?" I asked the genie.

Ridge's eyes went wide. "Umm. You didn't specify," he said.

"What are you saying?" I cried. But I was afraid I knew exactly what he was saying. "They're going to be our parents forever?"

It was Dad who answered. "That's generally how it works,

son." He bent low, his face between mine and Ridge's. "Now, there are a lot of people here. I need you to stay close. You know how your mother is with crowds."

This couldn't be happening! My wish for parents was supposed to be temporary. It was intended to get us into the park, not tie us down once we arrived. How were we going to find the cotton candy man and capture Thackary Anderthon if Mom and Dad were holding our hands?

This had to end now.

I stepped away from my dad's reach, turning to face both parents with Ridge by my side. "Mom, Dad . . ." I began. "You've always been wonderful parents. The last two and a half hours have been, well, inexpensive for Ridge and me. For that, we are very grateful. But I'm afraid it's time to part ways."

"Excuse me?" Dad shouted. "You two aren't going anywhere. . . ."

I turned to Ridge. "I wish they'd forget we were here." It was a simple solution, and didn't contradict the first wish I'd made.

My fake mom stepped forward, her face wrinkled with concern. "How could you wish that, Ace? We are your parents. . . ."

"If you want them to forget that we're here," Ridge whispered, "then your socks will get wet every time you laugh."

"Soaking wet?" I asked. "Or just damp?"

"Depends on how hard you laugh," Ridge answered. "A little chuckle will dampen them. But a full laugh will soak them. Like you dunked them in a bathtub."

"How long will this last?" I asked.

"The rest of the week," he answered.

I grumbled, not wanting wet socks, but knowing that we needed to ditch our false parents. "I guess I'll accept it. Bazang."

My hourglass watch clicked away as a dazed expression came over them. Then Mom pointed in the opposite direction, seized her husband by the hand, and they ran off toward some attraction.

"Bye, Mom. Bye, Dad," Ridge muttered too quietly for them to hear. He sighed. "Just when we were starting to get along."

"Come on," I said. "You know I was their favorite."

We wandered the park for quite a while. Ridge and I managed to spot three different vendors spinning cotton candy, but they didn't match the details we'd learned from the second page of the Anderthons' notebook. We were looking for a man with a pink mustache selling green cotton candy.

So we decided to do what any reasonable kids would do at an amusement park. We jumped in line for the nearest ride. It was one that lifted you straight into the sky and then dropped you in a free fall toward the ground.

By the time we got seated, the red padded security bars folding down over our heads, Ridge was having major second thoughts. "What if we hit the ground?" He was rubbing his sweaty hands together. "What if the safety bar comes up while we're falling?"

It was a little late for him to worry now. The seats were slowly rising to the top of the tower, giving us an aerial view of the amusement park. I saw the throngs of people growing smaller and smaller as we rose higher.

"What if a giant bird flies by and plucks me out of this chair?" Ridge was rambling now, but I wasn't paying him any attention. Through the narrow slits of my medieval helmet, I had seen something below. Tucked off in a corner where not many people passed by, there stood a man, hunched over a machine spinning sugar. I couldn't see if he had a mustache from up so high, let alone if it was pink. But I could see the color of the cotton candy as it spiraled around a paper cone in his hand.

It was green.

"There!" I cut Ridge off in the middle of describing a scenario that included a high-speed windstorm and us falling to our death. "See that guy down there?" I was pointing at the cotton candy man I had spied.

"Is that him?" Ridge squinted against the glaring midday sun.

"Hard to tell from up here," I replied.

"We need to remember where he is," said Ridge. "We can head over there as soon as we—AAAAAAHHHHHHHH!"

The ride dropped and Ridge started screaming like a baby. I felt my stomach heave as we plummeted. But that's what made it fun, right? You've probably been on a ride like that. But I bet you didn't scream half as loud as Ridge.

The ride was over before we knew it, and both of us climbed out of our seats and headed quickly in the direction of the green cotton candy stand.

"That was horrible," Ridge said. "It felt just like when Thackary pushed me off that cliff. Except, there was no chair at Mount Rushmore."

We had entered a walkway of carnival-style games. Hoops for basketballs, water pistols to shoot down targets, giant foam hammers to test your strength. The teenagers running the booths called to us, beckoning us to play.

Most of the prizes were stuffed bears. There must have been hundreds of them, ranging in size from mere inches to over five feet tall. Those seemed excessive. I mean, what would you do if you won something so huge? Carry it around and get extrasweaty for the rest of the day?

The cotton candy booth was at the end of the carnival walkway. Ridge and I moved with purpose toward it, watching the man, head bowed, spinning off another fluff of green sugar threads.

The man wore a red-and white pin-striped suit with a stiff-brimmed straw hat to shield his face from the hot sun. Ridge and I stopped just feet from his little booth, causing him finally to look up. Across his upper lip, the man had a bushy mustache. And it was bright pink.

"Hello, there," I said, once again extending my sleeves to the point that I could barely keep them rolled up. It was almost like knowing that I shouldn't say that word made me say it more often. "We'd like two, please."

My heart was racing. Ridge and I were about to complete the second task! This had gone so much better than Mount Rushmore. Eating cotton candy at the most joyful place on earth? It almost seemed too easy.

The cotton candy man looked at me, then at Ridge, then back to me. "I know what you are," he said, his voice sounding forced, and tinted with an accent I didn't recognize. All at once, he jumped backward, kicking over his cart and scooping up all his premade cotton candy. Then he was off, sprinting past us down the walkway of carnival games.

"Did I forget to say please?" I muttered, wondering how

things had suddenly gone awry.

"No, you definitely said please," Ridge answered. "This guy must not get many customers."

We darted after him, but we only made it a few steps before we realized what was happening.

Remember those huge, useless stuffed bears? Well, now they were coming alive.

CHAPTER 24

The teenage booth attendants ran off as the array of stuffed animals moved to charge us. They were Super-Fun-Happy Bears, the iconic mascot of the amusement park. When I'd seen them earlier, they looked snuggly and soft. Now that they were attacking, they didn't look superfun, or superhappy.

Getting mauled by stuffed teddy bears? You're probably wondering how bad that could be. I wasn't too worried about it at first, either. In fact, it sounded kind of fun. Like having a pillow fight. Only the pillows would be bear shaped. And alive.

A giant white polar bear holding a stuffed heart leaped over a counter and sent me sprawling to the floor. I would have shouted for Ridge, but the bear shoved the stuffed heart under the visor of my helmet, muffling my voice while punching me in the stomach over and over again. It was very annoying to be punched by a stuffed animal, but it didn't really hurt. I kicked

191

upward and sent the polar bear crashing into another incoming Super-Fun-Happy Bear.

Ridge had fallen beside the horse race game, swarmed by stuffed bears. He was screaming and thrashing in an attempt to shake his opponents. I ripped the plush heart from under my helmet's visor and thought about transforming Ridge into a shark. But doing so would cause me to be practically immobile. Instead, I ran over and slammed into Ridge, peeling away three stuffed animals before I saw a tiny pink bear leap from a shelf and grab Ridge's nose.

The enemy was probably only three inches tall, but it shoved a paw up one of Ridge's nostrils and clamped down. He howled, slapping his own face and sending the pink monster flying.

Ridge recovered, and together we raced down the walkway of carnival games. My eyes peered out of the helmet, searching for the man with the green cotton candy.

A grizzly bear came leaping out of a game tent. In its furry paws it clenched a heavy hammer, presumably stolen from the Whac-A-Mole game. I turned just in time to see it bring the weapon down with a crack right on top of my head.

The blow should have knocked me unconscious. But, wait—my helmet! It would seem that not everything about my consequences was bad.

The attack had knocked my helmet sideways so the eye-holes lined up with my ear. I stumbled, spinning it around until I could see straight again. The grizzly with the sledgehammer was on the ground and I delivered a hard kick before it could swing its weapon for my shins.

"There goes the cotton candy man!" Ridge cried, pointing off into the heart of the amusement park. "He's getting on a roller coaster!"

"Then so are we!" I shouted, breaking past a row of Super Fun-Happy Bears and sprinting in the direction the genie had pointed.

There was a long line to get on the ride, but the cotton candy man wasn't going to wait, so neither would we. He shoved and elbowed his way past the impatient people, creating a perfect pathway for us to follow. His bright pin-striped suit made him easy to spot in the crowd, and he held three premade cones of cotton candy above his head as he pushed his way through.

"We have to catch him before he gets on that roller coaster!" A few people tried to converge on us, probably thinking we were just some punk kids trying to cut in line. I considered using my air shark, but instead settled on ramming a guy with my helmet.

At last, Ridge and I reached the boarding platform, only to see the cotton candy man seated on the front row, pulling the security bar over his flat-topped boater hat. He turned to look at me and Ridge, cotton candy in hand, his bright pink mustache twitching when he saw how close we were.

There was something odd about him. Besides the pink mustache; that was obvious. But it felt as though the flamboyant facial hair was only there to draw my attention away from something even more unusual. Perhaps it was the look in his eyes, which seemed hollow and artificial. Or his movements, slightly mechanical and unnatural.

Whatever it was, the cotton candy vendor didn't let me stare at him for long. "Go!" he shouted. To my great surprise, the roller-coaster operator obeyed the man's command, inching the car on its way with our target as a single passenger.

"Come on!" I shouted to Ridge, pushing past the eager people on the platform.

Maybe it was because we'd had some practice with jumping onto the train in Wyoming, but Ridge and I successfully managed to leap onto the back row of the cart just as the chain began pulling it up the steep track.

We reached for the padded security bar, yanking it down as the ride edged upward. The cotton candy vendor swiveled his head around like an owl, grunting in frustration when he saw that we had managed to get into the cart.

"If we're lucky," Ridge said, "maybe some of his cotton

candy will blow off and land in our mouths." He stuck out his tongue to be prepared.

"That's how you end up eating bugs," I pointed out, causing the genie to promptly close his mouth.

"Wait a minute," Ridge said. "Couldn't we just have waited for him at the platform? Roller coasters go in a circle."

Huh. Why didn't we think of that before we climbed aboard? Too late now.

"We've got to stop him before the ride ends, or he might disappear again," I said.

Just then, the roller coaster reached the top of the incline. We stalled at the summit, long enough to take a deep breath of anticipation. Then we were plunging down the track, Ridge screaming by my side.

Upside down, around, sideways . . . the roller coaster was speeding us in every possible direction. I felt my mismatched eyes water and my stomach twist, but instead of enjoying the ride, my gaze was focused on the man in the front row.

"We have to get him!" I shouted, reaching down to try to lift the security bar. I didn't have a good plan. Maybe I could climb across the seats and take the vendor by surprise.

Ridge was aware enough to grab my hand. "Are you crazy?" he shrieked. "At least make a wish before you go climbing to your death!"

The ride wasn't going to last much longer. If I was going to wish something, I needed to do it then and accept the consequence. I couldn't risk letting the man get away when the ride came to a halt.

But what if it came to a halt in the middle of the track?

"I wish this roller coaster would stop!" I shouted, gripping the bar as we made a sudden twist.

"Good idea," Ridge said. "Trap him on the tracks!"

"What's my consequence?" I asked, wondering why he was delaying at such a crucial time as this.

"If you want this roller coaster to stop," Ridge said, "then every time someone says the name of a state, you must jump as high as you can."

"Jump forward or backward?" I asked. The last thing I wanted was to be standing at the edge of a cliff when someone said "Alaska," causing me to leap to my doom.

"Jump straight up," Ridge said.

It wasn't a perfect deal. The consequence could still be fatal if, say, I was standing under a helicopter and someone yelled "Illinois!"

"It'll only last for a year," he said.

"Bazang!" I answered, already dreading next year's U.S. geography classes in school.

Instantly, the roller coaster came to a grinding halt. It was exactly what I'd wished for, but my timing could not have been worse.

The roller coaster had stopped upside down.

Ridge and I dangled against the security bars, frozen in the middle of a loop-the-loop. Luckily, our cart was fused tightly to the track, so we just hung upside down. Like bats.

"Okay," Ridge said. "Now what?"

I had imagined things would turn out a little more right side up. In a perfect scenario, I would crawl across the seats, take a cone of cotton candy, and eat it. But the Universe never let things happen very easily.

In the front of the cart, the vendor in the pin-striped suit was wriggling out from under his safety bar, the cones of cotton candy smashed unappetizingly under one arm. I found it a little odd that his straw hat hadn't fallen from his head.

"What's he doing?" Ridge asked. "He's going to fall!"

"Hey!" I shouted to the stranger. "We just want some cotton candy! Is that too much to ask?"

Apparently, it was too much to ask. The man gripped all three cones in one hand while grabbing the security bar with his other. He slipped out of his chair, now dangling by one arm at a frightening height.

"I am a guardian of the Ancient Consequence. You may only receive the key if you prove yourself."

"It's just cotton candy, man!" I shouted.

"But what price will you pay to eat it?" He stared at me and Ridge for one brief second. Then he let go of the security bar and plummeted toward the ground.

"I can't look!" Ridge screamed, covering his eyes. But I looked. And you can imagine how surprised I was when I saw that the man with the pink mustache did not die.

There was a landing pad waiting for him below. A soft cushion comprised of countless stuffed animals. He fell into the mass of pillowy bears and they carefully passed him along, surfing the man over their furry heads and depositing him on his feet beside the bumper cars ride.

"He's part of the Ancient Consequence?" I repeated what the cotton candy vendor had said. "Do you think he's working with Roosevelt's head?"

"I don't know," Ridge said, his hands still over his eyes. "We'll never know. And now he's dead and we'll never get our cotton candy."

"Relax," I said. "He didn't die."

Ridge peeked out from under his fingers. "How did he get down?"

I pointed. "The same way we're getting down." I said it with my best action-hero voice to inspire Ridge.

The mass of stuffed animals below had turned into a frenzied mosh pit. They were pawing and stepping on each other, soft hands reaching up for us like zombies in some sort of pillow apocalypse.

"What?" Ridge shrieked. "We are not jumping into a pile of angry bears! It's way too far down."

"The cotton candy man survived," I pointed out. "The bears are soft. They'll break our fall."

"And then they'll break our bones!" said Ridge.

I took a deep breath. I wasn't going to let a few wild teddy bears stop me from getting that candy. "I'm going now," I said, pushing up on the security bar, which seemed to have released as though the ride had ended. "You can come willingly, or wait for the tether to pull you along."

Was I afraid? Definitely.

Did I scream? Probably.

But Ridge screamed louder.

CHAPTER 25

The two of us plummeted from the upside-down roller coaster, flapping our arms like useless wings. Then, umph! We landed in a soft pile of stuffed bears, instantly smothered by cuteness.

"Muumuu!" I tried to shout, but a flannel bear managed to slide its paw under the visor of my helmet and right into my mouth. I twisted and thrashed, spitting out the fuzzy hand and screaming again. "MUUMUU!"

This time, I felt the consequence pull me to the ground before I saw Ridge turn into a shark. My stomach hit the pavement, and I was now the very bottom of the Super-Fun-Happy-Bear doggy pile.

Then the stuffing started flying.

Shark Ridge erupted from the pile, his rows of razor teeth shredding through the stuffed bears. Darting through the air as though it were water, he batted the bears away with his powerful tail.

In a moment, the way was clear, but I couldn't stand up to make my getaway while Ridge was still a shark. "Muumuu!" I called, and he was a boy again. His mouth was full of polyester fluff.

We staggered to our feet, the bears chasing us again. There were angry looks on their cute furry faces.

Ridge kept spitting out stuffing as we ran. "We have to get out of here!" he said, as if I didn't agree. "This is unbearable!"

Really? That was the word he wanted to use?

With a wake of plush animals, we arrived at the bumper cars ride where I had seen the cotton candy man disappear.

Standing guard at the gate to the arena was a tie-dyed bear, about waist high. It put up its paws in a boxing stance and I kicked it as hard as I could.

Apparently, "as hard as I could" wasn't hard enough. The tie-dyed bear wrapped around my leg and held fast. I stepped back, but couldn't shake it. At least it was out of the way.

Ridge and I ducked inside. Running with a stuffed bear clinging to your leg was harder than I'd have imagined. We spotted the pin-striped suit and flat-top hat seated in one of the tiny vehicles, racing around in a tight circle.

The moment he saw us, he turned his car around and sped toward us on a collision course. I tried to back up, but stumbled into an empty car. Then, before I could step out of the way, the crazy cotton candy vendor struck.

My leg was pinned between the two cars. I expected to hear the sound of my shin snapping, accompanied by a crushing pain. But fortunately, I had a giant stuffed bear still wrapped around my leg.

My shin was saved, but the Super-Fun-Happy Bear wasn't so lucky. The stitching between its ears split and its head exploded in a puff of synthetic stuffing.

The cotton candy man reversed, his pink mustache twitching in a menacing way. Ridge and I had only one choice. Get into the empty car.

It was barely big enough for two boys our size. I shook

off the remains of the tie-dyed bear and we managed to slip into the padded seats before the man rammed us again. We bounced backward, spiraling across the arena and colliding with another empty car.

The Super-Fun-Happy Bears must have been doing a decent job of holding back the tourists, because we had the arena to ourselves. A few of the stuffed animals had decided to join us. They raced forward, laden with tools and scraps that they must have pilfered from other places in the park.

I stepped on the pedal, spinning the wheel and reversing around the approaching pests. But they didn't seem interested in us this time. They surrounded the cotton candy man's car like a multicolored pit crew. I craned my head to see what they were doing, hoping the little creatures had turned against him.

In a moment they were done. The Super-Fun-Happy Bears backed away from the car in an almost ceremonial fashion, allowing me and Ridge to see their handiwork.

The man's bumper car was now a shredding machine! The stupid bears had installed blades and spikes of scrap metal all around the small vehicle.

"We can't let that thing hit us!" Ridge said. "We'll get ripped to bits."

The vendor came racing toward us. I swerved at the last second and his armored bumper car tore into an empty vehicle behind us. I spun us around, but he reversed with intense speed, swinging sideways and slamming into our car.

The jagged metal that the teddy bears had installed sunk into our side bumper. One sharp blade pierced through the thin wall of our car, stopping just inches away from my hip.

Ridge screamed and I jerked the wheel, trying to spin away from the man. But in the collision, his deadly spikes had locked our cars side by side. We were stuck to him, getting dragged across the arena as he zoomed in a wide victory lap.

To make things worse, the Super-Fun-Happy Bears were climbing into the other empty cars, strapping on seat belts, and closing in on us, their adorable little faces twisted with road rage.

"We're doomed!" cried Ridge, throwing his hands up in the air.

I glanced over at the vendor. He grinned at me in a way that made me feel like it was a challenge. Beside him, lying on the seat, were the three paper cones, each wrapped with the green cotton candy.

"Take the wheel!" I shouted to Ridge. Our wheel was pretty much useless because we were anchored to the enemy car. But it seemed like the right thing to say. I reached out, my hand groping for one of the cotton candy cones in the next car.

"It's too far!" I said. "I can't reach it." My fingers stretched, but the man with the pink mustache swatted my hand away as he drove. I leaned farther, but the teddy bears started slamming into us, and I was afraid that a well-timed bump would throw me out of the car, only to be driven over by one of them.

"I need to get closer," I said to Ridge.

"You want to get closer?" he answered. "I want to get farther away!"

I gritted my teeth and reached out as far as I could, but the cotton candy was still five inches away. "I wish I could reach that cotton candy!" I shouted.

"Here's the deal," said Ridge, uselessly wiggling the steering wheel of our bumper car. "If you want to reach that cotton candy, then your tongue will turn green."

"How green?" I asked. There were at least a dozen shades of green. It might not be so bad if my tongue were just tinted a light lime.

"Really green," he said. "Like the color of grass at the park."

"How long will I stay that way?" I was still reaching for the cotton candy, hoping that I would be able to grab one naturally and not end up needing the wish.

"Umm . . . forever," said Ridge. "Sorry."

Green tongue forever? I glanced down at the hourglass on my outstretched arm. The white sands were nearly spent. "I . . . Bazang!"

I don't know exactly how it happened. Maybe my arm got longer. Maybe the cars got closer together. Whatever happened, the Universe fulfilled my wish and my fingers instantly closed around the nearest cone of cotton candy.

I gave a shout of success and flopped back into the seat beside Ridge, holding the airy treat aloft. Really, by this time, the cotton candy looked pretty nasty, all matted and barely holding on to the cone. But it was what we had come for, so in my mind it looked like victory.

I ripped off a bit and pushed it under the helmet to my lips, inhaling a bit of the sugary fluff. It melted instantly in my mouth. Eating candy like this would turn anyone's tongue green. But now mine had the unique privilege of staying that way.

The vendor slammed on the brakes and both our cars came grinding to a halt. The arena was quiet now. All the Super-Fun-Happy Bears that had been trying to ram us were unbuckling their seat belts and stepping out of their bumper cars. Something outside the arena seemed to be drawing their attention. They scampered off, uninterested in me and Ridge.

The man in the pin-striped suit looked over at me. "You walk a dangerous road, youngster." He picked up the two remaining cones of cotton candy and stepped out of his souped-up bumper car.

"Aren't you going to try to stop me?" I taunted, pushing

another bite of cotton candy up to my mouth, the green sugar melting on my tongue.

"I already tried," he said. "But you have completed the second task. There is nothing more I can do to stop you. But you must be warned. The Undiscovered Genie has a taste for chaos. He was locked away for a reason." He tipped his hat and raced off in the same direction that the Super-Fun-Happy Bears had gone.

"That guy was crazy," Ridge said, carefully climbing out of our damaged car.

"I don't think he was quite . . ." I didn't know how to say it. "Human." I still didn't know what the Ancient Consequence was, but it seemed the cotton candy vendor and Roosevelt's big head had both been charged with stopping people from completing the tasks.

Ridge nodded in agreement. Reaching over, he plucked a tuft of cotton candy off the back of the cone and folded it into his mouth. I wasn't too excited to share my treat when I was the one who had to bear all the consequences to get it.

At least the cotton candy was tasty.

CHAPTER 26

Ridge and I had just exited the amusement park when a large black pickup truck swerved onto the sidewalk to cut us off.

My first thought was that it was the FBI responding to the strange report of killer teddy bears. But the Universe would have shielded innocent bystanders from the bizarre truth. I don't know what park-goers thought was happening. Maybe the Universe made it seem like a strong wind was blowing the stuffed animals around.

My second thought was that Ridge and I were about to get abducted by whoever was in the truck. But then the window rolled down and my jaw dropped at seeing someone I recognized.

It was Tina!

"You two need a ride somewhere?" she asked. Her pink feather boa was gone, but otherwise she seemed unchanged.

I felt instantly relieved to see her, though I still remembered the betrayal I'd felt when she left us in the boxcar. "I thought you were on Thackary's team now."

"I tried that out," she answered. "That guy's a jerk."

"That's what I've been saying," Ridge mumbled.

"Did you save his life?" I asked.

"Not yet," Tina answered. "And now I really don't want to. Vale and I met up with the Anderthons at Super-Fun-Happy Place, but Thackary wouldn't even let us come near." She gestured over her shoulder. "Climb in."

Vale was in the passenger seat, but the cab was extended, so Ridge and I climbed into the backseats.

"Where's Thackary now?" I asked, as Tina reversed and then sped across the parking lot.

"Still in the park, I think," said Tina. I hated the thought of that despicable man on the loose in an amusement park full of kids.

"We lost him," said Vale. "We were buried under an army of stuffed bears. By the time we got free, Thackary and his son were gone."

"Ah," Ridge said. "You met the bears."

"And the man with the pink mustache," Tina said. "The cotton candy was just out of reach, and I had to wish to grab it." She stuck out her tongue at me. I thought she was being rude until I saw that her tongue was bright green.

Same wish, same consequence. The Universe was rarely fair, but it had given us equal treatment today.

"Same thing happened to my tongue." I stuck it out, even though she couldn't see it with my helmet on. "I tried a couple of tactics, but in the end I had to wish for it directly."

"What about Jathon?" Ridge asked. "Do you think he got the cotton candy?"

Vale nodded. "They were still working on it when we left. He even had his genie outside of her jar. Her name is Scree."

"What kind of a name is Scree?" I asked. "I thought genies were named after the location where their jars were first discovered." I glanced at Ridge, aware of how he had bent that rule.

"That's right," said Vale. "Her jar must have been discovered on a slope of scree."

"I thought scree was the sound a bird makes," Ridge said.

"No," answered Vale. "*Scree* is another word for a bunch of loose rock."

"Why didn't they name her Gravel?" I asked. "And while we're on the topic, what exactly is a vale?"

"It's basically a valley," she answered. "But *vale* had a better ring to it."

Hmm. Like *Ridge* versus *Kitchen*.

"Jathon and his genie are bent on protecting Thackary so he can get to the Undiscovered Genie jar," said Vale.

"Which makes me wonder," said Tina. "Where are we going?"

"You're the driver," I pointed out. "Which is actually super-illegal. And do I even need to ask where you got the truck?"

"I earned this truck, along with the know-how to drive it." Tina paused.

"And the consequence . . . ?" I pressed.

Tina scowled. "Now every time someone says my name I have to clap my hands."

"That's interesting . . ." Ridge said. Then he couldn't help but add, "Tina."

She lifted her hands from the steering wheel ever so briefly so she could clap them together once. I chuckled, and suddenly, my socks felt very wet. I glanced down to notice that Tina's clap had also caused my left shoelace to come untied.

"Not funny, Ridge," Tina said. "I have to put up with this for a year." Forcing her to clap had been sort of funny, but now I had wet feet, paying the consequence for my laughter.

"Thanks for getting the truck," I said, tying my shoelace.

"It wasn't the only thing we got," she answered. Vale reached under the seat, withdrew an item, and passed it back to me.

"My backpack!" I cried, taking the bag and peering inside.

I saw a bunch of smashed sandwiches, a couple of empty water bottles, and a very important peanut butter jar.

"Thackary didn't give it up willingly," Tina said. "But my wolf insisted." She smiled slightly. "Consider it my apology for leaving the way we did."

"Apology accepted." I rolled the magic peanut butter jar in my hands.

A white car blew past us. As per my consequence, I dropped the jar, my hand darting up and clanging against my helmet as I saluted through the window.

"Did you wish for that?" Vale asked.

"This old thing?" I knocked on the side of the helmet. "It was actually a consequence. But it's already saved me from at least one head injury. And with a twelve-year-old driving, I might be glad I have it on."

"We're not going to crash," Tina said. "That was part of my wish. And this thing won't run out of gas, either. But I really don't know where we're going."

"Don't look at me," I said.

"You don't know what was on the next page of the notebook?" Tina asked, a hint of annoyance in her voice.

"Oh, I get it," I said, a hint of annoyance in *my* voice. "You're wondering why I didn't accept another big consequence to find out what was written on the third missing page."

"How else are we supposed to know where to go?" Vale asked.

"Tina!" I pointed out. She clapped. My shoelace came untied.

"Don't put this on me!" she called back. "I got us this truck! You figure out where we have to go."

"Why don't you just rock, paper, scissors?" Ridge suggested.

I shot him a frustrated glance. The last time hadn't gone so well for me. You remember. I ended up with only one arm.

"Yeah," Tina said. "Rock, paper, scissors." She held out her fist to prove that she could play the game while driving.

I rolled my eyes. "Fine."

Tina beat me again. Her rock crushed my scissors, causing me to sit back in defeat, my backward pants wrinkling in half a dozen uncomfortable places. Pouting, I glanced out the window and saluted another passing white car.

"What are you waiting for?" Vale asked. "We could be driving in the wrong direction. The sooner you make the wish, the better chance we have at beating Thackary and Jathon."

Vale was right. Begrudgingly, I turned to Ridge. "I wish to know what was on the third missing page of Thackary Anderthon's notebook."

I felt my hourglass watch click out, but I didn't even bother looking down at it. I was getting better at gauging thirty seconds.

"If you want to know what was on that third page," said Ridge, "then you won't be able to tell left from right for the next year."

"Left and right," I said, gesturing left, then right, as if to prove that I currently knew the difference. I thought of all the times those directions were helpful. Like when monster rockmen were going to pound your friend and you shout, "On your left!" Or when evil stuffed bears are swarming, and you yell, "Look out to the right!" There would be none of that if I accepted the consequence.

"That's a tough one," Ridge said.

"If you accept it, we're never taking directions from you," Vale added.

"We have to know what was on that page," Tina stressed. And I knew she was right.

"I'll take it," I said. "Bazang." And as knowledge of left and right departed from my brain, knowledge of what was on the third page of the notebook entered it.

"Okay," I said, holding out my hands. "We have to go to Lake Michigan." At the mention of a state name, I jumped out of my seat, hitting the top of my head on the roof of the truck. Luckily, my knight's helmet prevented any harm, although my neck was growing tired of holding it up.

"What's in Lake Michigan?" Tina asked. I jumped again, this time ducking so my helmet didn't hit.

"There's a red fishing boat with a yellow flag," I said. "We have to dive under the boat and touch the bottom of the lake."

"Lake Michigan . . ." Tina mused. I jumped again.

"Why do you keep doing that?" Vale asked.

"Ace took a consequence," said Ridge. "Every time he hears the name of a state, he has to jump."

"So that's why he jumps when I say Michigan?" Tina said.

I jumped. "Not funny, Tina," I said.

She clapped. My shoelace came untied.

We drove in silence for a moment, afraid to say anything that would spark a reaction from the other. Then Tina struck up where we'd left off. "Lake . . . *M*," she said. "I'm guessing that's in the state with the same *M* name?" I was grateful for her careful phrasing.

Thinking back to my geography lessons in school, I remembered that Lake Michigan was one of the Great Lakes. "I think it's by Chicago," I said.

"So at least we're driving in the right direction," said Tina.

"How far is it?" asked Ridge.

Tina glanced at me in the rearview mirror and raised her eyebrows to indicate that she didn't know. "We'll have to check a map at a gas station," I said. "Chicago's probably not that far."

CHAPTER 27

Chicago was very far. The nice lady at the gas station said we were nearly thirty hours away! We had no choice but to drive on. By our estimates, we wouldn't arrive at Lake Michigan until dinnertime the next day. Talk about a colossal waste of time! But I wasn't going to wish for a faster means of transportation. Not while we had a truck that Tina was paying for.

Vale and Tina took turns driving. The girls didn't dare let me or Ridge behind the wheel, and I couldn't blame them. We drove fast, the no-crashing feature of the wish protecting us from harm, and the Universe's magical shield stopping us from getting pulled over by the police. I was sure we were shaving time off our travel.

But it was still a long ride.

Sometime in the dark, early hours of the next morning, I awoke from a horrible dream. I couldn't remember it upon awakening, but I knew it had been awful. You've had those, right? They're not the kind that let you quickly fall back to sleep.

I sat up and looked out the window. The two genies were asleep in the backseat. Tina was at the wheel to my right, or maybe it was my left. I couldn't decide.

"How you doing?" I kept my voice low, but it still sounded loud in the silence of the truck.

"We used to go on road trips," Tina said.

"We did?" I asked, still groggy from sleep.

"Not you and me," said Tina. "Me and my mom." She smiled. "She used to do the most ridiculous things. Anytime we stopped at a traffic light, she'd burst into some opera song at the top of her lungs."

"Is she a good singer?" I asked.

Tina raised an eyebrow. "Not at all. But it made me laugh." She shook her head. "Our house was a mess. Mama collected all kinds of weird things. I used to be embarrassed by the knickknacks she'd put on the shelves. Old buttons, a dirty sock, pebbles, toothbrush . . . I never understood why she did so many strange things. But that's part of what makes me love her."

I wasn't sure why Tina was opening up to me. Maybe she was overly tired. "You have a big family?" I asked.

She shook her head. "Just me and my mom now." She bit her lip and I saw her eyes glistening in the dark cab.

"It was your mom, wasn't it?" I said. "The woman in the hospital?" Now Tina nodded. But she didn't say anything more about it, so I pressed ever so slightly. "How long has she been there?"

Tina swallowed hard. "Going on three weeks," she muttered. "She got so bad we couldn't stay at home. And our little town didn't have the medical care she needed. That's what brought us to St. Mercy's."

"Where do you live?" I asked.

"Our house is a few hours outside Omaha," Tina answered. "But I've been staying in my mom's room at the hospital. Nowhere else to go. Doctors don't know exactly what's wrong with her. But she's . . . she's in a lot of pain."

I grimaced. "I don't know what it's like to have a mom," I admitted. "But it can't be easy to go through this." I didn't know what else to say, so I went for total optimism. "She'll probably start getting better soon."

"No," mumbled Tina. "No. She's getting worse, Ace." Tina gripped the steering wheel with both hands. "And there's nothing I can do about it."

I glanced toward the genies in the backseat. "What about Vale?" I said. "You could wish it."

218

"What do you think I tried, the moment I opened that lip balm jar?" Tina said. "I wished a dozen variations of the same thing. But it was just too heavy. Some consequences you just can't accept, no matter how badly you want the wish."

I knew exactly what Tina meant. It had taken me two days to work up the courage to ask Ridge about my past, only to be dealt an impossible consequence. And no matter how desperately I wanted answers, I thought it must have been worse for Tina to watch her mother suffer.

"This Undiscovered Genie that Jathon was telling us about," said Tina. "Do you think he can really grant a free wish?"

"I don't know," I said. "Jathon and Thackary seem to think so. There must be something different about him. Roosevelt's head said the genie was powerful. Like, scary powerful. And the cotton candy man said the jar was locked away for a reason. Don't you wonder what that reason is?"

She shook her head. "Does it matter? We're talking about a free wish, Ace. Anything you want."

"The matron at the orphanage used to say that there's no such thing as a free lunch." I lifted an eyebrow, wondering what she might say if she knew I had paid for a lifetime supply of lunches with a smudge of peanut butter on my cheek.

"What's that supposed to mean?" Tina said.

"That everything has a price—a consequence," I answered.

"Like cereal box toys. You didn't just get a free toy. You bought the cereal, didn't you?"

"You just compared the Undiscovered Genie to a cereal box toy?"

I shrugged. "All I'm saying . . . From the warnings we've heard, I get the impression that the Undiscovered Genie isn't exactly the kind of genie you want to work with."

This seemed to upset Tina. She scowled a bit, squeezing the steering wheel. "You don't understand," she whispered. "If our genies can't fulfill our greatest desires, then what's the use in being a Wishmaker?"

"Umm," I said, reminding her of the obvious quests. "Saving the world?"

"But did you really go with Ridge just because you thought the world needed to be saved?" she asked.

"Well, no," I muttered.

"Exactly," whispered Tina. "If our genies can't get us what we really want, then I have to believe there is another one out there who can."

I couldn't deny that the same thought had crossed my mind. It was no wonder Thackary Anderthon was so driven to find the Undiscovered Genie. If he could really do what Jathon claimed, wouldn't you want him to fulfill your greatest desire?

"That's a lot to think about," I said, feeling my heavy helmet clunk against the window as I rested my head. "I just need to focus on my quest and stop the world from ending. It's the only thing I have control over." I glanced at her. "And you should focus on saving Thackary."

She was quiet for a moment, and then she muttered, "I don't think I will."

"You can't give up!" I said. "There's still time."

"Time for what?" she asked. "If you succeed, Jathon fails. If Jathon succeeds, you fail. The world is going to end, Ace. Unless . . ."

"Unless?" I probed, but she didn't reply.

We drove in silence for a while and I felt sleepiness nipping at my eyelids once again. But I pushed past it, deciding instead to stay awake for Tina. In case she decided to say anything else.

She didn't.

CHAPTER 28

We got to Lake Michigan by seven thirty in the evening. I think we must have set a cross-country speed record, sustaining ourselves on peanut butter sandwiches and stopping only occasionally to stretch our legs. Thankfully, my medieval helmet had disappeared during the drive, and I think we were all feeling a bit more optimistic about the third task.

"Wow," Ridge said, as the four of us stood staring out over one of the Great Lakes.

"Yeah. This is a big lake." I couldn't help but state the obvious. The only lake I knew was a community fishing pond just outside town. It was a puddle in comparison.

I squinted across the horizon of water. There were plenty of boats out, but none was close enough to identify a yellow flag.

Tina turned to Vale. "I wish to know which boat is red with a yellow flag." She was wasting no time, and I felt like Tina had a steely determination after our conversation.

"If you want to identify the boat," said Vale, "then every time you hear the radio playing, it will turn to static."

"What about downloaded music?" Tina asked.

"Nope," replied Vale. "Just the radio."

"How long will it last?"

"You'll have static radio forever."

Tina took a deep breath, her face scrunched up in thought. "Okay. It's all about streaming, anyway. Bazang." I saw her hourglass watch close as Tina raised her arm to point across the water. "That's the one."

"Which one?" I asked. From my perspective, she was pointing aimlessly into the distance.

"I've got it figured out," Tina assured me. "We just need a way to get out there so I can give directions."

"Better you than me," I said. "I can't read, and I don't know left from right."

"We'll need a boat," Tina continued, pointing toward a nearby marina. It would be awfully convenient to borrow one without having to wish for it.

As the four of us drew closer, we realized that the docks were nearly empty. Only a single boat was lashed in place. And standing next to it were two despicable characters that I immediately recognized.

Thackary and Jathon.

"Ahoy, ye scallywags!" Thackary Anderthon shouted as we made a hasty approach. "I be commandeering this here vessel!" His pirate accent was actually quite fitting for our current situation. Although, I doubt historically there were pirates in Lake Michigan. Or motorboats.

Jathon stepped into the boat, taking his place at the controls as Thackary struggled with the lashing rope. I was the first to reach him, drawing to a halt when I was an arm's length away.

I scowled at Thackary in the evening light. The man's hair was stringy and damp, the black strands laid across his forehead like worms stretched out on the sidewalk after a rainstorm. His face seemed hollow and long, his chin ending in a cleft full of whiskers. He was rather pale, except for his ear, which looked puffy and red.

"Give us the boat!" I said. Behind me, I felt Ridge shrinking nervously. I tensed, preparing to transform my genie, though I wondered if he would be any braver in shark form. A cowardly shark would be just what I needed.

Thackary looked me in the eye, his face cracking into a smirk that exposed jagged gray teeth. When he spoke, his breath smelled like garlic. "You must be the ace of hearts."

I felt my body begin to tremble and I swallowed the lump in my throat.

"Me son told me all about ye," Thackary went on. "Poor little Ace. A story with no beginning."

My teeth were grinding together in an attempt to hold back my fury. Then I thought, Why hold back? This was as good a chance as any to complete my quest.

I lunged at Thackary. He took an agile step backward and dropped something to the dock. It made the unmistakable ping of a coin and I glanced down to see that it was a nickel. The second before I hit him, Thackary's foot came down on the coin and a column of silvery light erupted around him.

I hit the wall of light with a jolt that made me think I'd been electrocuted. The contact sent me reeling backward to collide with Ridge.

"Har-hardy-har," Thackary taunted, still encased in the column of protection with his foot on the coin. "Ye shan't be completing yer quest today, lad."

"How'd he do that?" Ridge muttered, propping me up as I glanced to Tina and Vale for support. But after that show of force, neither of them seemed anxious to take a swing at Thackary.

"'Tis called a trinket," Thackary said.

"Actually, it's called a coin," I corrected. I didn't know why his had magical powers, but at least he could call it by the right name.

"A trinket," Vale said. "It's a different kind of pay-as-you-play wish."

"Like Ridge's shark form?" I asked.

"The Wishmaker can wish for the trinket to have a special power whenever it's used," she explained. "They just have to agree up front that they'll pay the consequence every time someone uses it."

"Why am I just hearing about this now?" I cried. "It's day five!"

Vale shrugged defensively. "*I'm* not your genie."

I glanced at Ridge, who mouthed the word *sorry*.

"How can he use a trinket?" I asked, pointing back at Thackary. "He's not even a Wishmaker."

"Aye," Thackary said. "Trinkets can be mighty handy. And they be available for any scurvy sea dog to use. Not just Wishmakers. I have only to put me foot upon this here nickel and the Universe shields me from danger."

"But you had to pay a consequence," I said, hoping there was some fairness in the Universe.

"Nay," answered Thackary. "The Wishmaker pays the price." He pointed back to the motorboat. "And I gets the reward fer free!"

My eyes followed his gesture to the motorboat where Jathon stood at the prow. The boy was slapping himself in the face over and over again. Even from this distance, I could see that his cheeks were bright red as his flat palm smacked one cheek, then the other, at a steady pace.

I turned back to Thackary, my opinion of the man dropping even lower. If that was possible. "You're a monster," I said through clenched teeth.

"I couldn't be anything else," he answered. Thackary stepped off the nickel, bending to scoop it up as he leaped into the motorboat, the mooring rope falling to the dock.

"Onward to sea, boy!" Thackary shouted at his son. "Let that devil genie out of her jar. 'Tis time to take a wee dive!"

Jathon, breathing heavily and grimacing, grabbed the motorboat's wheel. With a spray of water across the docks, the Anderthon pair sped away.

"We've got to go after them!" Ridge shouted.

I saw Tina scanning the empty marina, muttering, "We need a boat. . . ."

"Or do we?" I asked. A grin spread across my face as a plan came to mind. I stooped to pick up a coil of rope on the dock.

"Ready?" I asked Ridge.

"For what?" he asked.

"Muumuu," I said. As the genie transformed into a shark, I flopped onto my stomach on the wooden dock. "We can tie ourselves to Ridge," I explained with my face on the planks.

"He can swim us out to the red boat so we can make the dive."

"There's just one problem," shark Ridge said. "I can't swim."

"Of course you can," I encouraged. "You're a great white shark!"

"Umm. You wished for an *air* shark," Ridge said. "So that's what the Universe gave you. If I go underwater I'll drown."

"Seriously?" I blew out a frustrated sigh.

"It might still work," Tina said. "We can tie the rope to his tail and hold on to it. Ridge can just . . . fly above the water and tow us along behind him."

"Let's do it!" I said. "Is that okay with you, Ridge?"

The genie shrugged with his fins. "As long as you think I'm strong enough."

"Definitely," I said.

Tina stepped forward and looped the rope around Ridge's tail. Then she offered me the other end of it while she turned to Vale, lip balm jar in hand. "The fewer people Ridge has to tow, the easier this will be."

Vale nodded, though her expression made it clear that she didn't love the idea of spending time in her jar, either.

"Vale," Tina ordered, "get into the jar." The redheaded genie disappeared in a puff of smoke, and Tina slipped the little glass jar back into her pocket, making sure it was secure.

I grabbed hold of the rope, Tina's hand just above mine.

Ridge tried to glance behind him, but it turns out that's rather difficult for a shark to do.

"Don't let go of the rope, Ace," I heard him say. "We could both drown if we snap the tether in the middle of the lake."

I was about to say, "Good point, Ridge," when the air shark lurched forward, dragging me and Tina off the end of the dock. The water felt cold as I plunged into it face-first.

I gasped, kicking my feet and trying to keep my head up against the pull of my belly being drawn downward.

"You'd better pick up some speed," Tina said to Ridge, "or your Wishmaker's going to sink like a stone."

Ridge sped forward and I felt the rope go tight in my hands. It almost slipped through my grasp, but I managed to hang on. Tina's body slammed against mine as we both dangled from the end of the rope.

You've seen a person water-skiing, right? That's what we looked like. Except, instead of a boat pulling us along, we had an airborne shark skimming across the lake's surface. And of course we didn't have skis. Instead, our bodies skipped painfully along behind the rope.

So, I guess we actually looked nothing like a person water-skiing.

"To the left!" Tina shouted. I didn't know how she could see anything in that spray of water. Ridge corrected his course

to the side, though I wasn't sure if it was actually left or right.

After a while, my entire body felt like one big welt. And I was surprised there was any water left in the lake, because I could have sworn I'd swallowed it all. Tina called a few more directions to Ridge, and then, finally, he began to slow down.

I started pumping my arms and legs, doing a strange variation of the dog paddle to keep myself afloat.

"Hey, Ridge," I called. "Can you swim?"

He clucked his tongue at me. "Of course I know how to swim, Ace."

"Muumuu," I said. There was a loud splash as Ridge fell into the lake. At the same time, I was finally able to get my legs beneath me and found it much easier to tread water that way.

Ahead of me, Ridge seemed to have quite a bit of difficulty swimming. He floundered with his arms, head bobbing in and out of the water.

"I thought you said you knew how to swim," I said.

"I do," answered Ridge, as he thrashed. "It's just really hard when you have a rope tied around your ankles!"

"My bad!" I called as I swam over to him. "Let me help you." But Ridge finally seemed to have gained control.

"I got it," he said. "My shark tail is a lot bigger than my ankles. I just had to kick the rope loose."

"Hey! There's the boat!" I said, finally spying the red vessel with the yellow flag floating just a few yards ahead. There was no sign of the Anderthons. Had they already completed the third task?

"That's why I stopped," Ridge said. "Looks like there's a fisherman onboard."

I squinted at the figure on the boat, who seemed to be squinting back at us.

"I see you swimming there!" the angler called. That's when I realized it was actually a woman—a *fisherwoman* with a thick brown beard. And there was something off about her. Besides the beard. Like the man with the pink mustache, she somehow seemed . . . artificial.

"Diving is not allowed here!" The burly woman pulled back

her arm and cast with a stout fishing pole.

Have you ever been fishing? All you have to do is put a little worm on a little hook, toss it into the lake, and wait for the fish to bite. Except this wasn't a little hook. The one that she cast was closer to the size of an anchor. And the worm on that hook was the most gigantic creature I had ever seen. It looked more like a python!

The oversized hook and monstrous worm splashed between Tina and me, rocking us back with the waves as it sank below the surface.

"Hey!" Ridge screamed at the fisherwoman. "That could have hit us!"

"I think that was the point," Tina muttered.

"She must be guarding the bottom of the lake," I said. "We better start diving!"

"This lake is deep, Ace," said Tina.

I heard Vale's muffled voice from inside her lip balm jar. "Two hundred and eighty seven feet."

"Two hundred and eighty-seven feet?" Way deeper than I'd thought! "How do you know?"

"I read it on a sign at the marina," Vale's voice answered.

Of course she did. . . .

One thing was sure, I'd need a wish to dive that deep. I had a hard enough time reaching the bottom of the deep end at the public pool.

Aboard the red boat, the large fisherwoman was preparing to cast with another sturdy pole.

"Ridge," I said, thinking of how I could complete the third task without making a direct wish for it. "I wish I could hold my breath for the next hour." I didn't know how long it would take to swim down two hundred and eighty-seven feet and back up again, but an hour seemed like enough time.

"If you want to hold your breath for the next hour," said Ridge, "then every time you walk directly under a lightbulb, it will explode."

"Whoa," I said. "That seems kind of dangerous. Won't broken glass fall down on my head?"

"Not if you move out of the way," said Ridge. "Besides, you can always weave around them so they don't explode."

"I'll always be looking up at the ceiling," I said. "What if I get a stiff neck?"

"Definitely don't look up," Ridge said. "Broken glass could fall in your eye."

"So how do I weave around lightbulbs if I can't look up to see where they are?"

Ridge pointed to my hourglass. "You'll have to work that out later. Besides, this will only last the rest of the week."

"Fine," I muttered. "Bazang."

Sure, exploding lightbulbs meant I'd be spending some time in the dark, but if accepting the consequence allowed me to keep up with Thackary, then don't you think it was worth it?

I turned to Tina, treading water beside me. "Did you wish for air?"

In response, Tina held up her little genie jar. "I didn't have to wish. Vale has enough air for both of us inside the jar. When I need to take a breath, I can put my mouth to it and breathe some of the air inside."

"Seriously?" I shouted. "That's going to work?" I suddenly felt as though I'd be destroying lightbulbs for nothing. I hadn't thought about air inside the peanut butter jar.

Tina drew in a deep breath and ducked under the water's surface. I reached around and unzipped my soggy backpack.

"Oh, come on," said Ridge. "You're going to jar me?"

"I didn't wish for you to be able to hold your breath," I pointed out. "And if the lake is really as deep as Vale said, then you'll have to come down with me."

Ridge nodded in understanding, and I quickly muttered, "Ridge, get into the jar."

Poof. He disappeared.

Down we went.

CHAPTER 29

Tina was already swimming downward. I saw her, maybe ten feet below, lifting Vale's genie jar to her mouth and taking a fresh breath of air. She might have been smart enough to come up with that trick, but my method seemed more foolproof.

I was holding my breath, and I felt perfectly fine. I could do this for an hour. That had to be a world record!

The water beneath us looked dark and foreboding, but things were going swimmingly.

And then I got hooked.

I was diving peacefully when my shoulder brushed past a cord of invisible fishing line. I ducked sideways through the water just as the huge hook passed me by.

I thought I had successfully escaped, when the massive worm suddenly lashed out like a sea serpent, winding its slimy body around my arm. There was a sharp tug and then I felt myself being reeled upward.

Since I was holding my breath, there was no possible way to get Ridge out of his jar to make a wish. Even if I could get him out, I knew talking underwater would mostly sound like "gurgle-gurgle-gurgle blub."

I punched the nasty worm, but if you've ever tried underwater punching, you know that it's not very effective.

I tried going limp and playing dead with the hope that I would slip through its grasp. While I was in this flaccid state, I saw Tina off to my left. Or maybe my right. She appeared to be having some trouble of her own.

Another hook and worm had found her, too. She was wriggling like a fish desperate to get free, but her demon worm had managed to wrap itself tightly around one ankle.

At last, I broke the water's surface. The bearded fisherwoman was leaning against the railing of the red boat, straining against the bent pole.

"It's a good one!" she shouted. "Look at the size of him!"

"Ridge!" I shouted, as the fisherwoman eased me closer to the boat. "Get out of the jar!"

The genie appeared in the water beside me, floundering for a moment as he realized where he was. "What happened?" he cried.

"What does it look like?" I shouted. "I need you to muumuu us out of this mess!"

At the mention of the trigger word, I rolled stomach down

in the water, giving up my last bit of resistance against the worm and the fisherwoman. At the same time, Ridge became a shark and shot through the air, his razor teeth snapping the line that was pulling me in.

The fisherwoman stumbled backward, slipping on the deck of the boat. As soon as the line was severed, the worm that held my arm seemed to dry up and unravel, sinking with the massive hook to the bottom of the lake.

The bearded woman recovered quickly, grabbing another fishing pole from a mount on the rail. "Fish on!" she cried, reeling hard. A second later, Tina broke the surface of the lake, gasping for air.

"Ridge!" I shouted, struggling to swim while facedown. "Cut her loose!" The air shark genie spun around, biting through the line that held Tina captive.

"Are you out of your mind?" Tina shouted at the burly fisherwoman.

"I am a guardian of the Ancient Consequence. I have been placed here to catch my limit!" the woman replied. "Whatever pain my hooks cause you will be nothing in comparison to what you will find in the Cave of the Undiscovered Genie."

It was another warning, similar to what we'd heard at Mount Rushmore and Super-Fun-Happy Place. I wanted to ask her for more details, but she looked to be prepping another fishing pole.

"I don't think she's going to stop," I shouted to Ridge and Tina.

Vale's voice echoed out of the jar in Tina's hand. "Let me out of here! I can help!"

"Yep," shark Ridge said. "She's itching."

"We're going to need something to cut the lines if we get caught again," I said to Tina. If only my shark could swim! "I wish for a knife!"

Ridge turned to me, his shark mouth opening wide to explain the consequence. "If you want a knife," he said, "then any time you sneeze this week, a grape will fall out of your nose."

"What?" I cried. "I don't have grapes up my nose!"

"I know," said Ridge. "But the Universe will cause one to fall out whenever you sneeze."

"Would it be a red grape or a green grape?" I asked.

"Does it matter?" Tina cried, ducking as the fisherwoman cast a giant hook and worm.

"It might!" I said.

"Green grape," answered Ridge. "The sour kind."

"That's gross," I said. "Bazang."

I felt something land in the back pocket of my pants. Since my pants were on backward, it was really the front pocket. Floating on my stomach in the water, I reached down and retrieved the item I had wished for.

"What's this?" I cried, holding it up. It was the smallest knife I had ever seen. Like the kind my foster mother used to cut olives. The blade was probably less than two inches long. "Why's it so small?"

"You didn't mention the size," Ridge said. "That's what the Universe gave you."

"Not cool, Universe," I muttered. "It better be sharp enough to cut the fishing line."

"Let's dive down and find out," Tina said.

"Aren't you wishing for something?" I asked her, wondering if she'd come up with some other brilliant plan to avoid getting hooked by the evil worms.

"We'll stick together," she said. "You can cut me loose with your knife."

I glared at her, feeling like she'd just used me. "That's a dirty trick."

Tina shrugged. "It's not a trick," she insisted. "I don't see why I should make a wish when we already have a perfectly good knife that would work for both of us."

"It's two inches long!" I shouted. We didn't really have time to debate. Every second wasted meant Thackary was closer to getting away. "Muumuu," I said. The shark turned into a boy, who fell into the water with a splash as I said, "Ridge, get into the jar."

A puff of smoke, Ridge disappeared, and I was able to float

upright again. Tina swam over to me, but I dove underwater before she could say anything. If she wanted my help with the knife, she'd have to keep up.

I darted straight down. Now that I knew what to look out for, I could see a few fishing lines, nearly invisible in the darkening water. One was close enough that I decided to test out my new knife. Sliding the tiny blade along the clear line, I felt the knife snap through, successfully severing the hook somewhere below.

Suddenly, an overgrown worm on a different hook whizzed past my head, leaving a trail of bubbles. I managed to dodge the reaching bait, but Tina wasn't so lucky. It took her around the middle, snugging her tightly against the huge hook. She was jerked upward, but I was there to cut her loose before she got far.

Tina took a breath of air from her lip balm jar and gave me a grateful look as we swam on. I cut through two more lines that brushed threateningly close. And once, a beastly worm managed to wrap on to my leg. But the knife, despite its miniature size, seemed to be sufficient defense against it.

I estimated we'd dived about a hundred feet when the fishing net got us.

It was so dark, I didn't see it until it wrapped around me. Tina was snagged up, too, and we collided underwater as the net tightened its grip. I used my little knife in hopes of slashing my way free, but the net was made of thick strands and I barely managed to saw through one as we were dragged upward.

Tina kicked and thrashed, but that didn't help at all. By the time we reached the surface of the lake again, our arms and legs were twisted and tangled in the net.

"What a haul!" cried the fisherwoman. "Bring them in! Bring them in!"

"Ridge, get out of the jar! And muumuu!" The genie suddenly appeared, instantly taking the form of a shark. I went belly down, but there was a bigger problem.

Ridge was inside the net.

My shark thrashed, but this only seemed to delight the fisherwoman even more.

"Can't you bite free?" I yelled.

"This is a fishing net!" he answered.

"So?"

"So, I'm a fish!" said Ridge. "This is designed to catch me!"

"Well, that turned out horribly!" Tina gasped as the bearded woman raked us toward the boat.

"How did Thackary get past this?" I cried, slapping the surface of the water. I had to assume he'd already accomplished the third task, or he and Jathon would still be nearby.

"Jathon must have wished for his dad to reach the bottom," Tina said. "Nothing can stop the Universe from fulfilling that kind of direct wish."

"Fine!" I yelled. "I wish to touch the bottom of Lake Michigan." At saying the state name, the Universe made me do my best to jump. But jumping is hard when you are floating on your stomach in a fishing net with a shark on top of you.

"Okay," said shark Ridge. "If you want to touch the bottom, then your breath will smell like fish until . . ."

"Until . . . ?"

"Until forever."

I cringed. "What kind of fish? Are we talking salmon? Tuna? Halibut?"

Ridge shrugged with his front fins. "Just general fishiness."

"Is there anything I can do to mask it?" I asked. "What if I brush my teeth?"

242

"Not going to help," Ridge said. "Besides, a few days ago you took a consequence that makes your toothpaste taste like cauliflower."

"Hmm." I had forgotten about the toothpaste, even though it wouldn't last. I had to complete the third task so I could catch up to Thackary Anderthon. That took priority over fresh breath.

"Bazang," I said. Suddenly, the net disentangled itself from me and I was able to swim free. Now that I had made the direct wish to reach the bottom, the Universe would have to remove all obstacles from my path to fulfill that wish.

I transformed Ridge and called him back into the jar, turning once more to Tina, who was still struggling inside the fishing net. "You're on your own this time." Tina couldn't mooch off my wish like she had done with the knife.

"Vale," she called. "Get out of the jar." The redheaded genie suddenly appeared in the net, getting soaked for the first time and gasping at the shock of the cold water.

"I wish to touch the bottom of Lake Michigan," said Tina, causing me to jump at the name.

"Same wish as Ace?" Vale said. "I could hear you from the jar, you know."

Tina shrugged. "We have to hurry. Being direct is the only way."

Vale nodded. "It's the same consequence."

"The fish breath?" Tina asked. Vale nodded. "Bazang."

The only reason I had stuck around to watch the exchange was because I needed a little bit of satisfaction in seeing Tina accept the same consequence that I had agreed to. Once I had received the reward of seeing her scowl, I took in a deep breath of fishy air and dove down.

The fishing lines were still there, slicing through the water with their giant hooks and demon worms, but they seemed to miss us. Twice, a fishing net pulled past us, but our wish had given us the assurance that we'd reach the bottom. Nothing could hold us back now.

It grew darker as we swam deeper. The pressure of the water was building around me and I thought my head might explode. I shut my eyes and continued diving, my fingers reaching out blindly before me.

I was seriously considering giving up and turning back, when at last, my hand plunged into a soft layer of silt that made up the lake bottom. I couldn't see Tina in the darkness, but I had to trust she was close behind.

I ran my hand through the muddy lakebed, a few small slimy rocks slipping through my fingers. I had completed the third task, taking me one step closer to receiving the key to enter the Cave of the Undiscovered Genie.

I didn't know how much time was left in my hour of breath, but it seemed like a good idea to get to the surface so I'd be ready to breathe air again. Kicking off the bottom of the lake, I streamed upward, finding this direction much easier than the dive.

When my head finally rose above the surface of the lake, the sun had just set and a cool wind whipped over the water. I had come up twenty or thirty yards from the red boat. In the dying light, I could see the bearded fisherwoman leaning against the railing.

Tina came up behind me, gasping and sputtering. "Did you touch the bottom?" she asked. I nodded, as the fisherwoman's voice sounded across the water.

"You have completed the third task," she called. "But before you seek the Cave of the Undiscovered Genie, I must warn you. He longs to breathe the free air, but his powers are fishy!"

"Ridge," I said, "get out of the jar." I wanted to be prepared if the guardian fisherwoman tried anything else. But just as Ridge appeared in a puff of smoke, the bearded woman slumped down on the deck of the red boat, as though suddenly fast asleep.

"Did you hear what she said?" Ridge asked.

"Yeah." More ominous warnings about the Undiscovered Genie. More incentive to stop Thackary from opening his jar.

Tina swam closer to me, still gasping for breath from her long time underwater. I turned my face away from her. "I'd offer you a breath mint," I said, "but it wouldn't help." And I didn't actually have one.

Tina splashed water in my face. "Mind your own consequences," she said. "You smell just like I do."

I couldn't help but laugh. And laughing should have made my socks wet. But guess what? They already were.

Ha! Take that, Universe.

CHAPTER 30

I destroyed most of the lightbulbs in our room at the Big Pillow Motel. I didn't mean to, but I had completely forgotten about that consequence when I went strolling into the room. Now there were bits of broken glass all over the carpet and bathroom, so we had to wear our shoes at all times.

Luckily, one small lamp on the desk escaped my destruction, because, well, it's hard to walk directly under a desk lamp.

At first, I think Tina was upset that we weren't pressing on to find Thackary, but after a hot shower and a moment of relaxation on the couch, she was seeing things my way.

We had been much too tired to go on after our ordeal in Lake Michigan. We'd ended up using some rope we found on the red boat to tie on to Ridge's shark tail so he could tow us to shore. There, Tina had proposed that we find out what was on the final ripped-out page of the notebook and continue our quests. I had proposed wishing our way into a motel room and actually getting a decent night's sleep before chasing down Thackary and Jathon.

I came out of the bathroom after my shower, damp clothes back on, complete with backward pants and overgrown shirtsleeves. Attached to the bottom of my foot was a fourteen-inch-long piece of toilet paper that I knew wouldn't fall off for an hour.

"This place is great!" Ridge said, thumbing through a binder on the desk. "They serve free breakfast in the morning."

"See?" I said. "Not only do we get a decent place to sleep, we also get a meal that isn't peanut butter sandwiches." I was getting very tired of eating those. I glanced at Tina on the couch. I'd heard her scream when she sat down. "I told you it would be worth it."

Vale, sitting cross-legged on one of the queen beds, answered. "Worth the mosquito bites?"

"Yes," I said, scratching at one on my arm. "Otherwise I wouldn't have accepted the consequence."

I had wished to find a key to a vacant motel room. In exchange, every time I saw a yellow flower, a mosquito would bite me. A year of potential mosquito bites actually seemed like a fair disadvantage for the comforts of the motel room.

I sat down on the couch beside Tina. The moment I

touched the cushion, I felt a force propel me sideways, landing me squarely in her lap.

"What are you doing?" she shouted, pushing me to the floor.

I thought back to the beginning of the week. I had forgotten about the consequence that forced me to bounce across couch cushions. In fact, I couldn't even remember what wish I had made to get it!

"Sorry," I muttered. "Consequence."

"I can't believe Thackary got away again," Ridge said, shutting the binder of motel amenities and leaning back in his desk chair.

"I didn't have a chance against that stupid trinket," I said. I turned to Tina. "If you knew about those, why haven't you wished for any?"

"Trinkets are risky because anyone can use them," she answered. "You saw what happened to Jathon on the motorboat."

I couldn't forget if I wanted to. The entire time his dad stood on that magic nickel, Jathon was forced to slap himself in the face. It was a horrible consequence.

"I see," I said. "So if you wished for a trinket and it fell into the wrong hands, someone could use it to affect you."

"Not worth the risk, in my opinion," Tina said.

"What *is* worth it?" I asked. "I've noticed that you don't make a lot of wishes."

"Not unless I absolutely have to," she said.

"Well, you're going to have to make a big one in a minute," I said. She gave me a puzzled look. "The fourth page of the notebook," I explained. "I think it's your turn to wish for the information on it."

Tina pursed her lips. "I think we should settle this the same way we settled all the others," she answered, putting her hand out for a rock, paper, scissors challenge.

"No thanks," I said. "You're way better than me."

"It's not really a game of skill," Vale pointed out. "How can Tina be better at it?"

Tina clapped at the mention of her name, and my shoelace came untied at the sound of her clap. Then her hands returned to the challenging position. "This is the last time," she said. "I promise."

Conveniently, it was also the last page in Thackary's note-book. I sighed and put out my hand to play.

I lost. Again.

Tina used paper to cover my rock. She folded her arms, though she didn't look as victorious as I thought she might. "You should make the wish now," she said.

I nodded. It might be helpful to know where we needed

to go tomorrow so we could make some sort of plan tonight. I turned to Ridge.

"I wish to know what was on that fourth ripped-out page of Thackary Anderthon's notebook."

He swiveled around in his chair. "If you want to know page four," he said, "then every time someone asks you a question, you will have to answer with another question."

"I'll have to what?" I cried.

"Exactly," said Ridge. "Just like that."

"What if I can't answer their question with a question?" I asked.

"It doesn't have to make sense. You just have to reply with a short question of your own. Then you'll be able to go on and say anything else you want. You can also choose not to respond at all. But that seems kind of impolite, if someone asks you a question."

"And this will last . . ."

"One year," said Ridge.

"I don't think I can," I muttered.

Tina cut in with an attempt to encourage me. "Come on, Ace! We're so close. This is the last thing we need to know."

I shot her an icy glare. It was easy for her to say. She wasn't the one that would have to bear the consequence. "Maybe we can find out another way," I said.

"How?" said Tina. "Thackary and Jathon are probably long gone. If there is any chance of catching up to them, we have to know where they're headed."

Ridge tapped his wrist, gesturing for me to take note of my hourglass. The white sands had almost expired from the top chamber. I needed to accept the consequence or let it slip away.

"Do it, Ace," said Tina.

"I can't," I muttered. "I have too many. I don't think I can manage another."

"Accept the consequence and I'll tell you a secret."

"What secret?" I asked. Why would Tina be hiding something from me?

"It's a secret that will even things out between us," Tina said, then promptly bit her lip as if she regretted saying it.

"Ace!" Ridge said, pointing to the hourglass.

"Bazang!" I squeaked out my answer just before the final grains of sand fell. Instantly, knowledge flooded my mind. I knew what was on that final page, and the answer both frightened me and gave me hope.

"This is it," I said. "We've completed the tasks."

"Then what was on the fourth page?" asked Tina.

"Do you want me to tell you?" Without even meaning to, I found myself answering her question with another question. "It's the cave," I added.

"You know the location?" Ridge asked.

"Would you stop asking me questions?" I answered. "The entrance to the Cave of the Undiscovered Genie is in San Antonio, Texas." I involuntarily sprang to my feet and jumped at the mention of the state. "I have an address," I said.

"The cave has an address?" Ridge asked.

"Why not?" I answered. "It's right downtown. Someone will be waiting for us at the entrance. We're supposed to ask him a question."

"What question?" Tina asked.

"'When is a door not a door?'" I said.

Tina, Ridge, and Vale exchanged puzzled glances. "That's the question we have to ask," I explained. "If we've correctly completed the tasks, then we'll be given a key and allowed to enter the cave." I sat down on the edge of the bed. "That's all I got."

"Hmm," Tina mused. "Texas is a long way from here." I jumped again. "If we hope to get there tomorrow, we'll need a faster way to travel than the truck."

"What about an airplane?" Ridge asked. "We could wish to catch a flight and be there in a couple of hours."

The thought of making another wish and accepting a new consequence made my head spin. I hoped I'd feel a little more optimistic about things in the morning. I lay back on the bed, stretching out just below Vale's feet, and closed my eyes. For a moment, I tried to forget my quest to save the world from zombie pets, and enjoy the softness of the motel bed.

"Hey, Tina," Ridge said, the sound of her name causing the girl to clap, which made my shoelaces untie. "Didn't you have a secret you were supposed to tell Ace?"

My eyes snapped open and I sat up sharply. I'd almost forgotten about that.

She waved us off and slouched into the couch cushions. "It was nothing. Nothing important."

"You said it would even things out between us," I added, remembering the words she'd seemed to regret. "What was it?"

"You're not going to like it," she answered. "It's just something I did to make the week pass a little smoother."

"Actually, I'm very interested," I said. "I could use a little tip to help me out."

"It won't help you," she muttered. "I'm afraid it's too late for that."

"Would you just tell me the secret already?" I cried. Vale sighed and lay back on the fluffy pillows, like she knew what her Wishmaker was about to reveal.

Tina swallowed hard, her gaze fixed on a jellybean-shaped stain on the motel carpet. "I'm not really that good at rock, paper, scissors," she finally said.

"That's your secret?" I was thoroughly disappointed.

"I mean . . ." Tina stammered. "I win every time." Was she gloating now?

"Not every time," I corrected. "I beat you the first time, just before we changed Thackary Anderthon's spare tire."

"I know," Tina said. "But I made sure you never won again." She took a deep breath. "I made a wish so that I would always win rock, paper, scissors."

I went numb, a feeling of gullibility spreading up from my toes. "You did . . . what?"

"I wished to win that stupid game," Tina said. "That's why I kept challenging you. I knew I couldn't lose, so you would have to bear all the consequences."

I didn't know what to say. Tina stood up, sat down, screamed, and then stood up again. Ridge had returned to the binder of amenities, pretending to read in order to remove himself from the awkward situation.

Tina had tricked me! I didn't care what consequence she had accepted to win rock, paper, scissors. I was sure it was something minuscule in comparison to what I had been dealing with.

"Wow," I muttered. "I'm having a hard time knowing who the bad guy is anymore." She didn't say anything, but slowly moved toward the door.

Tina pulled open the door and stepped out into the cool

night, forcefully muttering "alley-oop" as she passed through the doorway. Vale jumped off the bed and hurried after her Wishmaker, mumbling something about needing to take a walk.

As the door swung shut, I fell back into the big pillows of the Big Pillow Motel. Now that Tina had explained the truth, I felt every bit a loser.

And not just at rock, paper, scissors.

CHAPTER 31

I felt someone flop down on the bed next to me. Peering out from the pillows, I saw it was Ridge. Of course it was Ridge. He was the only one left in the room.

"You know, I don't think most Wishmakers take on as many consequences as you," he said.

"That doesn't make me feel any better, Ridge," I said. "That just makes me regret my wishes even more."

"Sorry," he muttered. "I guess what I'm trying to say is . . . hang in there, Ace. You're doing really well considering all the stuff you're dealing with."

"Consequences! Ahh! I don't want to think about them!" I scrunched my eyes shut and plugged my ears to block out all sound other than my own breathing. After a peaceful moment of ignoring everything, I opened my eyes. But when I went to remove my fingers from my ears, they wouldn't budge.

"Hey!" I said, sitting up, slightly panicked. "What's going on?"

Ridge reached up and tugged at my hand, but it was like my index fingers were fused into my ears. Then I remembered. Another consequence. In exchange for my wish to listen through Tina's door at the hospital, my fingers would be stuck in my ears for the next half hour.

"Can you hear me?" Ridge asked. His voice was muffled, but I had no problem understanding him in the quiet motel room.

"I can't take this anymore!" I said. "I've lost track of how many consequences I've had to put up with." I was feeling angry at the Universe for piling everything on my shoulders. "Let's see." I began to list them. In no particular order.

"I have a smudge of peanut butter on my cheek that I can't wipe off. I'll never be able to find the house of my foster parents. I ripped a door off its hinges, and got plastered in bird poop. I bounced across the couch to land in Tina's lap, and I haven't been able to read for nearly a week. I had to tell everyone my greatest desire, and each time I say 'hello' my sleeves grow an inch." As proof, my sleeves came unfolded as I said the word, the fabric spilling past my wrists and around my plugged ears.

"I know it's a lot to deal with. . . ." Ridge began.

"A lot?" I cried. "I'm just getting started! My fingers are

stuck in my ears. I have to salute every white car that passes. My left shoelace comes untied whenever someone claps. I sang 'Twinkle, Twinkle, Little Star' for a half hour straight. I've got a stupid piece of toilet paper stuck to my foot, and my pants are on backward. Every time you turn into a shark, I'm left belly crawling. My right eye is the color of pee, and my toothpaste tastes like cauliflower. I had to wear a heavy knight's helmet for a day. My socks get wet whenever I laugh, and I have to jump whenever I hear the name of a state. My tongue is green, and my breath smells like fish. I can't tell left from right. Every time I walk under a lightbulb, it explodes. If I see a yellow flower, I get a mosquito bite. I have to answer every question with another question. I sneeze green grapes, for crying out loud!"

"And your left arm fell off for a day," Ridge reminded me.

"Exactly!" I shouted. The fact that I didn't even remember to mention that my arm fell off shows you how crazy I was going. Don't you think it should be memorable if your arm falls off?

"It's been rough on you," Ridge said. "And you're probably counting the minutes until this week ends and I go away. But think of all the wishes, Ace. Think of all the things you've been able to do." He punched the mattress. "We're going to catch Thackary Anderthon. We're going to stop him from opening the Undiscovered Genie jar. You're going to save the world,

Ace. That's got to count for something, right?"

"Does it?" I answered him with a question. "I didn't want a genie," I muttered. "I didn't want any of this to happen."

Ridge tilted his head. "I'm afraid it's a bit too late for that. You chose to open my jar five days ago. Having me here is the consequence."

"I thought you were peanut butter!" I reminded him. "I probably wouldn't have opened the peanut butter jar if I'd seen the warning label." It didn't seem fair. "Sometimes I feel like this whole quest was rigged. Like the Universe already knows what's going to happen and it just wants to watch me suffer."

"I'm not sure if the Universe knows how everything will end," said Ridge. "But the Universe doesn't own you. It can't make you do anything. You push on to save the world because it's what you choose to do."

"Then why do I bother?" I asked. "All my choices just slow me down. We're always one step behind Thackary Anderthon, and I can't seem to do anything right. And if we succeed, it still means the end of the world because Jathon will fail. I wish . . ." I wasn't sure exactly how to phrase this one. But if I got it right, this single wish could save me from a lot of heartache.

"Easy now, Ace," Ridge said, looking a bit apprehensive. "Never wish angry."

"I wish I didn't have to make any more wishes," I said. "No more choices, no more wishes, no more consequences."

My white hourglass clicked out of my leather wristband.

Ridge exhaled long and slow, running a hand through his mess of black hair. "That's a . . . hmmm." He tapped his chin thoughtfully.

"What's the consequence?" I asked.

Ridge shrugged. "I don't know."

"What do you mean, you don't know?"

"I mean the Universe is silent on this one."

"So there's not a consequence?" I asked. Had I struck the jackpot? By giving up my wishes, could I accept this for free?

"No," said Ridge. "There's definitely a consequence, I just don't know what it is."

"Has this ever happened before?" I asked.

Ridge shrugged. How would he know? I was his first assignment. "I thought I was always supposed to know the Wishmaker's consequence." He scratched his cheek. "So . . . do you accept?"

"Accept what?" I asked. How could I agree to something that I didn't even know?

"I guess that's what the Universe wants you to commit to," Ridge said. "If you want to give up your wishes badly enough, you'll take the unknown consequence."

I shook my head. The whole situation felt like a trap, like the Universe was trying to manipulate me.

"I may not be the best Wishmaker," I said, "but I'm not

stupid. I won't accept a consequence I don't know. I mean, it could cause a giant meteor to hit the earth and kill everyone on the planet."

My hourglass snapped back into place and I slumped back down into the pillows, my fingers still jammed in my ears.

"That was strange," Ridge said.

"Stranger than sneezing grapes?" I asked.

"A wish with an unknown consequence," said Ridge. "I'll have to ask Vale if she's ever come across that. She seems to know everything."

"Her and Tina both," I said. I suddenly couldn't help but let out a laugh at how pathetic we seemed. "We're not very good at this," I pointed out, my socks wet from my laugh.

"We don't have to be perfect," said Ridge. "We just have to save the world."

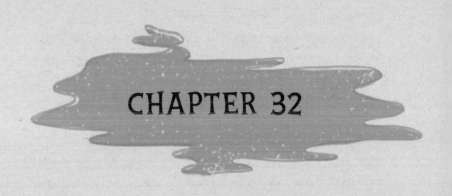

CHAPTER 32

The sixth day of my quest to save the world went like this.

I slept late and woke up with a stiff neck, because the big pillows at the Big Pillow Motel were too big. There'd been no sign of Tina or Vale since they walked out of the room the night before, so Ridge and I wandered over to the lobby for the free breakfast. We ate stale muffins and tangy orange juice, but anything was better than those smashed peanut butter sandwiches in my backpack.

I was going back for thirds when the lobby door opened and in walked Tina and Vale. I pretended like I didn't see them, draping a couple strips of flaccid, transparent bacon on my plate and returning to the small table where Ridge sat.

"You guys ready to go?" Tina asked, as though everything were normal between us.

"What makes you think we're going anywhere together?" I answered with a question. "I think Ridge and I will do just fine on our own." I refused to look up at her.

"Then I guess Vale and I will take the jet by ourselves," said Tina.

I finally glanced up. "Jet?"

"Yeah," answered Tina. "I was trying to think of the fastest way to get the four of us to San Antonio, so I wished for a private jet."

I had to admit that sounded pretty cool, but with Tina's track record, I wondered if it was just another trick. My defenses were up now. I wasn't going to fall for any yellow-eyed, green-tongued Wishmaker with a private jet.

Vale cleared her throat conspicuously. "Hey, Ridge. Why don't we go get some oatmeal?"

"I'm not really an oatmeal guy," Ridge answered.

"Then how about some yogurt?" Vale pressed.

"They don't have the flavors I like," he said.

"Ridge." Vale was growing impatient. "Why don't you come help me with the waffle maker?"

"It's pretty simple," he said. "Just put the batter in and close the lid—"

"Ridge!" Vale grabbed him by the sleeve and yanked him to his feet. "We're going over there for a few minutes."

I watched Vale pull my genie over to the buffet table as Tina sat down in Ridge's vacant chair.

"I'm sorry, Ace," she began. "I really am." I glanced across the table at her, but she was looking down. "I'm not proud of what I did. I shouldn't have tricked you like that. You're a brave Wishmaker. Braver than me."

I liked where this was going, but it didn't mean I was going to forgive her.

"I've been thinking about that consequence that Jathon accepted," Tina went on. "How he can't spend time with friends for the rest of his life. But I think I have it worse."

"What do you mean?" I asked.

"Jathon has no friends because the Universe won't let him," Tina said. "But I don't have any friends because of who I am all by myself." She sniffed. "I'm a liar, Ace. My whole life I've struggled with it. Keeping secrets from the ones I should trust. Maybe I am the bad guy."

"Hey," I said, setting down my bacon and turning to her. "I think you're being a little hard on yourself. I understand why you rigged rock, paper, scissors. I might have even done the same thing, if I'd been smart enough to think of it." I thought about putting my hand on her shoulder. "I don't think you're the bad guy, Tina."

At the sound of her name, she clapped her hands and my shoelaces untied. "I want to finish this together," she said, staring straight at me. "We have to finish this together. I thought about wishing to make you forgive me, but that seemed like another trick. Another lie."

"Yeah," I muttered. "Forgiveness wouldn't mean much if the Universe forced me into it."

"I know," Tina said. "It has to be something you choose."

I was sick of making choices. Choices that brought awful consequences. But maybe this one could actually bring a good consequence.

"You really have a private jet?" I asked. She nodded. "What consequence did you take for that?"

"Oh, several, actually," said Tina. "In order to get the jet, the Universe destroyed my three most favorite possessions." She paused, then decided to list them. "My guitar, a bracelet from Peru, and a blanket my *abuela* made for me."

I grimaced. I only had one real possession. And I'd be pretty upset if the Universe had destroyed my ace card.

"Of course, after I got the jet, I needed a pilot," Tina said. "As a consequence for that wish, I'll pee my pants anytime someone hugs me today."

I snickered, wetting my socks, and she shook her head, unamused.

"Lastly, I agreed to have my left elbow itch for the rest of the week."

"What was that consequence for?"

"That was for wishing that the jet would be able to take off from the motel parking lot," Tina said.

I stood up, grinning. "Seriously?"

She nodded, scratching her elbow. "We're all ready to fly to the cave. I just need to know if you and Ridge are coming with us."

It was hard to stay mad at Tina when I could see how sincere her apology was. And the fact that she'd taken on these consequences proved that she was trying to atone for the way she'd played me.

"Let's go stop Thackary Anderthon," I said. "Or save his life."

I moved around the table, waving the genies over. Ridge was just pulling a fresh waffle out of the iron, but he left it abandoned on the countertop.

"Thanks, Ace," Tina said. "Thanks for giving me a second chance."

"Just promise that you won't trick me again," I said.

Tina paused, and then opened her mouth to say something. Vale cut her off, gesturing toward the lobby exit. "This way to the jet, boys."

My gaze lingered on Tina for a moment longer, but she turned and strode after Vale, leaving Ridge and me to follow. I didn't know what to think. I could tell Tina felt bad about what she'd done. But she also seemed to think that lies and trickery were part of who she was.

I had forgiven her. And on a scale of one to ten, my trust in her was sitting somewhere around a seven. We were teammates, but I'd need to keep my eye on Tina.

The pilot greeted us as we boarded the private jet. Captain Steve. He was a cheerful fellow, but the Universe had really worked him over. To fulfill Tina's wish, he had suddenly appeared in the cockpit, with no need for an explanation of why he was departing from a motel parking lot and flying four kids across the country.

We settled into the big comfortable seats for takeoff. Once we were in the sky, I noticed Tina hunched over a tray table. Leaning forward, I saw that she was writing something on a pale blue sheet of paper.

"Catching up on your journal?" I asked, causing Tina to swipe a protective hand over the page.

"None of your business," she snapped.

I might have pressed the issue if Ridge hadn't suddenly arrived with a few sodas and a bag of pretzels.

"They've got a ton of snacks in the back in case you get hungry." He handed me a drink and seated himself beside me. Tina finished her scrawling and hastily folded the blue paper, tucking it into her pocket.

We talked. We napped. We ate.

The flight was extremely long. But this was traveling in style!

Finally, we made our descent, Captain Steve announcing our landing in sunny San Antonio. It wasn't until we got off the jet that we realized that we were definitely not where we needed to be. It was actually pretty cold outside—not at all like I imagined southern Texas to be in the dead of summer. And Ridge pointed out that none of the nearby signs were in English.

"Where are we?" I shrieked, climbing back into the jet.

"This sure isn't Texas," muttered Vale, causing me to jump at the state's name.

"I told the captain to take us to San Antonio," Tina insisted.

Captain Steve suddenly appeared from the cockpit. "This is San Antonio."

"Why is it so chilly out there?" Ridge asked.

"Because it is," he answered.

"Where are we?" I asked again.

"Chile," said the captain.

"I don't care about the weather," I said. "I need to know where we are."

"Chile," Captain Steve repeated. "San Antonio, Chile."

"What?" the four of us yelled in unison.

"We're in South America!?" I gasped.

"He's probably the worst pilot in the world," Ridge pointed out.

"We need to get back on track!" Tina yelled at the captain. "Fly us back to the States!"

"No can do," answered Captain Steve. "The jet only had enough fuel to get us here."

Tina grunted in frustration, whirling to find Vale. "I wish that the jet would have enough fuel to fly us directly to San Antonio, *Texas*." She emphasized the state name, causing me to jump.

"If you want to refuel the jet," said Vale, "then your armpits will be sticky for the rest of the week."

I cringed.

"How sticky?" Tina asked, scratching at her itchy elbow.

"Like you smeared honey in them," answered Vale.

Tina lowered her eyes as though she were embarrassed to accept the consequence. "Bazang," she muttered. Tina made a grossed-out face and slowly lifted her arms.

It took us some time to get approved for takeoff. When we were finally in the air, this leg of the journey felt even longer than the first flight.

Luckily, we got a good bit of sleep, and I was surprised to see that it was already morning when we began our descent into the real San Antonio, Texas.

Morning.

This was it. The seventh day. The final day. The day we would either succeed at stopping Thackary Anderthon from opening the Undiscovered Genie jar, or bring about the zombie pet apocalypse.

CHAPTER 33

We moved along the streets of downtown San Antonio, finally approaching the address of the cave, though I didn't see how a cave could be very secret if it was right in the middle of a big city.

I was nervous about the day. When my week had started with Ridge, it seemed as though it would never end. Now our time together was quickly drawing to a close. I glanced at the watch face on the top of the hourglass.

"Anybody know what time this all began?" I asked. If we were going to cut it this close, I wanted to know exactly when my quest would expire.

"I think it was just before noon," Ridge answered. "I remember because you were making lunch."

"I don't always eat lunch right at noon," I said.

"I opened Vale's jar at 11:47," Tina said. "I was down at the hospital cafeteria. I thought it seemed important to remember the time, so I checked the clock."

Of course she did. I agreed that it was important. I assumed that the exact time would be the deadline for my quest. "Ridge," I said, "I wish to know exactly what time you came out of the jar in my kitchen."

"All right. If you want to know what time I first arrived," said Ridge, "then whenever you go up or down stairs, you'll have to step with both feet on every stair."

"Oh, man! Like a little kid?" I had seen toddlers, not yet comfortable with stairs, making a half step at a time, lining up both feet before braving another.

"How long will that last?" I asked.

"Just the day."

Only a day? That wouldn't be too bad. It would be worth taking my time on the stairs so I could know exactly how many minutes I had left to complete my quest.

"Bazang," I said.

"It was 11:49," Ridge answered as my hourglass snapped away.

"Two minutes after me," Vale pointed out.

"See?" Ridge said. "I told you it was right before noon."

"That means we only have about an hour left," I muttered, suddenly regretting the way that I had spent the week.

"Maybe we can wish for more time," Tina said. "Maybe the

Universe will give us an extension to complete our quests."

"You can ask," Vale answered. "But I wouldn't mess with the seven-day assignment. I've never heard of a Wishmaker who could bear that consequence."

I was having a hard enough time accepting the little consequences. I wasn't in the mood to make any extra wishes. I just wanted to get to the stupid cave, find Thackary, and lock him down so he couldn't touch the jar.

"So, what will happen when the time expires?" I asked.

"It's over," said Vale. "No more wishing."

"But I'll still have the jar," I said. "Can't I—"

"It doesn't work like that," Vale cut me off. "We're with each Wishmaker for exactly seven days."

"What if someone completes their quest early?" I asked.

"Doesn't change anything," Vale said. "We just get to hang out and make fun wishes until the seven days are up. But you won't have the jar when the time runs out."

"What do you mean?" I said, holding out the plastic peanut butter container. "I'll just hang on to it."

"When the time runs out," said Ridge, "I will automatically go back into the jar. But the jar . . ." He trailed off, as if upset about the unspoken part of the sentence. But Vale, who seemed more hardened to the ways of the Universe, finished his thought.

"The jar disappears."

I looked down at the peanut butter genie jar in my hand. Even after just one week, it was hard to imagine life without it and its occupant. "Where does it go?"

"The Universe takes it," said Ridge. "The jar gets prepared to go into the hands of the next Wishmaker."

I looked at Ridge. "You're going into someone else's pantry?" I was surprised at the notes of sadness in my voice.

Ridge shrugged. "I won't always be peanut butter," he said. "The Universe disguises the jar into whatever it needs to be so that the next Wishmaker will open it."

"Who's the next Wishmaker?" I asked. I wasn't jealous. Just let down. After all we'd been through together, Ridge was going to disappear and fall into the hands of some other kid?

"Only the Universe knows," Vale said.

Tina suddenly stopped walking, her feet planted squarely on the sidewalk and her face turned up at the tall skyscraper building beside us as she absently scratched her left elbow.

"Isn't this it?" she asked, pointing to the numbered address hanging above the reflective glass doors. "Isn't that the address of the cave?"

I chose not to respond, since I'd have to ask a question back. How could Tina be right? Have you ever seen a cave that looked like a skyscraper?

"That's it, all right," Vale seconded, as I saluted a passing white car. "At least, that's the address Ace gave us when he made the wish."

"Maybe he told us the wrong numbers," Ridge offered.

"I didn't tell you the wrong numbers," I said, staring up at the meaningless squiggles above the door. It was good to know that I'd be able to read again in a little less than an hour. "What does it say?"

Ridge read the words. "'Museum of Cans, Crates, Cartons, and Containers.'"

I scoffed. "That sounds like the most boring museum ever."

"Containers don't have to be boring, Ace," said the genie. "It's all about what's inside them."

"It's probably just empty containers," I said. "Otherwise wouldn't it say 'Museum of Things Inside Cans, Crates, Cartons, and Containers'?"

"I don't think that would have fit above the door," Ridge said. "They had limited space."

"They could have used a smaller font."

"Does it really matter?" Tina cut in.

"Is the sky blue?" I answered with a nonsense question.

"It still looks orange to me," Tina answered.

"We should wait here and stop Thackary if he tries to go inside," I said.

"Unless he already went inside," Tina said. "We should go in and check it out."

Tina made a good point. We'd fail our quests for sure if we spent the last hour waiting on the sidewalk while Thackary made his way into the cave.

"I thought you said someone was supposed to be waiting for us," Vale said.

I nodded. "Whoever it is will probably be inside. And we're supposed to ask a question," I reminded everyone. "'When is a door not a door?'"

"What do you think that means?" Ridge asked.

"How should I know?" I shrugged. "Let's go find out."

The four of us strode through the shiny front doors of the museum, Tina muttering "alley-oop." We were greeted by an exploding lightbulb overhead, showering us with tiny fragments of broken glass. The radio was playing some soft classical music, but it quickly turned to static in Tina's presence. There was a little gift shop off to one side and the museum exhibits lay just ahead.

Acting as an entry gate was a reception desk with a nice bouquet of yellow flowers. The moment I saw them, I felt a mosquito bite my neck. I quickly slapped it away, and might have even killed the pesky insect. But then I made the mistake of looking back at the flowers, and I felt another mosquito bite my wrist.

Behind the desk with the dangerous flowers was a strange little man. He was barely my height, and very overweight. He wore thick round glasses with heavy red frames. The top of his head was mostly bald, and he had combed the remaining hair on both sides straight out. The effect made him look like he'd stuck his finger in the electrical outlet. But the strangest thing was his unibrow. The single bushy eyebrow was inching its way across his forehead like a fuzzy caterpillar.

"Good morning," I said, averting my gaze from the flower bouquet, as the four of us approached the desk.

The man seemed to jump at the sound of my voice. I didn't know how he'd missed us coming through the front door and blowing out a lightbulb. It was as if he'd been asleep while standing up with his eyes open.

"Oh, blimey!" cried the man. His hand darted up to his forehead, snatching his wandering unibrow and returning it to its rightful place above his eyes. "Welcome to the Museum of Cans, Crates, Cartons, and Containers!" His voice carried a whimsical British accent. "I am your friendly, knowledgeable curator!"

I peered past him into the exhibits, scanning for Thackary and his son. I didn't see anyone, but the museum seemed quite large. The Anderthons could be hiding.

Tina leaned forward, placing one hand on the desk for emphasis. "When is a door not a door?"

The curator exhaled sharply, his red glasses slipping down his nose and his unibrow suddenly leaping clear up to his former hairline.

"Oh, that's curious indeed," he muttered. Then, pushing up his glasses and pulling down his eyebrow, the curator stepped around the edge of the desk. Lowering his voice, he answered the question Tina had posed. "A door is not a door when it's ajar."

"A jar?" I asked, raising Ridge's genie jar. "Like this one?"

"Not a jar," said the curator. "Ajar."

I looked at Ridge, Tina, and Vale. "Is it just me, or does he keep saying the same thing?"

"Ajar," said Vale. "As in, the door is slightly open. It's ajar."

"Oh," I cried, finally understanding the riddle. "Ajar!"

The curator nodded impatiently. "I see you travel with genies," said the curator. I don't know why I was surprised to hear him speak so openly about Ridge and Vale. After all, we had just given him a secret riddle that we'd learned from the Universe.

I was anxious to get into the museum and search for the Anderthons. "Did anyone get here before us?"

"Oh, yes," said the curator, nodding solemnly. "Two visitors arrived not twenty minutes ago."

I felt my heart catch, and I tried to rush past the desk. But the curator clucked his tongue, reaching out with one pudgy hand and gripping my shoulder. He lifted me up with insane, inhuman strength and deposited me back on the other side of the desk.

"Before you enter the museum," the curator said, "you'll need to jar those genies for the duration of the tour."

"What?" I turned to Ridge, my only defense in an emergency. If he was in the jar, I'd be on my own. By the sound of it, Thackary and Jathon were already inside. I needed a backup plan. I needed a way to thwart Thackary Anderthon in case he got to the Undiscovered Genie while Ridge was still in his jar.

After the curator's impressive show of strength, I didn't feel right about trying to get past him.

"Would you excuse us for a moment?" I said to Tina, Vale, and the curator. Taking Ridge by the arm, I pulled him over to the museum's tiny gift shop, another lightbulb exploding as I passed under it.

"What are you doing?" Ridge asked.

"Can I tell you in a moment?" I studied the shelves of keepsakes, looking for something small that would easily tuck into my pocket. There were decorative pins, plenty of pamphlets, and a rack of cloth bags embroidered with the museum logo. "I'm strategizing," I said, picking out a fridge magnet from a little bin.

"Oh, really," said Ridge. "Because it looks like you're enjoying this museum so much that you want a souvenir."

I held up the little fridge magnet. It was the shape of a soup can with a label that had some writing on it. Even though I couldn't read it, I assumed the text said Museum of Cans, Crates, Cartons, and Containers.

"All right," I said to Ridge. "Here's my plan."

CHAPTER 34

Ridge and I stepped out of the museum gift shop and crossed to where Tina and Vale were waiting with the strange curator.

"What was that all about?" Tina asked.

"Wouldn't you like to know?" I answered with a question. "I was just doing some souvenir shopping." She rolled her eyes at me.

The curator cleared his throat. "If you are you ready to enter the museum," he said, "then you must put your genies in a jar."

"Do you mean a jar," I asked. "Or ajar?"

"Come on, Ace," said Tina. I knew we were in a rush, but there was always time for a good play on words. "Just put Ridge away."

I held up the peanut butter jar. "Sorry, Ridge," I said.

"Just hurry through," said the genie. "We don't have much time left, and I'd rather not spend my final moments in that itchy jar."

I nodded, then spoke the command. "Ridge, get into the jar."

There was a puff of smoke and Ridge disappeared. Vale also vanished at the words from her Wishmaker. Tina and I stood silently side by side as the curator reached behind the desk and produced two cloth bags just like the ones I had seen on the rack in the gift shop.

"Compliments of the museum," the curator said, handing one to each of us. I held it up like I wasn't sure what to do with it. "For your jars," the curator explained.

I set Ridge's jar into the souvenir bag and put one arm through the handles so it was dangling at my elbow.

The curator gestured for us to step past the desk and enter the museum. "Just to be clear," he said, "your genies must remain in their jars for the duration of this tour. Letting them out will automatically result in your expulsion from the cave."

At the mention of the cave, I shared a nervous glance with Tina. What if Thackary had already made it?

"We have to catch up to the visitors who came in before us," I said. "Take us to them."

"Right this way." We had only followed the curator a few steps, into an exhibit with a bunch of empty wooden crates, when he said, "Ah. Here they are now."

An elderly couple stepped around the corner, studying the

exhibits. The woman had a cane, and the man leaned on her for support.

"What?" I shrieked, as the old people moved out of sight into another exhibit. "*Those* were the visitors?"

"Indeed," answered the strange man. "The museum attracts at least a half dozen visitors every week." He said it like he was proud of the statistic.

Just then, the museum's front door burst open behind us. Wheeling around, I saw Thackary Anderthon and his son, Jathon, sprinting toward the front desk. It seemed the duo was not ahead of us, after all.

The fact that I didn't see Scree meant that Jathon's genie was probably still in her pickle jar. They passed the desk without difficulty, though the curator had moved forward to stop them, waving his short arms wildly, his wandering unibrow leaping across his sweaty forehead.

"You can't enter here!" he cried, but Thackary cut him off.

"When is a door not a door, matey?"

"A door is not a door," said the curator, "when it's ajar."

"Ajarrrrr!" Thackary repeated.

The curator glanced at Jathon. "Is your genie in the jar?" he asked. The bearded boy nodded and patted the pocket on his black leather jacket. "Then you may join us."

"What?" I shouted. "You can't let them in! The Universe told us to stop them!"

The curator shrugged. "I cannot stop anyone who has completed the three tasks. All are welcome to try their keys at the Cave of the Undiscovered Genie."

"Then I'll have to stop him myself!" I shouted, racing headlong at Thackary Anderthon. It would have been a lot easier if Ridge were allowed out of his jar. My air shark was much more threatening than me.

In fact, I never managed to reach Thackary at all. The curator stepped forward, deftly seizing my arms and throwing me to the floor like a ninja master. "There will be no fighting in my museum!" he shouted. "Another stunt like that and I will not hesitate to throw you out."

I pulled myself up off the floor. I didn't doubt the curator's threats. He was much stronger than he looked and I was no match without Ridge.

"I do not show favoritism among guests," he said. "If you are foolish enough to go ahead, you will all enter the cave together."

From inside his jar, I heard Ridge moan. If the curator was going to let Thackary and Jathon enter the cave, then we'd have to race every step of the way, neck and neck until the final moment.

"What are ye waiting for?" Thackary yelled at the curator. "Take us to the cave!"

The odd man adjusted his glasses and waddled off past an exhibit of empty plastic tubs. I, Tina, Jathon, and Thackary followed. The man was wearing some kind of cheap cologne that made my nose tickle. It was horrible to walk beside my enemies, knowing that the Universe had charged me to stop them. But without Ridge, I didn't know what to do. I'd have to bide my time and swipe the victory from Thackary at the last second.

"So Thackary was behind us, again?" said Ridge's voice, echoing up from inside his jar. "I thought we were supposed to be following him. So far, we've beat him to every location."

"That be no fault of ours," Thackary cut in, hearing my genie's voice. "'Tis a consequence we've been forced to endure. Me boy made a wish when we set sail to accomplish the three tasks."

"But a consequence followed," Jathon said. "If anyone else was seeking the cave, we were cursed to always arrive just moments behind them."

"That must have been irritating," Ridge's voice offered.

"Until now," said Thackary. "This be the final stop, and we have managed to catch up, despite all odds and consequences."

The curator guided us past a few more uninteresting

exhibits: bottles, barrels, cardboard boxes. Then we rounded a corner and stopped in a room that seemed secluded from the rest of the museum.

This exhibit didn't seem any more extraordinary than the last ones we'd passed. It had a low shelf, lined with lidless jars of varying sizes. Some were ceramic, others made of glass, metal, and wood. The wide tops were open and they all appeared to be empty.

"The door to the cave is not a door," explained the curator. "It's a jar."

"As in, it's slightly open?" I clarified.

The curator shook his head. "As in, a jar," he answered. "A series of three jars, to be exact." He gestured to the display on the shelf. "If you have completed the three tasks, you may now use the keys to enter the cave."

"Enough blabberin'," Thackary said. "I did what I was instructed to do. Let me have the key!"

The curator held up a hand. "These jars are unbreakable," he said. "But each of you must break them."

"How?" Tina asked. Thackary seemed ready to pounce on the shelf.

"The jars will break when you use the keys," answered the curator. "Each of you pick up a jar and peer inside."

Thackary pulled his son back as he stepped up to the shelf. "Not you, boy. I was the one who completed the tasks. The keys be mine." He picked a glass jar off the shelf, but I wasn't about to let him get ahead of me.

Leaping forward, I snatched up a wooden jar. I saw Tina moving beside me, but I couldn't worry about what she did. Squinting one eye closed, I lifted the wooden jar and peered into the empty space.

Immediately, the jar cracked. I didn't know wood could shatter, but the jar seemed to do just that. I jumped in shock as the container fell to splinters around my feet.

At the same time, something odd began happening around me. The museum suddenly seemed to fade. Tina and the curator remained normal, but the walls of the building, as well as Thackary and Jathon, took on a ghostly transparence.

As the museum began to fade out, a new environment seemed to fade in. Beyond the walls of the museum, I saw smooth stone. But the transition wasn't complete. In fact, it seemed to freeze partway between the two scenes.

The sounds around me had changed as well. The first thing I noticed was Thackary's pirate voice. He was facing us and screaming, but somehow he seemed farther away. Even the smell of his cologne dwindled, for which my nose was grateful.

"What is this?" Thackary threw his glass jar against the floor of the museum, but it wouldn't shatter. "How have ye tricked me?" He strode toward us, his face trembling. Thackary raised his arm to strike the curator. I was afraid for a second, but then Thackary's blow passed right through the strange little man.

"It's quite all right," the curator said to me and Tina. "We are now on a different plane from them."

"I can hear you, scurvy dog!" Thackary's diminished voice cried. "This be not fair! I did what was required. I was at Mount Rushmore and poked the eye of Roosevelt just as they did!" He pointed at us. "Jathon, me boy. Vouch for yer father. Tell this scallywag curator that I did what was needed."

But Jathon wasn't listening to his father. The bearded boy had crossed to the shelf and lifted a ceramic jar of his own. Raising it to his face, he peered inside. Instantly, the jar shattered and Jathon's ghostly figure came into full view. He was now on our plane, much to the surprise of his raging father.

"What?" Thackary called. "How did that happen?" He plucked another jar from the shelf and slammed it against the floor with no result. "Me son didn't do any of the required tasks. 'Twas I who touched the stone eye, ate the cotton candy, and reached the bed of the lake. This is me moment! Yarrrrr!"

The curator turned to the three of us. "Quite a sore loser, isn't he?" I was glad to know that other adults found Thackary just as awful. Though the curator didn't really seem like a normal adult.

"I don't understand," Jathon said. "My father is right. I didn't do any of the tasks."

"Oh, but the tasks were quite unnecessary," said the curator.

"Unnecessary?" I cried. We had spent almost all week doing something that was useless? "What do you mean?" Even Thackary had fallen silent to hear the explanation.

"You see," said the little man, "anyone can touch the faces of Mount Rushmore, eat candy from a park, or scuba dive to the depths of a lake. The Universe wasn't interested in what you could do. It was interested in what price you would pay to do it."

"Our consequences," muttered Tina.

"Precisely," said the curator. "The three of you share a trait that no other possesses." His glasses slipped down his nose and he pointed at his eye.

Of course! It made sense now. The consequence we had all paid to reach Roosevelt's eye was a change in our eyeballs. Now unnaturally yellow, the jars reacted when we looked inside. We had paid the price to be there.

The Universe had told us that we would receive the keys to the cave when we needed them. Little did we know that the keys were with us all along, disguised as useless consequences.

"But as you can see," said the curator, gesturing around the room, "we're not quite there yet." He pointed to the ghostly jars in the museum. "Each of you take another jar from the shelf. It is time to use your second key."

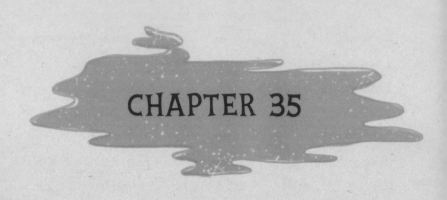

CHAPTER 35

Tina, Jathon, and I stepped forward. I picked a metal jar from the shelf this time. I wondered how I would be able to pick up the ghostly-looking jar, but when I touched it, the metal object seemed to cross into our plane, becoming as solid as a regular jar should be.

"Ye can't leave me behind, Jathon!" Thackary cried. "The Undiscovered Genie jar is not for you to open! Yer quest is to help me. Don't ye forget that!"

"I won't, Father," answered Jathon. "I'll bring you the jar."

The curator clapped his hands to get everyone's attention, causing my shoelaces to come untied. "Your eyes were changed by a choice you made," said the curator. "Now let us see about your tongues. Everybody give the jar a lick."

The jar in my hand didn't taste like anything whatsoever. But then, the point of doing this strange activity wasn't for

the flavor. It was for my tongue. A tongue that had turned bright green ever since I'd eaten that cotton candy at Super-Fun-Happy Place.

And the Universe must have recognized my discolored licker, because as soon as my tongue passed over the metal, the jar shattered.

The room around us faded further as I continued into another plane. Things in the museum, namely Thackary Anderthon, continued to grow transparent, while beyond the walls, the image of a spacious cavern seemed more real.

Thackary now looked like a ghost, running around the room like a maniac and waving his arms in disgust. He was definitely shouting, but I could hear only the faintest sound.

"I can't believe you'd help that guy," I said, turning to Jathon. "I mean, I know he's your father, but . . ."

"But he's a horrible person," Jathon answered. I was surprised to hear him speak so bluntly. Perhaps the fact that his dad was out of reach made him more bold. "I can't stand him."

"You don't have to go through with this," I said. "Give up on the Undiscovered Genie."

"I can't give up," Jathon said. "My dad has lived a hard life. Never had anything he wanted. I've never met a single person who could tolerate him. I wished for things to be different," he said. "I wished that I could like him. But the Universe wouldn't let me. . . ." He trailed off, stiffening. "Besides, I have a quest. I have to save the world."

"So do I," I whispered. "And I will stop you." Either way, it seemed that the world was about to end. But I wasn't going to let it end on my watch.

"Before we go on," interrupted the curator, "let me be the final voice of warning. Nothing good will come from this cave. If only there were something I could say to convince you to turn back now."

There was nothing he could say to convince us to turn back now. With less than thirty minutes remaining, I had to beat Jathon to the jar so he couldn't deliver it to his rotten dad. I had to stop the world from ending with a gory woof and meow.

"The Undiscovered Genie came into existence over three thousand years ago," the curator continued. "But the original Wishmakers who found his jar perceived that he was far too dangerous to be handled. They made a wish—the Ancient Wish—that his jar would be locked away in an unknown cave, never to be discovered by anyone."

"But aren't we discovering it now?" I asked.

"There was a loophole," answered the curator. "The Ancient Wish was not phrased perfectly, which allowed the cave to be discovered if someone sought for it specifically."

"So that's how the cave has stayed hidden in the middle of a big city," Tina said. "Because no one is looking for it."

"Correct," said the curator. "The Ancient Wish put the cave in a place that was, at the time, completely uninhabited. The wish demanded that it be a place that would never be discovered. So in the midst of the desert, I was created as a guardian."

"No offense," said Ridge's voice, "but when I saw you at the desk, you didn't seem too intimidating."

"I wasn't always like this," said the curator. "I began as a deadly serpent, a sort of desert dragon."

"Okay. That would have been way cooler," I said.

"But as the world expanded, a city was formed," continued the curator. "This city, San Antonio. But I couldn't very well survive as a desert dragon in a thriving metropolis. So the

Ancient Wish adapted, and I adapted with it. Ultimately, this museum was constructed as an elaborate illusion to conceal the cave that you are about to enter."

"You went from a dragon to a museum curator?" I said. "Man, that's a downgrade."

"I had several forms in between," said the small man. "Not all of them were quite as flawless as this one." As he said it, his single eyebrow danced across his forehead. He was hardly flawless.

"The Ancient Wish protected this place and its awful jar." The curator looked down. "But for every wish, there is a consequence."

"The Ancient Consequence." I remembered hearing about it while trying to complete the tasks. "What was it?"

"The original Wishmakers wished for the cave to be locked tight, but the Ancient Consequence provided a key to those who completed a series of tasks. The Sculpture, the Vendor, and the Fisher were guardians of the Ancient Consequence," he explained. "For three thousand years, they have been adapting to fit their changing environment, as I have with mine. They have been waiting for Wishmakers like you to attempt the three tasks."

"They kept warning us," I said. "They were trying to stop us from getting here."

The curator nodded solemnly. "They were giving you a choice. And when you decided to persist, they did whatever it took to force you into a wish that would yield a specific consequence."

"The yellow eye and the green tongue," Tina said.

"And lastly," said the curator, "the fish breath." The little man clenched his hands, a grave expression on his round face. "Three thousand years of wishing have tried to prevent this moment from happening. If you go on, you will discover the Undiscovered Genie. What you do with his jar is your choice alone. I will not be going with you, and your genies must remain in their jars until the Undiscovered Genie has been removed from the cave."

"We're ready," Jathon said. But I suddenly felt very uncomfortable about our decision to continue. How many voices of warning had urged us not to find this cave?

"Each of you pick up a new jar," instructed the curator.

Tina and Jathon stepped over to the transparent shelf. One of the glass jars that Thackary had thrown lay near my feet, so I stooped and lifted it.

"With this final key, the cave will appear in full reality," said the curator. "But know this—the Undiscovered Genie is not like other genies. He will give you what you want without a price. But your life will never be the same."

I glanced at Tina, but she was staring at the ground.

"Take a deep breath," said the curator. I heard Tina and Jathon inhale, so I did the same. The curator sighed deeply, eyes momentarily closed. "May the Universe save us all," he muttered. Then he looked at us. "Breathe into the jars."

I lifted the glass jar to my mouth and exhaled all my nasty fish-smelling breath right into the open top. It shattered, though I think that had more to do with the magic of the Universe than my awful breath.

As the shards of broken glass fell to my feet, I saw the curator dissolve into a puff of smoke. The final ghostly remnants of the Museum of Cans, Crates, Cartons, and Containers vanished, taking Thackary Anderthon with it.

Tina stood on my left and Jathon on my right. All around us, ominous stone walls shimmered into perfect clarity as we moved through the final plane and entered the Cave of the Undiscovered Genie.

CHAPTER 36

The cave had an unnatural glow. It was as if the walls and ceiling had been rubbed with broken glow sticks, making the whole area shine in an eerie multicolored light.

It was a vast cavern that seemed both ancient and new. Ancient, because I know it takes millions of years to form a cave. But new, because we were the first human beings to set foot in this place in thousands of years.

Tina, Jathon, and I didn't need to spread out, searching for the undiscovered jar among the luminescent cave formations. Our eyes were instantly drawn to a feature right in the center of the cavern.

There was an island. Now, this wasn't the pleasant kind of island surrounded by an ocean where you might want to vacation. This was an island of stone, surrounded by a deep chasm on all sides, like a pillar that was cut off halfway to the ceiling of the cave.

I couldn't tell how deep the abyss was, but a single rope bridge spanned the distance. In the center of that stone platform was a dais, with at least half a dozen stairs leading up on all sides to a slender pedestal. And there it was, displayed upon a black stand. It looked to be made of hardened clay, and it glowed with a deep crimson aura.

The Undiscovered Genie jar.

The three of us sprinted for the rope bridge. Jathon was in the lead, but that was only because he was playing dirty. He knocked into Tina and stuck out his foot to trip me as we ran. I hit the ground hard, sliding across the smooth stone as Jathon stepped onto the narrow bridge. Scrambling, I came up just behind him, with Tina hard on my heels.

I wasn't sure who'd designed the bridge. I guessed it was the Universe, since it seemed totally unsafe and definitely not made for kids. The bridge was constructed of wooden boards, strung together with a coarse rope. It sagged just slightly, spanning about twenty feet across a bottomless abyss. The bridge's planks were only about three feet wide, and to make matters worse, there was absolutely no railing on the sides.

Have you ever crossed a rope bridge before? How about a rope bridge without a railing? How about a railingless rope bridge that drops off into nothingness on both sides?

"What's happening?" Ridge shouted as the three of us

Wishmakers moved slowly across the terrifying bridge. The boards swayed dangerously underfoot. Jathon's weight ahead of me and Tina's weight behind me made for a very precarious experience, which soon had me crawling on my hands and knees.

"You want to know?" I answered my jarred genie with a question before going on. "We're on a bridge! I'm stuck behind Jathon."

"Slide past him," Ridge said.

"It's not that kind of bridge," I answered.

Ahead of me, Jathon stopped, but he hadn't quite reached the other side yet. He seemed rooted in place, knees bent so the motion of the bridge didn't buck him off to his doom.

I didn't understand why he had frozen. From his vantage point, there would be no contest in reaching the Undiscovered Genie jar first. He slowly turned back to me, his bearded youthful face determined.

"It isn't for me," he said, his voice echoing in the huge cavern. I didn't know what he meant, and my confusion must have shown, so he continued. "I have to help my dad achieve his greatest desire."

"It's too late," I said. "Your crazy dad isn't here. And you can't get the jar to him before your time runs out." I shook my head. "The quest's over, Jathon. You'll never make it."

He reached into the pocket of his horrible leather jacket and withdrew a pencil. It looked perfectly ordinary. Jathon twirled it between his fingers once, like he was debating whether or not to do something. Then he grabbed the pencil in both hands and snapped it in half.

As it turned out, the pencil was a trinket. Jathon discarded the broken halves, and they tumbled into the black chasm. But my attention didn't linger on the spent trinket.

Jathon was paying a consequence. The Universe seemed to pick him up and slam him against the ground. Except, at this moment, the ground happened to be the rope bridge.

Jathon slammed into the planks, half a dozen times, like he was trying to body-slam the wooden boards. The repetitive action caused the rope bridge to undulate like a wave.

Luckily, I already had a death grip on the boards, but behind me, I heard Tina scream. Whirling around, I saw the girl barely hanging on to the coarse rope, her legs dangling over the edge of the bridge.

I performed a quick backward crawl, reaching her in a second. As Jathon's beating came to an end, the bridge calmed and I hoisted Tina onto the safety of the planks.

Jathon was lying facedown on the boards, just feet from the end of the bridge. He had paid the consequence for the pencil trinket, and now I saw the wish that went along with it.

Thackary Anderthon had appeared. He was standing on the stone platform just behind his fallen son, face twisted in a snarl. "Ha-ha!" His laugh seemed slightly frenzied at finding himself in the place he had been seeking. "The trinket has brought us togetherrrr, son!" he cried. "And I told you the consequence wouldn't kill you!" He nudged his son with his foot.

Jathon slowly raised his head. His nose was bleeding and there was a cut across his forehead from the pounding he had accepted.

"It will all be worth it, boy!" cried Thackary. "Once I have what I want, I can be the father you've always wanted me to be." He turned away from his injured son, laying eyes for the first time on the jar of the Undiscovered Genie.

It fell silent in the cavern. Only Jathon's ragged breathing split the quiet as Thackary Anderthon stepped across the raised stone platform and climbed the steps, reverently approaching the crimson jar.

"Ace?" Ridge's voice rang out from my museum bag. "Ace, what's going on?"

"You want to know how bad it is?" I whispered. "Thackary's here. He's almost to the jar."

"Do you have it ready?" he whispered back.

I chose not to reply to his question, grinning instead, as Tina gave me a questioning glance. "We thought of a little something in case this happened," I explained to her.

On the stone platform, Thackary Anderthon reached out and lifted the genie jar from its pedestal. For a brief second, he cradled it close, showing more care than I'm sure he ever showed to Jathon. Then he burst out in maniacal laughter and lifted the jar above his head.

I'm sure his next move would have been to pop off the lid and take control of the Undiscovered Genie, but I had a trinket I was dying to use.

I knelt high, pulled a fridge magnet out of my pocket, and hurled it at Thackary. The consequence of using my pay-as-you-play trinket displayed itself immediately. I reached behind myself, grabbed the elastic of my underwear, and gave myself the biggest wedgie you could possibly imagine.

Hey, I didn't want to. The Universe forced my hand. But it was a price I was willing to pay. And as quickly as I paid the wedgie consequence, the magnet hit Thackary Anderthon and worked its magic.

Remember when Ridge and I had stepped into the museum gift shop to pick out a souvenir? I thought it would be a good idea to wish for a trinket for a situation just like this. The magnet forced the person it touched to drop whatever they were holding. In this case, that was Thackary Anderthon. And the item he was holding was the clay jar.

My trinket was simple but effective. And it caused Thackary to scream in surprise as the crimson jar toppled from his grasp, bounced down the steps, and rolled across the stone platform. It hit the little ledge where the bridge was anchored into the stone, and popped up, rolling just a few more inches until it came to rest between the first two planks of the rope bridge.

The jar was two feet from Jathon. Had he not been so stunned, he might have taken it. Instead, I risked rising to my feet, sprinting the final distance, and leaping over Jathon's injured form.

I halted at the edge of the stone platform, stooping quickly to snatch up the clay jar. I wasn't sure exactly what my intentions were, I just knew I needed to keep the jar away from Thackary Anderthon for a few more minutes. I could have run around the cavern, stalling for time. I could have tossed it back and forth with Tina, like a game of keep-away that could save the world. I could have hurled it into the abyss at my feet so no one would ever find it again.

But the moment I had the jar in my hand, all those ideas were replaced by a single all powerful thought.

Open it.

I could finally find out where I came from, who my family was. No heavy burden to bear. No unpleasant consequence. I could ask, and the genie would grant it.

Did it matter that Roosevelt's head, the cotton candy vendor, and the fisherwoman had warned against opening the jar? Did it matter that the curator had explained that nothing good would come from this cave? I had the answer to my biggest question. It was right in my hand.

Come on. You would have wanted to open it, too.

Slowly, my hand moved to the ceramic lid of the jar. My fingers tightened, and all it would have taken was the slightest tug. But before I could finish the action, a certain trinket fridge magnet struck the back of my head.

Two things happened at once. The hand that had been about to pry off the lid instead reached back to further the wedgie I had given myself. And my other hand, which seemed to have a solid grip, suddenly lost control of the jar.

It tumbled forward. And from my position at the edge of the bridge, there was only one place for it to fall.

Into the chasm.

I cried out, releasing my wedgie and reaching desperately for the jar I had so carelessly dropped. I was furious at myself. Vale had warned me about the risks of a trinket, and my own trick came back to bite me!

I thought for sure the Undiscovered Genie jar was a goner, tumbling over the edge, when Jathon's hand suddenly shot out and grasped it mid-fall. He had been lying so still at my feet, so beaten and defeated, that I wasn't even sure he was still conscious. But his reflexes didn't seem slowed by his injured state.

"That's me boy!" Thackary shouted from behind me on the stairs. I whirled around to face him. His hand was still poised from throwing my fridge magnet. Thackary stretched out his other hand, beckoning hungrily for the jar his son had just rescued.

But I wasn't going to let that slimeball touch it. I glanced down at the watch face on top of my hourglass. I had only like fifteen minutes left until my quest expired. And I didn't intend to let the world get ruined now!

"Tina!" I shouted. Her single clap echoed through the cave, so I knew she could hear me. I'm sure my shoelace came untied, but I didn't have time to worry about that. "Get the jar from Jathon!"

I sprinted directly at Thackary, taking him by surprise as I turned my back on Jathon and the jar. When I hit the bottom stair, one of my recent consequences kicked in and I suddenly found the need to take two steps per stair.

The wiry man fumbled for something in his pocket. I assumed it was his coin trinket, the one that would encase him in a force field. Whatever he was reaching for, I was going to make sure there wasn't time to use it.

I didn't let my double-stair-stepping curse slow me down.

Leaping from the second stair, I plowed into Thackary and sent us both to the ground in an impressive tackle.

"Are we fighting now?" Ridge shouted from inside his jar in the museum bag. He was probably piecing things together from the sounds of our scuffle. "Are we winning?"

"Isn't it obvious?" I answered with my obligatory question. "I've got him pinned!" I quickly maneuvered myself into a position where I was kneeling on Thackary's chest. I had one of his arms clasped tightly in both of my hands, but the other one was wriggling free from where it was trapped against the stair.

"We don't have much time left!" Ridge called.

I blame Thackary's bad cologne for this next part. My nose twitched. I drew in a sharp breath.

I sneezed.

A green grape, much larger than my nostril, came shooting out of my nose. It pelted off Thackary's forehead, leaving a somewhat slimy smear above his eyes.

Sneezing out a grape was certainly not a pleasant experience. But if it had to happen, I was glad it occurred when it did. The distraction of the disgusting grape caused Thackary to falter, and I managed to wrangle his other hand down against the stairs.

The fact that I had successfully pinned him was a miracle. But I seriously doubted that I'd be able to sneeze enough grapes to keep him like this for the next fourteen minutes. I needed help.

Glancing down the steps, I saw Jathon on his feet at the edge of the rope bridge. To my surprise, the crimson jar was still in his hands. I wondered what Tina had been doing while I was tackling the mean dad, and then I saw. She had stepped up beside Jathon, her hand on his shoulder for support.

"What are you doing?" I shouted. "Take it and go!" But Tina seemed to have no intention of following my advice. She looked at me, her gaze piercing the distance across the stone platform.

From beneath me, Thackary angled his head to see the two kids on the bridge. "Bring me the jar, boy! Bring it to yer old man! This is the moment we be fighting for!"

Jathon stepped toward his dad, but Tina held him fast. "You can't do this, Jathon," she said. "You know you can't. We talked about this."

"What are you saying?" I muttered. "When did you talk about this?"

Tina looked at me. "The night in the train," she said. "Jathon and I made an agreement before I let him go."

"What kind of agreement?" I asked, my insides turning to mush.

"There was only one way this could end," Tina said. "But I

knew you wouldn't like it, Ace. I knew you'd try to stop me, so I couldn't tell you."

I felt my grip on Thackary relax as my muscles wanted to give out. Instead, I channeled my anger to hold him tighter.

"Don't be a fool, Jathon!" Thackary screamed. "Think about what that jar could do fer me! I promise I'll be the father you've always wanted!" Then his teeth clenched in a rage. "Bring it here!"

Tina released her grip on Jathon's shoulder and held out her hand instead. "It's the only way, Jathon."

"What are you talking about?" I shrieked. "What's the only way?" I wanted nothing more than to sprint over to the bridge and shake some sense into Tina. But I wasn't sure what would happen if I released my grip on Thackary. I was trapped, and my only option was to shout my logic.

Jathon closed his eyes, one already swollen shut from his pounding on the bridge. He drew in a deep breath, as if hoping that the air could make the choice for him. Then his eyes opened. He looked across the stone platform and muttered two words.

"Sorry, Dad."

Then Jathon handed the jar to Tina.

CHAPTER 37

Tina stood on the rope bridge, her eyes fixed on me, and my eyes fixed on the Undiscovered Genie jar in her hand.

"This is what I came for, Ace," she said. Her voice wasn't very loud, but it resonated in the stone chamber better than it did in my head.

"No!" I cried. Now that I wasn't the one holding the jar, the warnings we'd received from the guardians seemed much clearer. "You can't!" I had felt the allure of the jar. The promise of a free wish. But now that I was seeing someone else on the brink of decision, it seemed like opening that jar was a very bad idea.

"I have to do this for my mom," she answered. "It was always about my mom."

"But . . ." I stammered. I didn't know what to say to convince her to stop. With only minutes left to fulfill her quest, I realized that Tina must have given up. There was no way she could save Thackary's life because we'd never found him close to dying.

"Don't quit," I urged. "There has to be a way!"

"I'm not quitting," she said. "I'm fulfilling my quest."

I gave her a confused look, my fishy breath catching in my throat as her hand moved to the lid of the jar. Then Tina explained everything with a single sentence.

"My mother is an ex-Wishmaker."

Her words hit me like a battering ram. I thought of the woman I'd seen in the hospital room. Tina had told me that her mom was quirky. Singing opera every time the car stopped? Collecting odd knickknacks? They weren't just quirks. And I had assumed that her upside-down ear was part of her condition, but now it made more sense. Tina's mom was still carrying consequences from years ago. From when she was a Wishmaker.

"How long have you known?" I asked, wondering why she would keep such important information from me.

"Since the night in the train," Tina answered. "Jathon told me."

"How did he know about your mom?" Ridge's voice called from inside his jar.

"We went to the hospital," Jathon said. "I had wished to

know if there were any other Wishmakers in play and where I could find them. The answer led us to St. Mercy's Hospital, room 214. By the time we got there to investigate, you guys had already left. But my dad recognized the woman. He knew her from a long time ago. They were Wishmakers together."

Thackary Anderthon and Tina's mom had crossed paths in their youth? Had they worked together on their quests like us?

"I didn't know that she was Tina's mom until we started talking after you fell asleep on the train," Jathon finished.

"I have to save my mom, Ace," said Tina. "It's not just what I want. It's my quest."

"What about my quest?" I asked, struggling to keep Thackary contained. "I can't hold him much longer."

"This will fulfill everything. If I open the jar," Tina whispered, "it means Thackary never can."

"If you open that jar," I yelled, "then Jathon fails his quest and the world will end anyway!"

The injured boy answered me this time. "My quest was to help the person I'm closest to in achieving their greatest desire."

"I know!" I shouted. "I have him pinned. You'll fail!"

"The person he's closest to," Tina said, reaching out and touching Jathon's shoulder, "doesn't have to be his dad."

Ridge had once pointed out that our quests contradicted each other. Three Wishmakers were in play: me, Jathon, and

Tina. We all had quests, and failing any one of them meant the end of the world.

I suddenly realized what it all meant. In this moment, Tina was standing closest to Jathon. He had given her the jar so she could achieve her greatest desire, therefore fulfilling his quest. By opening the jar, Tina would prevent Thackary from ever doing so, therefore fulfilling my quest. And once the jar was open, Tina could make her one free wish and save her mother's life, therefore fulfilling her quest.

Tina was right. This was the only way for all three contradicting quests to be completed.

The guardians of the Ancient Consequence had told us that the Undiscovered Genie would bring chaos. The curator had told us that nothing good would come from this cave.

Tina was prepared to sacrifice herself, and in the process, she was saving the world three times over. But I didn't like it. And I couldn't accept it.

If I couldn't convince her to drop it, maybe I could trick her into it.

"Tina!"

I said her name, knowing that her consequence would make her clap. But she managed around it, her hand moving right back to the unopened lid as the sound of her clap resonated in the huge cave.

"I have to, Ace," Tina whispered. "It'll be all right." Then she ripped open the jar.

I didn't care about holding Thackary anymore. I sprang to my feet, moving down the stairs at a painstaking rate with both feet on each step, careful to avoid tripping on my untied shoelace.

A silence enveloped the cavern. More than a normal silence. It was as though the red smoke venting from the opened jar was absorbing sound.

Then there was a loud crack, and a new figure stood before Tina on the rope bridge. I froze.

The Undiscovered Genie was not at all like Ridge, Vale, or what I'd seen of Scree. He was a man. Not a boy, but a fully grown adult. His head was shaved, his chest was bare, and his muscles rippled in the creepy glow of the cave walls. Black-lined tattoos networked his exposed skin, like cracks in his flesh. Around his right wrist was a thick leather band.

He scanned the room, his dark eyes taking stock of his surroundings while a demonic smile tugged at his mouth. "I," he began, his speech low and almost inhuman, "I am Chasm!"

Then the genie tilted back his head, upraised fists clenched, and sang a bellowing note like a Broadway star into the spacious cavern. His voice was thunderous and seemed to shatter the stillness that had descended upon us all.

He pounded his chest with one hand and when he spoke again, his voice wasn't nearly so freaky. "Whew," he said. "Sorry about that introduction. Totally creepy. I haven't spoken in, well, forever. But I think we're good now."

Thackary and I stood side by side at the bottom of the stairs, no longer the struggling enemies we had been but momentarily stunned into a mutual audience.

Chasm clapped his broad hands together. "So, who's the lucky Wishmaker?"

Jathon, several feet behind the new genie, had fallen to his knees. Tina stood alone to face him, and from her place on the rope bridge, I thought she seemed to cower.

"Well, well, well!" he said, opening his fists as if to flex his fingers for the first time in centuries. "I'm Chasm. You can call me Kaz." He reached out like he wanted to shake her hand.

Tina was stunned for a moment, but she finally went to accept her new genie's handshake. "I'm Ti—"

"Heigh-ho! Don't care," he said, pulling his hand away and pretending to smooth the hair he didn't have. "Make your wish, little sister. Anything you want in all the world. No quest. No consequence." He sang this last part. "No strings att-att-attached!"

As genies went, this dude was pretty weird. Ridge had some odd things about him, but this was a new level. Chasm seemed to think he was a contestant on a reality show.

Tina nodded, clutching the crimson jar in both hands now that the lid had turned to smoke. She cleared her throat, squaring her shoulders as she faced the tattooed genie. I knew exactly what she was going to say. I thought of that hospital room and the woman I'd seen lying pain stricken in her bed. I couldn't imagine what Tina was feeling.

"I wish," she said, "with all my heart. I wish you would heal my mother."

"Let's hear that magic word," Chasm said, cupping a hand to his ear.

"Bazang," Tina whispered.

Chasm waved a large hand over the deep abyss before him. "G-g-g-granted!" he sang. "Your mother is now healthier than a veggie platter!"

On the bridge, I saw the glimmer of a hopeful smile spread across Tina's lips. *"Mamá,"* she whispered.

"Now let's get down to business." Chasm put his hands on his hips. "Your free wish is spent. And now, our partnership truly begins."

Tina took a deep breath. "Does the Universe have another quest for me?"

Chasm shook his bald head. "Oh, don't be a naive turkey on Thanksgiving. The Universe has little say in what I do next." He stepped toward Tina. "Okay! Your second wish will be to lose your voice." The thick leather band on his wrist suddenly opened up, an hourglass appearing just like the ones Tina and I wore.

I didn't know why he was wearing it. And instead of white, Chasm's hourglass was full of blood-red sand.

"What?" cried Tina. "No! I didn't wish for that!"

"Hey, now! You haven't even heard the consequence. Let me explain. Okay! If you wish to have no voice," said Chasm, "then your mouth will always be agape."

"No!" Tina shouted. "I didn't make that wish! I don't accept! You can't do this!"

"Oh, very well," said Chasm. And he sang the magic word. "Baz-a-a-ang!"

Tina suddenly fell silent. Her lips were still moving, but no sound came out of her mouth. The moment she realized what had happened, her hand went to her throat. She attempted to shout something again, and then tears began rolling down her face. Her jaw hung slack, mouth agape, just as Chasm had explained.

The Undiscovered Genie turned, dusting his hands as the red sand hourglass snapped out of sight.

"The Universe created genies so you could wish," he said to his audience of me, Thackary, and Jathon. "Your genies allow you to choose and to act. To be the Wishmaker. But what is a Wishmaker who cannot make her own choices?" Chasm looked back at Tina. "She's a little dancing puppet."

"Whoa, Ace," Ridge's voice whispered from inside his jar. "This guy's freaking me out."

"You can't do this!" I shouted, finding my voice for the first time since Chasm's arrival. "The Universe has rules! This isn't how a genie works!"

"Oh, but I am something altogether different," Chasm explained. "I am both genie and Wishmaker. I am the consequence that the Universe had to accept when it created the other genies. Dear Tina received what she wanted. Her mother is alive. And now the girl is mine."

"But the wish was supposed to be free!" I screamed. "Tina wasn't supposed to have a consequence."

"Healing her mother was free," answered Chasm.

"But it wasn't!" I cried. "You've enslaved her!"

"She was enslaved the moment she chose to open my jar," said the muscular genie.

It could have been me.

I had been standing on the rope bridge with the jar in my hand. I had my hand on the lid! If Thackary Anderthon hadn't used my own trinket against me, I would have opened Chasm's jar. I had been only seconds away from being in Tina's position. I would have been his slave.

Thackary's voice hissed out from behind me. "Take me!" he

shouted at Chasm. "I would gladly be your slave if you would take away my curses."

I glanced back at him, disbelief on my face. Here I was, thanking my lucky stars that I had narrowly missed Tina's fate, and Thackary was bemoaning the fact that he wasn't Chasm's puppet. How demented was he?

"I like that attitude, skinny britches," Chasm snapped and pointed at Thackary. "Soon. Soon I will find a way to bring more puny human beings under my control. But for right now, I'm a bicycle built for two. The girl will have to suffice."

"Hang on, Tina!" I shouted. "He only has you for seven days. You can fight him!"

Chasm's laughter resonated through the cavern. "Seven days?" he mocked. "Those are the rules of a common genie. This girl is my servant until the end of her piddly little life. Together, we will wish for marvels, and she will accept the consequences until they are too much for her tiny human form to bear."

This bit of news caused Tina to collapse to her knees, silent sobs coming from her open mouth.

"Now," Chasm said, turning back to Tina. "For your next trick . . . you wish for a way out of this cave. Much too damp and dark for my taste." The hourglass on his wrist emerged. "In exchange for a way out, your right foot will be replaced with a roller skate." He waved his hand at her. "Don't you worry.

Won't hurt a bit." Then he sang the command. "Baz-a-a-ang!"

Tina stooped over, suddenly clutching at her right foot. At the same time, a terrible tremor began to pass through the cave. I covered my head as stalactites shook free from the ceiling, falling like deadly spears. Across the rope bridge, on the far wall of the cavern, a huge crack had opened, with daylight spilling through.

Chasm strode onto the rope bridge, scooping the weeping form of Tina over his shoulder as he passed. I saw her foot, now replaced with a bright red roller skate.

"That's our cue," Chasm said. "It's time to see this world of yours." He inhaled deeply through his nose, as if smelling the potential that the world had to offer. Then, in several bounding steps, he was across the bridge. Tina's museum gift bag slipped from her arm, falling at the threshold. Daylight reflected on Chasm's shaved head as he climbed through the exit, a silently screaming Tina draped over one shoulder.

"You fool, boy!" Thackary's voice pealed through the crumbling cavern. At first I thought he was speaking to me, but then I saw that he had strode past. The man stood over Jathon, berating his injured son for letting Tina open the jar. "You have failed me! What have ye done?"

Thackary seized Jathon by the neck and pulled him to his feet. For a terrible moment, I thought he might toss his son into the abyss. Instead, he dragged him across the rope bridge, shielding his balding head from bits of crumbling rock.

I stood there, the last one to flee this terrible place. But I wasn't alone. Ridge's voice echoed out of his jar. "Ace! Ace! It sounds bad out there!"

I reached into the museum bag and withdrew the familiar peanut butter jar. The curator had forbidden our genies from coming out of their jars until the Undiscovered Genie had departed the cave. Chasm was gone. He had taken Tina. Thackary and Jathon had escaped, and the entire cave was about to crash down on my head.

I needed a friend.

"Ridge, get out of the jar."

My genie appeared beside me, his hands instinctively going up to cover his head as debris rained down. "Yikes, Ace! We've got to get out of here!"

I knelt on the cold stone, my hands shaking at the turn of events. "It doesn't matter," I said. "We lost."

"But the quests . . ." said Ridge. "I thought Tina fulfilled them all."

I shrugged. "We completed the quests," I said. "We saved the world. No zombie pets, no lemonade flood, no raining pianos. But I think we've released something even worse!"

"You don't know that," Ridge said. "We can stop Chasm."

I shook my head. "You didn't see him!" I cried. "He's going to use Tina to . . ." I didn't know what he was going to do. Enslave the human race? That's what Chasm had hinted. "We can't stop him, Ridge."

"Chasm took Tina," said Ridge. "Don't let him take you, too."

"What do you mean?" I looked up at my genie friend.

"Chasm took away Tina's ability to choose, but he didn't take yours." Ridge extended his hand. "Get up, Ace. Let's get out of here."

I reached out and took the genie's hand. The determined grip of my friend seemed to send a surge of energy through me. Ridge hoisted me to my feet and pushed me forward in the direction of the rope bridge. As I ran, I set the peanut butter jar back into the museum bag on my shoulder.

With every step, I grew more determined. Ridge was right. Chasm had defeated Tina, but he hadn't defeated me. As long as I had the power to wish, there was hope.

"We have to save Tina," I said. As the words left my mouth, I'd never been more sure of anything. If it hadn't been Tina, it could have been me. Or Thackary. Though I don't think I would have felt so strongly about saving him.

And then it dawned on me.

"The Universe knew," I said to Ridge as we reached the far side of the rope bridge. "Once knowledge of the Undiscovered Genie came out, the Universe knew that his jar would get opened. It couldn't stop our choices, Ridge. All it could do was try its best to control the way that the jar was opened."

I leaped over a crumbled rock formation. "The Universe knew that if Thackary Anderthon opened that jar, we wouldn't make any attempt to save him from Chasm. Worse, we'd probably think he was getting what he deserved. But not Tina."

I felt emotion choking my throat. "The Universe knows that we'll try to save her. It's the only way to stop Chasm. By letting someone we care about open his jar." I clenched my fists. "We have to save Tina!" I said again. "The Universe is depending on us, Ridge!"

My genie didn't answer, so I glanced over my shoulder.

He was gone.

I skidded to a halt, sunlight from the exit spilling down, feeling warm on my neck. Ridge was gone. Our time was finally up. I glanced down at my wrist. The leather band had disappeared, and with it, the hourglass. My hand flew to the museum bag over my shoulder, but it was empty.

The jar, like my genie, had vanished.

I was paralyzed for a moment, feeling more alone than I'd ever felt before (which is saying something, for an orphan who didn't even know his own name).

At my feet was Tina's discarded museum bag. Vale was surely gone, too, but I couldn't help but lift it from the rubble and peek inside.

No little lip balm jar. But there was something else—a folded piece of paper with my name written on the front.

I could finally read again now that my quest was over. And I recognized the sky-blue paper. It was the note Tina had been writing on the airplane. I shouldn't have taken the time to read it there, with the cave roof coming down at any second. But my trembling fingers unfolded the page and my eyes scanned across the words.

Dear Ace,

If you are reading this, then something probably went wrong in the Cave of the Undiscovered Genie. Even though it goes against all the warnings, I've decided to open his jar. If something bad happens to me, I'm relying on you to help.

I've created a trinket.

I didn't dare use something nearby, so I wished it on my mother's favorite necklace. You need to find her and break the necklace chain. When that happens, Ridge's jar will come back to you.

Best wishes,

Tina

"Tina, that's brilliant!" I said aloud, wondering why I hadn't thought of such an ingenious fail-safe. I couldn't help but worry about what kind of consequence would accompany such a powerful trinket. But with Chasm, Tina was now in the throes of bad consequences. Amid all the despair, this was at least a glimmer of hope.

Crumpling the letter in my hand, I turned my face toward the sun.

Ridge was gone.

Tina was taken.

And it was up to me to get them back.

Acknowledgments

I came up with the wish/consequence idea more than six years before this book was published. Since then, many people have influenced the story and inspired me to keep going.

Thanks to Chris Schoebinger, Heidi Gordon, Lisa Mangum, and Rob Davis. Also to my parents and siblings who are always so supportive and encouraging. The biggest thanks goes to my wife, Connie, for listening and talking me through every part of this book (and the next).

Thanks to Chris Hernandez for his diligent and thorough editorial skills. And to Jessica Warrick for her fun illustrations.

My agent, Ammi-Joan Paquette, believed in this story from the beginning, and worked tirelessly on its behalf. It was a roller-coaster ride worthy of Super-Fun-Happy Place. Thanks, Joan!

Speaking of Super-Fun-Happy Place . . . thanks to my old

band buddy Tristan Wardle for making up that name many years ago. It is now immortalized.

And thanks to you, reader! Being an author is a wish come true for me. I hope you enjoy Ace and Ridge's next adventure!

Wish you could know what happens next?
Here's a special look at the sequel to *The Wishmakers!*

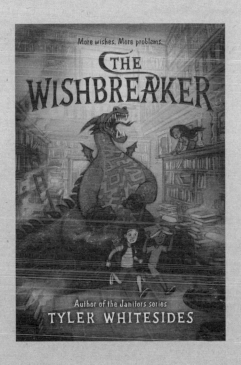

It's not every day you get a second chance to save the world.

CHAPTER 1

There was a giant robot dinosaur smashing its way toward me.

You might be wondering how I got here, sitting in a pile of peanut butter jars in the grocery store while people ran screaming in every direction.

I'll tell you.

It had been ten terribly lonely days since I lost my genie, Ridge, who disappeared back into his jar once our quest was over. Chasm, the newly freed all-powerful genie bent on world domination, escaped his cave prison—and I got left behind. Luckily, the hole he had blasted to get out of the cave led to the street right outside the Museum of Cans, Crates, Cartons, and Containers, and that strange curator guy was still around. Apparently, he no longer needed to guard the museum, since the undiscovered cave had been, well . . . discovered.

He took pity on me and asked where he could drop me off.

I told him Nebraska, assuming Tina's mom would still be there and that she had the magic trinket I needed to set everything right.

The curator drove me the whole way in the museum van, which was actually a very frightening experience, since he didn't really know how to drive. It shouldn't have taken us so many days, but I was terrible at giving directions since I still couldn't tell left from right.

I went to St. Mercy's Hospital first, made some inquiries, and eventually found the rural town that Tina and her mom called home. From there it was pretty easy to locate the correct house. There really weren't that many to choose from. I thanked the curator and told him that I needed to do this next part on my own. The strange man wiggled his unibrow and drove off into the sunset.

Right as I was about to knock on the door, Ms. Gomez pulled out of the garage. Lucky for me, she wasn't going far. I chased her a few blocks to the neighborhood grocery store and followed her inside.

But how was I supposed to start this conversation?

"Hi, Ms. Gomez. You must be Tina's mom. I know, because I spied on you in the hospital when you were terminally ill. My name's Ace. I'm friends with your daughter. Or at least I was before she got enslaved by an evil genie called Chasm. Anyway,

I'm here to break your favorite necklace. . . ."

No. It would be easier to avoid such a conversation altogether. It would be easier to corner Maria Gomez, take her by surprise, break the chain, and run for it. Tina could explain everything to her mom after I saved her. But first, I needed to get my genie back before Chasm did anything crazy.

I hadn't seen any major catastrophes on the news, so Chasm seemed to be biding his time. I knew the evil genie was somewhere out there. But where? I was sure Chasm had hundreds of nefarious plans cooked up from his millennia of entrapment inside his jar. So, what was he waiting for?

I watched Ms. Gomez pick out a shopping cart, tucking a strand of jet-black hair behind her upside-down ear. As an ex-Wishmaker, she still carried consequences like that from her youth. I could relate. I, too, had a few unfortunate consequences that would be sticking with me forever.

As I looked at her now, it was hard to believe she'd ever been sick. Tina had cured her mom's illness with a wish, and she looked perfectly healthy. Ms. Gomez wasn't very tall, and pleasantly plump, but seemed plenty strong as she yanked apart two shopping carts that had been stuck together.

I crept up behind her as she stopped to pick out a loaf of bread. Tina's note said she had made a wish to turn her mother's necklace into the trinket that would reunite me with my genie.

3

I saw the thin chain glinting around Ms. Gomez's neck. A sharp tug should easily snap it. Of course, Tina would suffer some kind of nasty consequence in the same moment, but she'd known the risks when she wished for the trinket.

I glanced from side to side to make sure no one was watching. Only then did I realize which aisle we were in. Where fate (or the Universe) had brought me.

The peanut butter aisle.

I moved in as Ms. Gomez stooped to set the bread into her cart. She turned as I leaped toward her, but I was too fast. My fingers brushed her neck as I snatched the chain. My momentum kept me going down the aisle. I heard her gasp, felt the necklace go tight in my grasp.

The chain snapped.

I thought for sure I was safe, but Ms. Gomez whirled with surprising speed, the shopping cart rolling away as she caught me by the arm. I was jerked around, barely getting my feet under me as we came face-to-face.

I probably looked really sick to her. Old consequences meant that my ragged breath smelled like fish, my right eye was yellow, my tongue was green, and my face was smudged with a bit of dried peanut butter.

"Do you have any idea what you've done?" Ms. Gomez whispered, her voice carrying a definite Spanish accent.

"Do you like toast?" I said. Not because I wanted to sound like a smart aleck. The Universe forced me to answer any question with another question. I still had the rest of the year until that consequence let up.

My mismatched eyes fixed on the necklace dangling from my fist. Good. I could see where the chain had broken. Ridge's jar should be on its way.

"You can have it back," I said, opening my fingers and letting it fall from my sweaty hand. Behind me, there was a thump as something fell to the hard floor of the grocery aisle. Craning my neck against Ms. Gomez's iron grip, I saw what had made the sound.

It was a solitary peanut butter jar that had seemingly leaped from the shelf like an anxious volunteer.

A grin spread across my face as the jar wobbled upright. I could see the bright warning label from where I stood. No other peanut butter jar came with a warning. That was it. Ridge! All I had to do was twist off that lid and my genie would be back!

"It's okay," I said. "I'm a Wishmaker. Or, I *was* one. And I'm about to be again."

"That necklace was a trinket," Ms. Gomez cut me off, still holding my arm.

"I know," I answered. "That's why I had to break it. That was the only way to find my genie again."

"That's not what it does!" Her face twisted in confusion, but her grip finally relaxed enough for me to pull free.

"What?" I replied, crossing to pick up Ridge's jar. "The trinket worked perfectly." It felt right to hold the jar again. But my grip also brought back the dreaded responsibility of being a Wishmaker. The power of the Universe at my fingertips . . . in exchange for consequences.

"But the necklace," Ms. Gomez said, pointing at the broken chain on the floor. "I took that trinket from a very bad Wishmaker nearly eight years ago."

What was she talking about? I picked nervously at the edge of the jar's warning label, feeling the edge of the sticker begin to peel up.

Ms. Gomez's eyes suddenly grew wide. "Fudge ripple!" she shouted, stooping to lift the chain from the floor. "It's a double trinket!"

"Double trinket?"

"You wished for this necklace to become a trinket," she said.

"Not me," I replied. Should I tell her about Tina? "It was—"

"What does it do?" Ms. Gomez interrupted me.

"Didn't I already say?" I answered with a mandatory question. "Breaking the chain reunited me with my genie." As proof, I held up the jar of peanut butter, the half-peeled warning label curling up like a scroll.

"Then you better open that quickly," Ms. Gomez stated. "We're going to need a genie to get away from the trinket's original purpose."

"What was its original purpose?"

"The Wishmaker I took this from loved chaos." Ms. Gomez gave a worried glance down the grocery store aisle. "When the chain breaks, the trinket releases a creature capable of mass destruction."

I swallowed hard. "What kind of creature?"

And that's how the giant robot dinosaur got there.

The shelves behind Ms. Gomez erupted. She crumpled to the floor as bagged loaves of bread flew like shrapnel. The force of the impact tossed me backward and I slammed into the rack behind me.

Plastic jars of peanut butter cascaded upon my stunned form, burying me nearly to the neck. I shook my head against the blow and lifted my hands, only then realizing that I had dropped Ridge's jar. No worries. I just needed to find the jar with the warning label on the lid.

Oh, right. The label was stuck to my thumb.

There was another loud crack, and a nearby shelf exploded, sending deadly canned goods flying in every direction. That's when people started running from the store, screaming. I don't know what they thought was going on. The Universe always shielded ordinary people, making magical things seem somehow explainable. But I was no ordinary person. I was an ex-Wishmaker.

So, I think that catches you up on my current situation. Now, any ideas on how to get away from a robot dinosaur?

CHAPTER 2

You probably think dinosaurs are cool. I do too. But I prefer the ones that aren't trying to crush me.

The one in front of me looked kind of like a T. rex, except totally made of metal. Its head scraped the high ceiling of the grocery store as mechanical feet slammed down with enough force to crack the smooth floor.

Robo Rex paused, tilted its head, and let out a roar that sounded like nails in a blender. A row of multicolored LED lights flickered across its razor teeth, and both eyes flashed red and yellow. On a TV show, it would have looked ridiculously cheesy. But in real life it was really quite terrifying.

If it didn't bite me in half, it would stomp me with those iron feet. At least it had tiny, useless arms.

Lasers suddenly shot from Robo Rex's arms, blasting another shelf to bits. Okay, not so useless after all.

It was time to find Ridge and take this punk down.

I grabbed one of the peanut butter jars from the pile around me and twisted off the lid. This time, there was no puff of smoke. But what if Ridge was trapped beneath that papery protective seal? I jabbed my index finger through, feeling it sink in creamy peanut butter up to the second knuckle.

I dropped the jar and grabbed another, repeating the process. The second one was not a genie, either. It was chunky.

A short distance away, I saw a bit of rubble rousing. Ms. Gomez! She pushed aside a broken shelf and painstakingly rose to her knees. Her black hair looked gray with dust, and her movements were slow but determined.

Ms. Gomez looked up at Robo Rex defiantly. Its animatronic eyes fixed on her and I thought I saw the tiny laser arms recharging.

"Hey!" I shouted, leaping to my feet and hurling the ordinary jar of peanut butter at the robot dinosaur. It pinged harmlessly off one of the metal legs. "Pick on someone your own size!"

In response, Robo Rex turned its gaze on me, pointing the lasers in my direction.

"Not me!" I shouted, backing up. "I'm way smaller than you!"

Ms. Gomez looked at me as I tripped on the array of peanut butter jars and fell hard on my backside. "Adios, muchacho!"

she said, sprinting toward the store's exit.

"You're not going to help me?" I screamed.

"*I* didn't break the necklace!" I heard her shout as she ducked out of sight.

I managed to stick my fingers into three more jars of peanut butter before the dino's lasers powered up again. It fired and the floor in front of me broke apart, debris flying with a cloud of smoke and the smell of toasted bread. Well, at least Robo Rex had terrible aim.

With the sound of grinding gears, it came toward me. I scrambled away from the pile of peanut butter jars, grabbing two on my way out. I was counting on one of them to house Ridge, because the mechanical dinosaur's foot promptly pulverized the rest of the pile.

That giant stomper came down right where I'd been sitting. I heard the plastic jars popping like grapes under its metal foot. Peanut butter spattered everywhere. I felt a big gob of it hit me square in the back as I staggered away.

Cleanup on aisle twelve!

I sprinted around the end of the shelf and ran down two more aisles before making a brief stop next to the spices.

Okay, jar number one. Please have a genie inside.

Tucking one jar under my arm, I quickly twisted the lid off the other. I stabbed my finger through the quality seal and came up with nothing but sticky spread.

Grunting in anger, I tossed the useless jar aside. Behind me, I heard the giant robot dinosaur smashing through shelves, coming my way. . . .

Okay, jar number two. It had better be you.

I slipped it out from under my arm, grabbed the lid, and gave it a sharp twist.

Nothing but peanut butter. Organic.

I hurled it down the aisle. Now my only hope was to circle back around to the scene of the peanut butter massacre and try to find Ridge's jar in the mess. I might have stomped my feet in frustration if Robo Rex's head hadn't suddenly appeared over the spice shelf.

As I dove forward, the light-up teeth snapped at the spot where I had been standing. I ran aimlessly, painfully aware that I was moving away from the peanut butter squish and any hope of finding Ridge.

Hmmm . . . How to stop a robot dinosaur without some magical assistance?

One time, a kid in my class ruined his remote-control car when he dropped it in the toilet. Not sure why he had it in the bathroom, but it was clear that electronics and water didn't mix.

A laser blast went over my shoulder, striking the refrigerated dairy section and melting twenty pounds of butter.

That's it! Milk!

Maybe I could short-circuit Robo Rex with a couple gallons of milk. At least that might slow it down so I could get back to the peanut butter aisle.

I grabbed two jugs of skim milk and turned to face the dinosaur. I really hoped this guy was lactose intolerant.

I threw the first jug, hoping it would break open when it hit, but I missed altogether. Turned out I was just as bad at aiming as the T. rex. And I had full-sized arms!

My second jug got him right under the chin, breaking open and showering the robot. But instead of throwing sparks and slowing him down, the milk bath just seemed to enrage him. Robo Rex's foot came up for a mighty stomp, higher than any one before. And then I saw it.

Ridge's genie jar.

The peanut butter container was lodged in the bottom of the dinosaur's foot like a thorn. The metal was ripped and folded back, and I could just see the plastic lid sticking out.

Any other container would have been smashed to bits, but a genie jar was unbreakable.

I acted out of sheer impulse, leaping forward as the foot started to come down. Dropping to my knees, I slid across the wet, milky floor. My hands came up, scraping the cold metal and groping blindly. I caught the lid and felt the jar fall into my grasp, clearing the foot just as it came down to crack the floor.

I was on my feet, sprinting down the nearest aisle that still had shelves intact. Behind me, the dinosaur's metal tail swiped around, utterly crushing the dairy section.

Gasping for breath, I came to a halt. My fingers were still messy with peanut butter, and I slipped twice while trying to twist off the lid. At last, I felt it turn in my hand.

There was a loud bang and a puff of smoke, and I felt the lid disintegrate in my grasp. I let out a victorious laugh, peering through the smoke to see my long-awaited genie friend.

Across the aisle, I thought I saw his silhouette, but his back was to me. And his voice . . .

"Behold, mere mortal!" cried a gravelly voice. "I stand between you and the power of the Universe. Your wish is my command. But beware the costly consequences that come with . . ."

The smoke cleared and the genie turned around.

"Oh, hey, Ace! It's you!" It was indeed Ridge, and now his voice had returned to the squeaky timbre I was familiar with. "You're my Wishmaker? What are the odds that the Universe would put us together again?"

"The Universe didn't," I said. "It was a trinket. And what happened to your voice a second ago?"

"Oh, that." Ridge scratched self-consciously at his curly hair. "I was trying something new. You see, when I appeared to you the first time, I didn't do a really great job of explaining anything. I figured I should lay down some of the basics for my new Wishmaker. Maybe try out a more intense voice to get some respect."

"It sounded like you had a cold," I pointed out.

"I was going for ominous."

There was a bright flash of lasers and the shelf behind Ridge exploded. He screamed good and loud, but I was past that by now.

"What was that?"

"That's the robot T. rex," I explained. "He's got laser arms."

"Why is there a robot T. rex in the grocery store?"

"Um . . . I blame Tina's mom." I could tell the dinosaur was making its way toward us, demolishing anything in its path. It was wishing time.

Don't miss these books by
TYLER WHITESIDES!

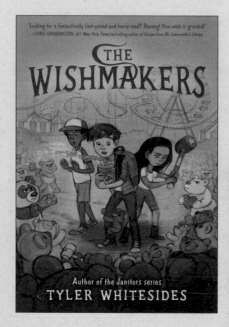

More wishes.

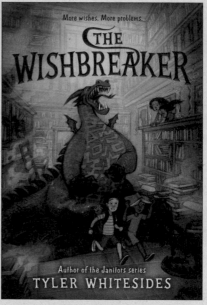

More problems.